Adv_____gs

"A gut-wrenching plunge into the supernatural, *Broken Wings* reveals Dittemore's skilled, elegant prose and her prowess with compelling characters! Tangible fear and violent beauty collide in this page-turning sequel in the Angel Eyes Trilogy. Simply unputdownable! Tear the veils from your eyes—*Broken Wings* is one of the best YA novels out there!"

—Ronie Kendig, award-winning
author of the Discarded Heroes
Series and Trinity: Military War Dog

"This is one of my favorite series! Dittemore has accomplished a rare feat with *Broken Wings*: she's written a sequel that's as good as or better than book one. Beautiful, romantic, and fascinating. I couldn't stop reading this enthralling page-turner. I'll be the first one in line for book three."

—Jill Williamson, author of *By
Darkness Hid*, *Replication*, and *Captives*

"Powerful, honest, and emotionally gripping. I read it in one sitting!"

—C.J. Redwine, author
of *Defiance*

Acclaim for *Angel Eyes*

"*Angel Eyes* has everything I look for in a novel—gorgeous prose, a compelling heroine, humor, and an intriguing plot—and two things I dream of finding—permission for brokenness and the promise of hope."

—MYRA MCENTIRE,
AUTHOR OF *HOURGLASS*

"*Angel Eyes* is a fine debut. A touching and exciting romance with celestial implications."

—ANDREW KLAVAN, AWARD-WINNING
AUTHOR OF *CRAZY DANGEROUS*

"Stunning. A captivating read with all the intensity necessary to keep me turning pages well into the night."

—HEATHER BURCH, AUTHOR OF THE
CRITICALLY ACCLAIMED *HALFLINGS*

"Shannon Dittemore gives us a classic tale of good versus evil with an authentically contemporary feel—and the assurance that beautiful writing is back."

—NANCY RUE, AUTHOR
OF THE REAL LIFE SERIES

BROKEN WINGS

BROKEN WINGS

Book Two in the
ANGEL EYES TRILOGY

SHANNON DITTEMORE

THOMAS NELSON
Since 1798

NASHVILLE   DALLAS   MEXICO CITY   RIO DE JANEIRO

Published in Nashville, Tennessee, by Thomas Nelson. Thomas Nelson is a registered trademark of Thomas Nelson, Inc.

Thomas Nelson, Inc., titles may be purchased in bulk for educational, business, fund-raising, or sales promotional use. For information, please e-mail SpecialMarkets@ThomasNelson.com.

Library of Congress Cataloging-in-Publication Data

Dittemore, Shannon.
  Broken wings / Shannon Dittemore.
      pages cm. -- (Angel eyes trilogy ; book 2)
  Summary: "When the Prince of Darkness pulls the demon Damien from the fiery chasm and sends him back to Earth with new eyes, the stage is set for the ultimate battle of good versus evil"-- Provided by publisher.
  ISBN 978-1-4016-8637-6 (trade paper)
[1. Supernatural--Fiction. 2. Angels--Fiction. 3. Demonology--Fiction. 4. Fate and fatalism--Fiction.] I. Title.
  PZ7.D6294Br 2013
  [Fic]--dc23
                                        2012032528

Printed in the United States of America

13 14 15 16 17 18 QG 6 5 4 3 2 1

For Mom and Dad,
who taught me that broken doesn't mean alone

"The light has come into the world, and men loved darkness rather than light, because their deeds were evil."

—JOHN, THE APOSTLE

1

Pearla

Hell is loud.

Talons scratch at the stone floor and clack against the pillars circling the chamber as the great hall fills. Hisses and snarls sound all around, but the noise doesn't unsettle the Cherub.

She's been here before.

Carved into the earth, deep against its core—in a realm undetectable by human technology—lies the stronghold of Satan. A massive structure formed out of darkness, molded and hardened into stone, Abaddon sits at the very center of the Prince's domain.

Pearla's velvety black skin goes unnoticed as she slides behind a chunky pillar, pressing against the outer wall.

But the cherubic spy isn't deceived by the darkness that surrounds her. This place was created for the Prince, given to him by the Creator. And while the light of the Celestial won't permeate these walls, even here the Father cannot be escaped. Unlike the demonic crowd scratching and biting at one another, this created one experiences peace.

Her celestial feet are silent against the icy floor, her wings folded tight against her back. She keeps her white eyes pinched tight. Nothing draws attention like shards of light piercing the darkness.

And darkness is everywhere.

Pearla slinks from pillar to pillar, feeling the rough rock with her hands, searching for a familiar crevice. When at last she reaches it, she slides inside, deep into the rock wall. Facing away from the chamber, she opens her eyes just wide enough to guide her climb. She's nimble and fast, scaling the wall with precision. Pearla locates a crag high above the pillars circling the room, high above the crowd of demons pushing and shoving and jockeying for position, and wedges herself far into the wall. The silky black wings—characteristic of cherubic spies—whisper against rock as she unfurls them and covers herself. Her gaze penetrates her wings and she watches.

And she waits.

The circular hall is ringed by rows and rows of demons. She's seen some of their grotesque faces before. As members of the Prince's guard they rarely leave Abaddon without the Prince; if they do, they do so in small numbers. His guard is made up of the most loyal, the most trusted demons. But there are others here: fallen angels with smaller, less important roles in the devil's stronghold. With so many in attendance, Pearla wonders if the Prince himself will preside over this assembly, a task he normally delegates.

Rumors lend credence to this idea—reports that indicate the entire Palatine legion is on the move. Sources insist they've returned to Abaddon to receive new orders. But it defies logic. Why return thousands and thousands of the Prince's best warriors to their fortress when a small council would suffice? But the rumors persist, and as the commander of the Creator's forces, Michael is giving them due consideration. If they're true, a movement like this indicates an attack of ambitious proportion.

But where?

With a victory in Uganda imminent, the legion of light will be ready to move. And there's no Warrior better suited for a war against the Palatine than Michael, the Commander himself.

Pearla closes her eyes against the chaos below and imagines herself back in the Throne Room of the Father. Magnificent in its beauty with everything in good order. The Father glowing bright, a river of gold flowing from His throne. The Thrones—wisest of the angels—wrapped head to toe in feathers of white, hovering about the Father, singing His praises, echoing one another back and forth. Pearla fights to control her lips as memories of the Creator's goodness well up in her soul.

Worthy! Worthy! No one else is worthy! she thinks.

And then another sound, a terrifying sound, pulls her back to hell. It's the sound of bondage. Of slavery. She wills herself to remain steady as the hiss and spit of fiery chains against the cold, moist floor draws excitement from the Fallen crowded about.

A lone demon is led into the hall by a small band. They prod and poke at him like a wayward cow. When they reach the center of the room, they latch his chains to the floor. With little ceremony they leave him to stand alone before a pathetic replica of the Father's throne.

The Prince's seat of power is not without grandeur, but where the Father's throne is constructed of the purest gold and gemstones, here an extravagant dais has been carved out of rock. Behind it, a slab rises high with strange symbols and designs cut into the stone. Chief among them is a dragon, his teeth menacing, his scales polished to a shine. His tail wraps around the platform, and clutched in his serpentine coils are thousands of brightly jeweled stars. The image, a symbol of the great dragon's rebellion, has always disturbed Pearla.

And with the prisoner chained before the throne, it seems Pearla was right.

Lucifer himself is expected.

2

Brielle

I'm alone.

The room is full of people, but I don't see them. Not clearly. They're a blur of summer colors and shadowed faces as my legs push me across the stage. My arms bow and curve, matching my inhales and exhales. Flutes, clarinets, and instruments I can't even name trill from the speakers, the music telling a story. The dance sharing a journey.

My journey.

Getting back to the stage was not an easy path, and my mind is full of the circumstances and the players that brought me here. I rise to my toes and I think of Ali, my closest friend. I think of the life that was taken from her. I think of her boyfriend, Marco, and the case built against him: smoke and mirrors to hide what really happened.

But truth is stronger than lies, and as the music slows, my black skirt whispers against my knees and I remember the first time I saw the Celestial. Light and life everywhere, and on every surface colors that never stop moving.

I think of the first time I saw Canaan, not as Jake's guardian only, but as the angel he really is—his outer wings spread wide, Jake wrapped tightly in his inner wings and pressed safely against his chest.

The music changes, dropping into a minor key, and my movements become more ghost-like. I think of the fear that nearly destroyed me six months ago, of the doubt that ate away at truth and hope.

I think of Jake.

The music is all but silent now. My body moves slowly, deliberately, but my heart trips over itself at the thought of his fiery, hazel eyes, his healing touch.

It's only right that my first performance is here, in Stratus, with him in the audience. With my dad and Canaan looking on, with Miss Macy cheering my feat from the wings. With Kaylee chattering away to Mr. Burns, telling him which pictures to snap.

The song builds, thundering drums that urge my legs faster and faster. The music crescendos and I spin, again and again. My hair pulls free of its knot, wild and free, like an angel in flight.

This choreography is my story. I let it swallow me, stretch me.

Cymbals crash like waves against rock—my doubt against the Father's will—and I drop low, bending to it, letting my fingers brush the floor, allowing myself a moment shrouded in the darkness of my curled torso before I rise once again to my toes. Light streams through the windows, turning everything around me a vibrant gold.

And then it's over. The music, the dance, my trip down memory lane. All of it. I drop into a bow, and the room erupts with applause.

When I rise I see the place clearly. The newly painted basketball court, the groupings of people here and there, standing, clapping, toasting me with plastic cups of red punch. Dad swipes at his eyes with gigantic paws, his ruddy face flushed. Jake stands near the back, whistling, cheering, a tiny orange tutu over his jeans.

I snort.

Where did he get that?

Hilarity joins exhilaration, and I laugh. And laugh.

Kaylee, friend extraordinaire, skips up the stairs and wraps her arms around me.

"You were amazing," she says. "I can't believe you almost gave that up!" She stumbles toward the microphone at the front of the stage, pulling me with her. "Wasn't she fabulous?" she asks the audience. The crowd claps harder, and I smile as the tears fall.

The gathering here is humble—just my friends and neighbors—and the Stratus Community Center is not nearly so grand as the theatres I toured last summer.

But I did it. Really and truly.

It's impossible not to think of Ali now. Not to remember her childlike laugh or the way she pushed and pulled me, made me believe I could conquer the world.

She'd be proud of me.

The tears are thick now, drenching my face, running down my leotard, so I wave my thanks to the crowd and duck into the wings. Miss Macy grabs me before I get too far. She pulls me into her arms and presses her cheek against mine. She's crying too.

"You are grace personified, sweetness. I know that wasn't easy, but . . ." Her voice catches and she pushes me away. "Oh, go. Kiss that boyfriend of yours and get back up here before our little fairies fly away."

I glance at the youngest of our students, lining up backstage.

Their mamas are busy corralling them, smearing sparkles on their cheeks, securing tiny wings to their backs. An ache passes through me—the same ache I always get when I realize I never had such moments with my own mother.

What would she have thought of my performance today?

I pull Miss Macy in for another hug and then make my way down the stairs. Kaylee's still speaking into the microphone. She thanks everyone for coming to Stratus Community Center's Grand Reopening, tells them her Aunt Delia's slaved over the pies in the back and to help themselves.

I weave through the crowd, looking for Dad, looking for Jake. I accept pats on the back and words of kindness. From the stage the crowd looked small, but on the floor with their familiar faces and words of congratulation ringing in my ears, I'm impressed by the turnout. When I agreed to open the celebration for Kaylee, I had no idea she'd rallied so many to the cause. Canaan towers over the crowd at the back of the auditorium, so I angle toward his silver hair. The crowd is dense enough that I don't see Jake until I'm right in front of him.

He spins in a circle, showing off his tutu. "You like?" he asks, that boyish scratch in his voice endearing.

He has no idea how much I *like*. "Does this mean you're ready for that dance lesson?"

"Does this mean *I'm* ready? You're the one who's been hiding all the tutus."

I haven't. Not at all, but there's something of the truth to his words. Sharing ballet with Jake would be like admitting I'm ready to move on. That I'm ready to let dance be more to me than my big break in the big city. And that's a hard thing to let go of. At least it used to be.

I flick the orange tulle at his waist. "Apparently I didn't hide them well enough."

"Canaan got me this one."

"Garage sale," Canaan says, diving into a slice of cherry pie. "I honestly didn't think he'd put it on. Had I known . . ." Canaan winks at me.

"You have to admit, omniscience would have been helpful here."

Jake feigns offense. "What are you saying? That I'm not tutu material?"

"Don't be sad," I tell him. "You're good at so many other things."

"I blame you for these two left feet."

"Me?"

"Yes. You said if I got a tutu you'd teach me to dance."

"So?"

"So. Teach." He scoops me into his arms and spins me full circle. "Am I doing it right?"

"Not even a little bit." I laugh.

We bump into a slew of people. I try to pull away and apologize, but they're kind and clap for us. Spurred on by their support, Jake prances me around the food table, around the easels set up promoting the various programs, refusing to stop until we reach center court. He dips me, all dramatic and ridiculous, but I play along, snapping up hard and fast, our faces just inches apart.

More clapping. More whistles.

"Has anyone ever told you how hot you are?" Jake says, his words nearly inaudible in the chaos.

I'm breathless and heady and trying far too hard to come up

with a new response to Jake's favorite question. Before anything remotely intelligent occurs to me, I feel a hand on my elbow.

"Elle, could you come over here for a minute?"

It's Dad. And he doesn't seem nearly as amused as the rest of the room.

"Um, sure."

Jake loosens his grip and nods at my father. "Mr. Matthews."

"Kid," Dad says, his lips a tight line. He takes my hand, pulling me from Jake. I do my best to cast Jake an apologetic look, but Dad places a hand on my back and leads me away.

"Everything okay, Dad?"

He squirms, twisting his neck against the top button of the dress shirt I bought him for Father's Day. He's already shed the new tie. "Everything's great, baby. I just wanted you to myself for a second. I'm so proud of you, little girl. You know that? Most people wouldn't have been able to do what you did up there today. Not after . . ."

"Dad."

"No, Elle. I'm serious. You were . . . heck, kid, you were . . ." His eyes glaze over. "You remind me so much of your mom."

The thought makes my throat tight. He's been talking about Mom a lot lately. A lot.

"I wish I remembered her."

He sniffs. "Come on. There's someone I want you to meet."

The woman Dad steers me toward is dressed in a designer pencil skirt and a starched white blouse. A red belt cinches everything together over an impossibly small waist. She's older than I am, by a decade probably, but she's got that racially ambiguous beauty thing going for her, all olive skin and caramel eyes.

Standing here in our community center she looks far too . . . expensive. Her black heels alone retail for seven hundred and fifty dollars. I know that because my ankles were featured in the ad campaign for them last summer. They place her a good three inches taller than I am, which bothers me for some reason. The euphoric state I've been reveling in fades as we step closer. My toes squirm in my ballet slippers.

My repulsion surprises me.

Am I intimidated by her?

I don't think so. I've done the model thing dozens of times, been surrounded by hundreds of gorgeous women. I know what intimidation is, and this feels different. Maybe it's the haughty look on her face, or the way her eyes keep flitting to my father.

I scratch at my empty wrist, wishing with everything in me that I could see this woman with celestial eyes.

"Sorry, Keith. No beer," she says, handing Dad a glass of punch.

"Of course there isn't," he says, yanking at his collar. The sloppy motion pulls my attention off the woman and back to Dad. I'm irritated that he wasn't kinder to Jake, but I have to admit that he looks rather dashing in his suit—or would if he'd stop trying to crawl out of it. "Baby, this is Olivia Holt."

Ah, Olivia. *The* Olivia.

"Liv is fine," she says.

"I'm Brielle," I say, extending my hand to the stranger. Her grip is cold, clammy. A startling contrast to the collected demeanor she exudes. "How did you two meet?"

"Just met her. Turns out Liv here is the one who saved the day. Swooped in at the witching hour."

Somehow that's not too hard to believe. I release her hand and resist the urge to wipe mine on my tights. "I've heard about you, of course. Kaylee's convinced you hung the moon."

"I'm impressed with your friend Kaylee," Olivia says. "She's done a noteworthy job here."

Olivia Holt's not wrong. With the Peace Corps taking forever to get back to Kaylee on her application, she decided she needed a project to take her mind off the wait. The Stratus Community Center was nothing but a rental hall before Kaylee petitioned the city council and gained permission to organize programs and seek out volunteers. And she did it all while juggling graduation and final exams and everything else that comes with the last semester of high school.

But there was little money, and the center was falling apart.

Enter Olivia Holt and the Ingenui Foundation.

"Kay's awesome," I say.

Olivia turns her attention back to Dad, closing me out of the circle. I bristle at the snub, but I'm more intrigued by the fact that Dad hardly notices. Olivia asks about his job and the state of the economy here in Stratus. He tells her things are rough, wiping his mouth with the sleeve of his suit jacket. Classy.

"The foundation could lift some of the strain, Keith. We have resources," she says, placing a freshly manicured hand on Dad's bicep.

Is she flirting? With my dad?

My head spins at the thought, and I lose track of the conversation. Dad's dated here and there, but always women I knew. Always women from town and never anything serious.

"Brielle's getting ready to head off to college, right, baby? Dance scholarship."

My stomach clenches. I avoid his gaze and smile as sweetly as I can at Olivia.

"Oh, congratulations. I do envy you." Her eyes drift off. "College was one of the happier times in my life."

There's a break in the crowd, and I catch sight of Miss Macy. Talk about saving the day. She winks at me and tilts her chin toward the stage.

"Excuse me. I've got a little thing to do."

"Don't let me keep you," Olivia says, waving my dismissal. "Your dad and I can figure out how to pass the time. I'm sure of it."

They laugh, Dad's face turning fire-truck red. "Break a leg, baby."

Anybody's leg? The thought flies through my head unchecked. Dad's voice carries across the gym floor as I make for the stage. He's stammering a bit, bragging on me. To Olivia. He tells her about all the colleges I've been accepted to. About the dance scholarship from that "fancy school on the East Coast."

He doesn't tell her about my doubts. That the idea of leaving makes me ill. He doesn't tell her, because he thinks it's nothing but jitters. Cold feet. He thinks if he keeps talking about it, I'll feel better about leaving Stratus for school.

To pursue dance. Again. 'Cause that turned out so great the first time.

Jake materializes out of the crowd and slides his hand into mine. "Where'd Jessica Rabbit come from?"

"That's Olivia Holt," I say.

"Kaylee's favorite person in the world, Olivia Holt?"

"Yup."

"I assumed she was just one big checkbook," he says.

Wouldn't that be nice?

"Everything okay with your dad?"

I blow a hair out of my face. "I guess. He keeps pushing college."

We take a good seven steps before Jake says anything.

"It's worth considering, Elle."

Three more steps.

"I know."

Jake stops and turns me toward him. "We're still on for tomorrow, right?"

"Yes, absolutely."

"Good. 'Cause I have a surprise."

My mind flies to the shiny black chest in Jake's house. The one the Throne Room uses to communicate with Canaan. It's cut from some sort of glorious-looking onyx and inside it sits a diamond engagement ring. My engagement ring.

I shake off the thought. It's too soon. We're too young.

And if Dad gets his way, I'm leaving town.

I start walking again, pulling Jake with me.

"*Another* surprise?" I ask, gesturing to the tutu he's now holding. "What can compete with that?"

"Well, it can't, right? I mean, this thing is orange. And sparkly."

We're at the stage now. Miss Macy is there, prodding a wayward fairy princess back up the stairs.

"Whenever you're ready for that lesson," I say, "you slide that tutu back on, okay?"

"Bu-arf," Kaylee says, pushing past me and grabbing the waist of my skirt. "Stop being so dreamy, Jake Shield. Twinkle Toes has a show to do."

"I'll be here," Jake says, "holding my tutu."

"And my heart," I tell him, as theatrically as I can muster.

"I really am going to vomit." Kaylee shoves me, and I slide toward our little dancers, all fidgeting and waving at the crowd. I take my place at stage right. Miss Macy takes stage left. Feedback screams through the speakers as Kaylee turns on her microphone.

"Sorry, sorry," she says. "Again, I can't thank you all enough for coming. So many of you helped get this place open again. You donated your time to teach workshops. You helped sandbag the place when the rains got to be too much. And then, when it looked like safety concerns were going to shut us down, Miss Holt stepped in and kept the dream alive."

The room fills with applause. Olivia smiles and waves it off. *Is her arm looped through Dad's?*

"Seriously, Miss Holt, it's been a ride and a half, but we couldn't have done it without you, without the foundation. Please pass our thank-yous on to the board." Kaylee takes a sip of water, spilling half of it down her shirtfront. "So, behind me, right? *What's all this dancing about?* Well! Miss Macy's Dance Studio has agreed to offer a few classes here at the center free of charge." She pauses. "You should totally be clapping right now. Miss Macy's is one of the premier"—air quotes around *premier*—"dance studios in Oregon. She suggested that an introductory class here at the center would allow more of our kids to participate in the arts. You're clapping, right? Yes? Clapping?"

The crowd obeys, bursting into rambunctious applause yet again. I shake my head in amazement. Standing here on the stage, watching Kaylee in her element, I find Miss Holt is not the only one impressed by my friend. The girl may be clumsy, but she's great at rallying people.

"Miss Macy has brought one of her classes here to show you what they can do. After the performance, please take a minute to visit the other art rooms to see all that your support has made possible. Thank you, thank you for coming."

Feedback screeches through the speakers yet again before the microphone can be silenced. After an agonizingly long pause, the "Dance of the Sugar Plum Fairy" begins. The room fills with oohs and ahhs as our little ladies sashay right and left, adding a spin here and there as whim would have it. Miss Macy and I do our best to keep our dancers onstage—a task far more exhausting than my own performance earlier but equally as rewarding.

When at last the song is over and the parents collect their children, I grab my bag and slip into the restroom. I trade my leotard, tights, and skirt for jean shorts and a green flouncy top. Then I hop on the counter and pull my duffel bag onto my lap. I dig around until I find the halo. It's near the bottom, tucked inside a legwarmer, warm and waiting.

I slip it onto my wrist and pull a light sweater over it. It's warm out, and the halo's sure to make me warmer, but Dad gives me grief every time he sees it.

"*High school boys don't give their girlfriends gold bracelets, Elle.*"

"*Sure they do.*"

"*Not bracelets like that, kiddo.*"

I had no response to that.

My skin soaks up the halo's presence, and I lean against the mirror. Today was a good day. A very good day.

So why do I feel like I've been socked in the stomach?

Someone knocks on the door, and I jump.

"Coming. Sorry." I slide off the counter and twist the doorknob. "Sorry, I was—" The door swings open, Olivia Holt on the other side. "I was changing."

All at once, I know exactly why I feel like I've been punched in the gut.

"Not a problem," she says. I step out of her way and into the hall. "A girl without a wardrobe change could never be the belle of the ball, right?"

She tilts her head at me, scrutinizing me from beneath those long—probably fake—lashes.

"Your dad, Keith . . ."

"I know my dad's name."

"Of course. He tells me you're multitalented. Modeling, right? And some acting."

I heft my bag higher on my shoulder. "Not so much anymore."

She taps her teeth with a red fingernail. "Shame. The foundation's looking to do some publicity in the near future. I wonder if I could convince you to help us out with some print work, maybe a commercial or two?"

She's not the first one to ask. My agent's called no less than a billion times over the past several months. I tell Olivia the same thing I tell Susie.

"I don't think so. Dance is really my thing. I can get you the numbers of a few girls in Portland who might be interested, though."

She shrugs off my offer. "Models in the city are easy enough to come by, but I'd like the opportunity to work with *you*." She produces a business card. "Take it. If you change your mind, give me a call."

I don't want her business card. I don't plan to change my mind. Still, politeness demands I take it. But the minute her fingers touch mine, I jerk away. The halo flames red-hot against my wrist—angry hot.

Her face pales and her caramel eyes narrow.

She felt it too. She balls her hand into a fist but leaves it hanging there, the business card wrinkled.

"Probably just static electricity," she whispers. "This dry weather and all." But her eyes are on my hand, and I have a sick feeling, like I've just given up a friend's secret. I slide both arms behind my back and twine my fingers together.

"There," she says, placing the card on the bathroom counter. "Don't want another shock, do we?" And then she takes a step back and grabs the door. "I'd appreciate you taking the card, Brielle. Just in case."

But I leave the card on the counter and walk away.

Because she's right.

Another shock is the last thing we need.

3

Pearla

earla watches the demon chained to the floor. He struggles to stand as the Fallen assembled round about bite and snap at him from a distance.

The Fallen are a species who eagerly devour their own kind. Cannibalism, the humans call it. Yes, they specialize in cannibalism. Only here, in the depths of hell, the beings are spirit. Not flesh and blood. And death doesn't come easily to spirit beings.

The chewing lasts for ages.

But the blistering, smoking wounds on this one weren't inflicted by another demon. The Fallen don't use fire as a weapon. They fear it. The demon waiting below is nursing wounds that could only have come from the pit.

The abyss.

The eternal fire created for the devil and his angels.

Pearla's seen it—navigated the cavern on occasion. It's a place that cannot damage her. When the Prince's stronghold was formed, the Creator confined the celestial light that was displaced to a chasm just beyond the black walls of Abaddon.

There holy fire reflects itself eternally, magnifying in that ever-brightening divide.

The pit is a glorious thing to the angels of light. It is God's goodness multiplied. But for those who chose darkness, the abyss is feared above all. Because even the Fallen heal.

Angelic beings are eternal; regardless of the damage they sustain, their spiritual bodies cannot be destroyed. Those sent to the abyss for punishment are burned by the Father's radiance again and again, only to spontaneously adapt and scar, healing in their own twisted way to be singed and charred once more.

It's hell.

And ironic, really. The very thing that energizes Pearla and the other angels of light is devastation to their adversaries. All because of a choice they made long ago. A choice none of them has the capacity to regret.

Pearla has surfed the abyss, searching for answers, for clues. She's watched the Fallen count their time there in licks of flame, wondering, between screams of misery, when and if the Prince will summon them from its cavernous depths.

Silence consumes the assembly now, imposed on them by the sight of an icy white figure dropping into the hall from above. His wings, spread wide, are white, save the tips, which retain a char he's never rid of.

Black-tipped wings for the Prince of Darkness. Healthy wings. Strong wings. His skin shines like polished marble. His hair lies in curls of midnight around his face—still fresh, still bright, still retaining the beauty that seduced a third of the angels. Human eyes would have a hard time distinguishing the Prince from a Warrior like Michael. But the absence of light behind those pale blue eyes hints at the creature's true nature. And they are pale, so pale the blue seems buried far below, glinting like coins at the bottom of a well.

He's exquisite. Majestic.

And he's afraid.

Celestial light has been banned from this place, but even here among the arctic shadows, fear cannot hide. Its blackness swirls in a controlled spin down his right arm, over his well-formed bicep, around his elbow, circling around his forearm, and sliding from his palm down his middle finger where it puddles beneath his throne. Tendrils branch out across the stone floor seeking, seeking.

He cups his hand, allowing the fear to pool there. His fingers close around the sticky substance and he prods it, molds it like a human child playing with a handful of clay. All the while, his eyes rip into the demon before him.

After a slow descent, the Prince's feet touch upon the seat of his throne—the graven dragon behind him. His legs and waist are wrapped in cords of white. His torso and arms are bare. Very little separates him from the other archangels. And yet so much.

Pearla watches the Prince. The Creator gave him beauty—a beauty unrivaled—and he's taken great pains to preserve it. His time here in Abaddon has kept him from the damage his hordes have suffered in the light of the Celestial. Pearla's heard stories of the Prince venturing above, but his untarnished appearance alone is proof that his time to heal greatly exceeds that of his minions.

"Sit." His celestial lips are still, unable to vocalize anything but animalistic rages—like those assembled, like the demon chained to the floor, like every angel he led astray—but they all hear. They all obey. It's sad, really. His song, like his face, was far superior to all others. Now his mouth is good for nothing.

Wings rustle and talons scratch as countless demons crawl and flap toward rough shelves cut into the cliffs surrounding the hall. The demon chained to the floor drops to his knees.

Humility, even false humility, is appreciated here.

The Prince doesn't sit, though. No. He stands on his throne, his legs spread wide, looking down at the demon trembling on the floor.

"It's unfortunate, brother, to see you in chains. Again."

His voice—sincere, seductive—vibrates through Pearla's small being.

He's opened his mind to the entire assembly, which makes her job much easier, but the Prince's voice is dangerous, his lies far too easy to believe. She draws her legs more tightly into herself, ready to launch up and away should occasion call.

"Let us relieve you of that burden." A small flick of his hand. "Please, friend, release Damien from his chains."

From the darkness beyond the throne emerges another soul—coal black, his shoulders broad and thick, his arms and legs muscled. Scars zigzag across his body, the largest—the one gracing his chest—bears the undeniable shape of a Shield's sword.

Pearla knows this one. This is Maka. Confidante of the Prince. His wings snap on approach, taunting his demon brother. Strange. The rumors had him suffering the pit. It seems he's been shown mercy. A rare thing here.

Damien stands and offers his hands. Maka draws his scimitar and slices through the binds, wrists first and then waist and ankles. His icy blade rubs against the chains of fire, sending up a haze of steam, but Pearla can still see Damien's wings unfurl as the chain around his waist is cut through. They spread wide, like sails released after a storm's confinement. Relief shivers through him, a growl escaping his lips and sending tremors through the hall.

Maka turns and marches away, his talons clacking against the stone floor. The Prince examines Damien like a bird eyeing the worm beneath its feet.

"So subservient, so docile you are, Damien—here in my fortress. And yet, it seems, you cannot be trusted beyond these walls."

Damien stands tall. "I can be trusted."

"Can you?" Dark brows lift over those pale eyes, but the Prince's voice remains silken. "I do not recall asking you to rally your brothers for a heroic battle. Nor did your assignment require it."

The Prince squeezes the ball of fear in his hand. Like sickly blood, it clots and coagulates inside it, oozing between his fingers.

"If I'm not mistaken, and correct me if I am, you developed a fascination that pulled you from the enslaved. Am I mistaken, Damien, or are your ears as damaged as your eyes?"

Silence.

"I require an answer."

"You are not mistaken, Lord Prince."

"Ah." The Prince flings the ball of goo from his hands and twines his fingers together. He peers over loosely bound knuckles at Damien as the fear continues to drip. "I didn't think so."

"You must admit, there was ample cause for my fascination."

Damien's outburst is dismissed with a shrug. The Prince drops into his seat, his wings lowering him slowly.

"I admit nothing. I've spoken to Maka, to Javan. I've spoken to the Twins, Damien. I know what it is that captured your imagination."

"Then you know I was right." Damien is shaking now. Fear, rage. It all seems bottled inside this one. "That boy can heal, Lord Prince. If corrupted, his value to darkness is insurmountable."

Fear trails from the Prince's elbow now, running down the arm of the throne. He watches it.

"Others claim to heal, Damien. He is not the only one."

"But this boy can do it with a touch. He's different, Lord Prince. Like me. Like you."

The Prince stiffens. His nose flares and his eyes narrow. The idea of another being approaching his glory in any manner has always unsettled him.

"Oh, I doubt very much he is like me."

"No, no. Of course not, but beyond the gifts bestowed to other men, this boy has *something*, Prince. Something."

The Prince glances sideways to Maka, who has established himself against a pillar. Maka seems uncomfortable with this line of questioning, but nods slowly.

It seems they're holding a private conversation: Maka and the Prince. The ability angels have to control just who hears their thoughts is a frustration to the cherubic order, to those who gather information. Pearla grows frustrated that they've closed out the assembly. She's not the only one: growls and hisses sound all around, and the twitching wings of the accused say they've closed out Damien as well.

Finally, with a decidedly more curious expression on his face, the Prince opens his mind to those gathered.

"I see." He stretches his wings luxuriously wide so they gently brush the arms of his throne. Then he settles back and raises a fear-streaked hand before his face. "Hands like ours."

"Yes, Lord Prince."

The Prince doesn't sigh, but everything about his posture says he'd like to. "It is now widely known, Damien, that you and your brothers allowed a Shield to claim the victory that night."

Before Damien can unleash an argument, Maka intercedes. "There were two, Lord Prince. Two Shields."

"Two? Well then." The Prince turns his eyes on Maka, quelling him with sarcasm. "I'll not patronize you, Damien; this information is valuable and something must be done with the boy. And yet the question begs to be asked: of what value are you to me? You, with eyes so frail and weak . . ."

"You could fix that."

They're dangerous words for Damien to utter, and the assembly reacts as such. Pearla expects nothing but satanic fury at the near-demand, but is surprised at the Prince's docile treatment.

"I could, yes, but I'd prefer to return you to the pit for a millennium or two while another of your brothers—Maka, maybe—handles this boy."

"Lord Prince—"

"What's to stop me from doing that, Damien?"

"Because this thing, whatever it is, has grown beyond just the boy, and I deserve a chance to make it right."

"Deserve?" It's Maka.

But the Prince interrupts. "Beyond the boy?" His mawkish voice is low now, rough. He tilts his head, the icy shadows pulling his nose and chin into darkness. "Tell me, Damien. Regale me with a tale that will change my mind."

Pearla considers Damien. His straightened gait, his squared shoulders. He has the look of a gambler throwing his final card to the table. The one he's hidden up his sleeve.

"She saw me," he says. "The girl."

The Prince stands. His face, once passive, is now rigid as stone, a sense of urgency pulling his wings tight.

"Saw. You."

"Yes, my celestial form. This girl, this Brielle, saw through the terrestrial veil with understanding. It was like, like . . ."

"Like Elisha's servant. In Dothan. The site of your last great failure."

"Yes, Lord Prince." Damien averts his eyes, but only briefly. Then he steps forward, toward the Prince, his face set. "She knew where I stood and what I did. She knew what the greatest expression of love looked like in the Celestial. Somehow, some way, Lord Prince, mankind is breaking into our realm."

Even Pearla gasps at this revelation.

Yapping phrases like "the beginning of the end" begin to permeate the great hall. "Cataclysmic." "Armageddon."

The Prince stands silent for what seems like years, while the raging of the assembly builds. And then with measured, sound-less footsteps, the Prince of Darkness crosses the floor. He lifts his hand toward Damien's face—an offer of healing, it seems—and Damien steadies himself visibly for the honor. It's not like the Prince to offer healing—even to one of his own—and Pearla is perplexed by the gesture.

But before the Prince can make contact, a noisy clatter echoes through the hall.

From the shadows, a small, blackened creature scurries—all four of its limbs moving one after the other. It's an impish spy, the fallen counterpart to Pearla's cherubic order, and she recoils at the sight of her traitorous kinsmen. His small, bat-like wings lift him here and there on his chaotic trot across the stone floor. When he reaches the river of fear running in a sticky trail from the Prince's arm, the creature groans in delight and swims through it toward his master.

The Prince's hand, so close to Damien's face, drops away, reaching down and allowing the imp to latch on to his fingers. It scurries up the Prince's arm and shoulder, leaning past the lush black curls and into his ear.

The Prince's face hardens at whatever he hears, and with pale fingers he pinches the imp like a naughty cat and drops him to the floor. The imp chirps and gurgles, sliding in the train of soupy fear, finally springing from the hall.

The Prince waits until the hall is free of the imp's clamor, his face a carved stone. When at last silence returns, he reaches out a near-perfect hand, placing it on Damien's eyes. Fear drips from the Prince's arm and onto Damien's chest, mingling with the thin coat of terror the Fallen always wear. With the lightest touch, the accuser of the brethren restores the demon's celestial vision.

A swift movement, and his hand is gone.

Damien's eyes snap open and the Prince watches him, awaits his response. Damien flinches, his large hands grip the sides of his head, and he wails in agony.

"Yes, Damien?" the Prince asks.

"You are . . ." His mind sputters. "You are beautiful."

The Prince's lips part in a specious smile. "But I will not forgive again."

A flick of his wrist brings a scimitar to the Prince's hand, its frostiness smoking. He slides it into the sheath at Damien's waist. "Bring them to me at Danakil, Damien. The girl who saw through the veil and the boy with hands like *mine*."

This order surprises Damien. "To Danakil?"

"You question me?"

Damien cowers now, his hands raised in surrender. "No, Lord Prince."

"If these two are as *special* as you say—if they bear angelic gifts—I should very much like to meet them myself. Give their . . . abilities . . . a little test."

The Prince's wings flutter softly and then snap open. Grace and force.

"If you fail, brother," he says, stepping into Damien's face, "the cavernous pit will be nothing compared to my rage."

Damien nods—a soldier ready for battle.

The Prince turns toward Maka. "Maka, are you ready to redeem yourself?"

There is something very, very wrong with the Prince of Darkness using the word *redeem*, but Maka stands tall, rising to the opportunity.

"I am. You know I am."

"Good, then."

The Prince's wings take him back to his throne, where he hovers high above. Damien and Maka look on, the assembly growing restless.

"Hear me, brothers." The Prince waits for silence. "Hear me! You who love freedom, arm yourselves. Prepare for battle."

Pearla's wings twitch as the Prince reaches his arms wide, his pale eyes roaming over hell's manic hoard.

"The Sabres have been released."

And like that, the chamber is a torrent of angry noise and skitter, of spastic movement, claws and wings and snarls. Pearla's mind is just as chaotic.

"Calm yourselves!" the Prince cries, and silence permeates the hall once again. "This is not the first time the veil has undergone attack. You remember, yes? The Sabres have torn through it before, but we repaired the damage. We were victorious. We will be victorious again."

The once-slow trickle of fear leaking from beneath the Prince's wing has spread, and now a waterfall of terror pours, hiding the bottom of both wings and covering the Prince's lower body in the black tar.

Now he looks like darkness's prince.

"The earth is mine. My domain. My veil. Mine to control. War is upon us."

The noise is raucous, but the anger is tinted with celebration now. Amidst the chaos, Maka draws near the throne.

"Where, Lord Prince? Where will the Sabres attack?"

A terrifying smile splits the Prince's face. "Can you not guess?"

Maka bows his head. He *can* guess, it seems, but his silence is nothing but an ache in Pearla's chest. The Prince turns his eyes to Damien.

"You have fourteen days, brother. Fourteen days to secure the boy and the girl. After that—hear me, brothers—after that, the first demon to bring either of them to Danakil will be rewarded. And you, Damien, will never again see beyond the chasm."

"Y-Yes, Lord Prince."

"General Maka, I am putting the Palatine under your command. Have you confidence in yourself?"

"Pride, my Prince. I will not fail."

"With ten thousand of my finest at your command, I don't imagine you will. A defeat of that magnitude would demand consequences of severity."

"I will. Not. Fail."

"That pleases me. What say you about our brother Damien and his task?"

"I say fourteen days is too long. Surely he can secure them in less time."

The Prince shakes fear from his wings. "It will take some days before your war band is ready, General."

But Maka's muscled form is taut. He's not satisfied. "And the Sabres?"

The Prince places a pale white hand on Maka's massive black shoulder. "Their progress will be slow, friend. I know them well, and they will not risk harming the humans. We have time. But, Damien," he says, rounding on the fallen one, "come that fourteenth day, I will send the Palatine into Stratus to destroy the work of the Sabres. And I will have my prize whether you bring it to me or not."

"Yes, Lord Prince."

"Make your arrangements, then. And, Damien, keep your new eyes open. I imagine our old friend Michael won't be long."

Damien's wings falter. "Light is already on the move?"

The Prince shrugs. "If not, they will be soon."

"My lord?"

The Prince's pale eyes search the cliffs. "You are not so naïve as to believe our walls don't have ears, are you?"

Maka and Damien turn, following the Prince's gaze.

"If their King doesn't tell them, their Cherub will."

Pearla's legs tense.

"But what does it matter?" the Prince says. "The skies over Stratus will be ravaged. The boy with hands like ours and the girl who sees will be brought to me, yes? And the veil—"

"Will be restored." This time it's Maka who answers.

"Good, General Maka. This matter is now in your hands. Now go."

Pearla doesn't need to be asked again. Up, up, up and through the rocks, through the very earth itself she flies. Toward the Commander and the only army capable of handling the deadly forces of the Palatine.

4

Brielle

When I wake Sunday morning it's early. The sky's still black and my sheets are drenched with sweat. I take a raspy breath, but my chest feels tight, like my ribs are closing ranks. My heart presses against them, crowded.

It's the first nightmare I've had in months. The twilit morn paints smears of color on my wall. I stare at them, trying to remember the details, but everything's fuzzy.

A girl, her clothes torn, her skin burnt.

And fear. So much fear.

Shadows walk like men across my ceiling, and a shiver runs the length of my spine. The girl wasn't alone, but with my waking eyes I can't recall anything more. After another minute, I roll onto my stomach and press my hands beneath my pillow.

The halo's gone.

I reach for my side table, feeling with my fingers. I drop to the floor, my quilt tangled about my legs. My knee falls on something hard. Something hot. I feel it through the blanket. I must have knocked the halo to the floor. Before the nightmare or during? I don't know.

I shift and pull it from beneath my knee. There's not much light to be found, not much light for the halo to grab and reflect, but it seems to have found every bit of it. I slide it beneath my pillow and climb back onto the bed. The minute my head hits the pillow, colors swirl on the insides of my eyelids. Red and orange, blue and green, purple. Again and again, lulling, mesmerizing me until at last I'm asleep.

This time I don't dream.

But I don't sleep long either. A couple hours at most. When I wake, it's to the sound of the Beach Boys and the smell of bacon.

Dad's singing, which should really never happen. He drums dual spatulas on my quilt-covered bum for ninety-eight seconds solid before his rendition of "Surfer Girl" gets so bad I lose count. I curl into a ball, hoping to burrow through my mattress to a place where there are no singing, drumming lumberjacks.

But he's incorrigible.

"Stop drumming. Stop, stop, stop. I'll get up. I will. Hey! I will."

He ignores me, moving the spatulas down to the exposed soles of my feet, where they make a slapping sound. "Do you love me, do you, surfer girl? Surfer girl, my little surfer girl. Surfer girrrrlllll . . ."

"Please, please stop singing."

I throw the pillow over my head, but he continues on and I'm forced to plot his demise. My plan requires a well-aimed ninja-kick to distract him and catlike reflexes to grab the makeshift drumsticks. But he's fast for such a big guy, and the moment I throw my halfhearted kick, he's across the room, smiling at me from between the slots of a spatula.

"Mornin', baby," he says. "I made pancakes."

I shove the hair out of my face, trying to huff and puff, but I'm a sucker for pancakes.

"You know you want some."

I shove at the sheet and blanket, trying to find my legs. "Can I shower first?"

"Sure," he says, his red freckles brightened by his performance. "Made bacon too, but that's been disposed of." He taps the spatula against his brawny gut.

"That's all right," I say, finally freeing my right leg. "I've had more than enough ham this morning."

"Hardy har."

"Hardy har yourself. Now, out. Let me shower." Left leg's finally free. "And just so you know, I'll be mad at you until after I've had my first pancake. You put chocolate chips in them?"

"Nah, we ran out."

"Then I'll be mad until I've had at least two pancakes."

"Fair enough," he says, closing the door behind him.

I'm a mess, I feel it. My neck is sticky with dried sweat and my head aches. My sheets are knotted and my quilt's flipped sideways.

I hate waking up like a zombie. Especially the mean kind. I zone out for a sec, the poster above my desk catching my eye. The child Cosette stares back at me, the words *Les Misérables* a banner over her sorrow. It's my absolute favorite musical. There isn't a lick of dancing in the whole production, but something about it swirls in my gut, rallying me to the cause of freedom. I can't watch it without weeping, without feeling the need to sweep up a flag and wave it madly.

Ali tried to convince me to try out for it once, but there's so much singing. The whole glorious thing is singing. And, well, I sing like my dad, only with far less bravado and never, ever with spatulas.

Ali was brilliant as Eponine. I must've watched her onstage a zillion times during the run, but I'd do just about anything to watch her play it one last time.

I flick away the tear that's cooling on my lashes and move toward my desk. Something about the child Cosette pulls me closer. She hasn't changed, the girl. She's sweeping away just like always, but for a moment I see Olivia Holt. That same tragic expression Olivia had when our fingers brushed stares back at me from the battered child's eyes. I turn away, refusing to feel sorry for the drop-dead gorgeous woman who gets kicks out of parading her wealth before the less fortunate. I can't think of a single person who needs my pity less.

I unknot my sheets and make my bed, not because I'm dutiful, but because I need to ensure the halo's tucked under my pillow while I shower. It takes longer than it should for me to sort out the mess, but once I'm sure the halo's safe, I head to the bathroom, yawning and sticking my tongue out at Dad as I pass through the kitchen.

"You look beautiful, baby. That hair. Those eyes!"

A quick glance in the bathroom mirror and I see Dad and I are thinking the same thing.

That hair. Those eyes.

Ugh.

Twenty minutes later I'm sitting at the counter, wrapped in my fuzzy zebra-print robe, a Christmas gift from Kaylee. I cringed when I unwrapped it, but it's actually very cozy, and this morning it improves my mood by leaps and bounds. That and the sudden appearance of chocolate.

"Thought you said we were out of chocolate chips?"

"I had an old Hershey bar in my lunch box," he says, tucking the spatula in his back pocket and pouring a glass of milk.

"Can't even tell the difference," I say, my mouth full.

"That's because I'm good." He sets the glass next to my plate and leans into the counter. He *is* good. I dip a square of pancake into a blob of butter on the plate and slide it into my mouth. A few bites later I realize Dad's staring at me. Squinting, really, his bushy brows merging into one gigantic caterpillar.

"What's up, Dad?" I say, my mouth full.

"I have a date."

I chew slowly, thinking about that caterpillar—how I could flick it with my fork, the fork I still have in my hand, suspended over a plate of chocolate yumminess I suddenly have no appetite for. Dad's had dates before, of course, but I'm pretty sure I know who he's planning to take out. And I'm pretty sure I'm not going to like it.

"With Olivia. Olivia Holt."

I hear, *Bond. James Bond.* And I have to mentally slap myself before I start cataloging the similarities between the two.

I set my fork down and take a swig of milk. "Okay."

"Okay?"

I bob my head. What else am I going to say? He's not asking my permission, and he shouldn't have to. I hack at my pancake, cutting another pizza-shaped slice. It doesn't taste as good as the others, but I swallow it down.

Dad whips the spatula from his pocket and scratches at the dried batter on the griddle.

"You don't like her," he says.

"I don't know her."

He jabs the spatula in my direction. "But you still don't like her, do you?"

My stomach's all twisty and turny with this conversation. With the idea of my dad out with someone the halo clearly has qualms with. But crafting an answer to the question takes longer than it should, and now the bushy caterpillar is offended and all puckered across Dad's forehead.

"Why don't you like her?" he asks, flicking dried batter across the room.

Because the halo . . .

See, Dad, there's this Throne Room . . .

You remember God, right?

Yeah. This conversation's going places.

"You don't like her," he says. "I get it. You don't have to, Elle, but is it okay if I do?"

I set my fork down. There's still half a pancake steaming on my plate, but I'm done, my appetite officially dead with Dad's ridiculous request for permission. I should tell him he has my blessing or some other such nonsense. That's what I'd have done in the past. Heck, that's what I'd have done if the halo hadn't nearly blistered my arm yesterday.

But as kind—and superfluous—as my blessing would be, I still can't offer it. Not even as a sign of goodwill. It doesn't feel right.

"Dad . . ."

I can think of nothing to say, at least nothing appropriate. So I'm grateful when there's a knock at the door, Jake smiling at us through the windowpanes. Dad mutters something about needing a curtain on that blasted window, but Jake's standing there all handsome and clean-shaven. And that means . . .

"Oh geez. What time is it?"

Dad swings the spatula over his shoulder, wielding it like a weapon. "I'm guessing it's time for church."

Dang. I slide from the barstool and fling open the door.

"Five minutes," I say, pulling Jake inside. "Just five and I'll be ready."

"Good morning to you too," he says, all warm and smelling like coffee. He looks rather dashing in a green dress shirt, his eyes brighter for the color. I resist the urge to brush my lips against his, because Dad's already in a bad mood. "Good morning, Mr. Matthews."

Dad grunts and pours another pancake on the griddle. He hates that our Sunday morning routine has changed. Hates it.

"You coming with us this morning, sir?" Jake asks.

Oh, boyfriend. Oh, brave, brave boyfriend.

"Dad has a date," I say, trying my hardest to make it sound like *shut up*. I drag him to my barstool. "Sit. Eat a pancake. Three minutes, I swear."

I run from the kitchen, holding my robe closed. Jake's doing his best, trying to engage Dad, making small talk. I'd give most anything for the two of them to find some common ground, to find something neutral they can discuss. I whisper a prayer.

"So you have a date, huh?" Jake's voice carries through my bedroom door. "That's cool. You could bring her to church too, if you want."

I pray harder.

The first time I remember stepping foot into a church was this past Christmas. It was the same church, in fact, that Dad had recently helped repair. After a massive storm knocked an evergreen onto the roof, an improvised patch was thrown together until a roofing company could get a team out there—a team willing to work through the rain.

So that's how I spent my Christmas morning. Sitting between Jake and Canaan on a wooden pew that had suffered quite a bit of water damage itself. Dad wasn't happy about my interrupting our Christmas morning, but he didn't protest much. I asked him to come with us. I even begged a little, but he declined. Still, the look on his face wasn't nearly so bitter as it is these days.

Looking back on it, I think he figured my desire to attend stemmed from my crush on the new boy. And while there's an element of truth there, he had yet to understand how deep the transition truly was.

Even without Dad, that church service was an hour and a half I'll never forget.

I was nervous. I'd been dreading it, really. Christmas without Ali. I just wasn't sure I could do it, and I knew I couldn't tackle the day without celestial eyes. So I selected my outfit with careful precision: a black sweater dress with metallic silver threads woven into it over black tights. On my head was a beanie—a crocheted beret, really. But it had fancy silver buttons on the side and it looked dressy.

Underneath my cap, nestled snug to my crown, was Canaan's halo.

I didn't tell Jake or Canaan that I'd decided to wear it, and they didn't ask. But by the look of amusement on Canaan's face as we exited the building that day, he'd figured it out.

I'm not sure what I was expecting, but the minute we pulled into the parking lot I knew that I didn't know anything. Not about church or the people who filled the pews week after week. Nothing about this new family I'd suddenly become a part of. And while I've come to understand that no congregation is perfect, that one Christmas morning was enough to endear me to the people of God in a way that still breaks my heart.

I stepped out of the car, my hand warm inside Jake's, the world all fire and light to my celestial eyes. From atop the church strange tendrils of color curled. Like the wafting of incense, the bending colors lifted higher and higher, disappearing into the celestial sky.

I turned my eyes back to the building and focused. As I did, the stained-glass windows, the planters full of Christmas roses, the tarp tacked up to prevent rainfall from damaging the church further—all of it disappeared, and I saw the source of the spiraling wisps of color.

It was the pianist.

Stephanie something. Older than I was, but not by much. I'd seen her around—her mom owned the fabric store in town—but I'd never seen her like this. Her eyes were closed, her lips silent, but as her fingers struck each key, the music rose like campfire smoke into the sky.

And then I smelled it.

For the first time ever, I smelled adoration.

I smelled worship.

Deep and earthy. And sweet. Like the lily of the valley that blanketed Gram's front lawn, the fragrance spread through the sky with the intensity of her praise. I wondered if she had any idea how sweet her devotion was in the heavenlies. How fragrant, how honeyed, how pleasing.

The rest of the service brought many similar questions. So much to see and smell, to take in. To process. And through it all Jake was there on one side and Canaan on the other. They didn't try to explain; they didn't ask me if I was okay.

They let me see.

And that was enough. They kept busy worshiping alongside the other believers—believers who hadn't seen what I'd seen and had still chosen to follow.

Would I have believed if I hadn't seen?

It was a question I couldn't answer.

We shook hands with these other believers, learned their names.

And then I shed brand-new tears when the minister, Pastor Noah, stepped to the pulpit and opened his Bible. I've since learned that he's Dad's age, but with a clean-shaven chin and callous-free hands, Pastor Noah looked a good decade younger than my father. Until that morning, I thought the Christmas story began with "'Twas" and ended with "and to all a good night."

I'd seen nativity scenes, of course, and knew about baby Jesus and the Virgin Mary, but it was all so childish, so implausible.

But that morning I heard the story—I really heard it—the pastor shining like the great star above Bethlehem as he explained. I saw the truth of it in his eyes, in the eyes of the believers around me, and I understood why a Savior had to be born. I choked with joy as I played connect the dots with a series of Bible verses and finally understood just why that tiny baby had to grow up and die.

Every Sunday from then till now has been filled with the same wonder. I like the stories, especially the ones about angels, but I don't understand everything I hear or read. Canaan's been good to put things in historical context for me, and Jake's made it his mission in life to help me memorize Scripture. He says we've been given weapons and we have to know how to use them.

Try as I may, I can't imagine my words doing much to a demon. Not one so massive and terrifying as Damien. But there were a lot of things I couldn't imagine before. So I'm doing my best to learn.

Stephanie sits at the piano again this morning. The halo's on my wrist, so I'm not seeing or smelling the worship like I did that first Sunday, but I'm enamored nonetheless. I've never heard the song she's singing, but the words feel at home in my head and in my heart.

May the vision of you be the death of me. And even though you've given everything, Jesus come.

I don't sing. That would ruin the song entirely. But I close my eyes and imagine what these words would look like on the dance floor, what the melody would demand of my arms and legs, of my torso and the tilt of my head.

"Shane & Shane," Jake whispers quietly. "They wrote this." Shane & Shane is Jake's favorite band. He'll have a copy, then. Good, because I simply must dance to this.

After the service, Pastor Noah cuts through the crowd. He shakes Jake's hand and squeezes me lightly, leaving the scent of aftershave hanging about my shoulders.

"And Canaan?" he says. "Where is he this morning? I was hoping to have a word with him."

"He's working," Jake says. "Out of town for a couple days."

"Could you have him call me when he returns? I'd like his thoughts on something."

"Sure."

I make small talk with Becky, the pastor's wife, while Jake types Pastor Noah's number into his phone.

"We'd love to have you over again, Brielle," she says. "Your father, too, if he's up for it."

"Oh, thank you. I'd like that and, um, I'll let Dad know. You believe in miracles, right?"

"I do," she says with a laugh. "I absolutely do."

The ride home is quiet. I lean against Jake's shoulder, tired, the nightmare taking its toll. Sunlight presses through the dirty windows of his beat-up Karmann Ghia, settling around me like a blanket.

"You're making tired noises," Jake says.

"That's 'cause I'm tired. Didn't sleep very well last night."

"That's weird for you, isn't it?" he asks.

"I had a nightmare. First one since the halo, I think."

"And you had it with you?"

"I put it under my pillow like I always do, but this morning it was on the ground. Probably knocked it off the bed."

Jake's quiet, and that means he's thinking. Dissecting. Trying to solve the Rubik's cube of life.

"Don't overanalyze, okay? I had a busy day. I was restless."

But Jake doesn't look convinced. "You've never been restless before with the halo."

"Canaan said I'd eventually grow more accustomed to it, right? That it won't always affect me so intensely."

He scans my face. "Yeah, I guess. If it happens again, though . . ."

"You'll be the first to know."

"Thank you." He kisses my forehead and then settles back in the seat. "You going to nap the day away then?"

"I wish. I told Kay I'd meet her at Jelly's for lunch. You want to come?"

"I can't," he says. "Phil called. They need me at work."

"Again?" Between my classes and his extra shifts we haven't had much time together, and I'm all needy and crave-y right now. We could use a date. I nestle closer, trying to hold on to the last minutes I'll have with him today. "So does that mean no surprise?"

"Would you mind waiting? I could give it to you now, but—"

"No, you're right. I'd rather have time to thank you adequately. You have time for a quick bite at least?"

He kisses my forehead again, apologetic. "I have to be there at one."

I groan, but only a little. It's not his fault they're shorthanded, and if the Throne Room is to be trusted, we'll have the rest of our lives to be together.

"Good thing you had pancakes for breakfast."

"Yeah," he says, his shoulder suddenly rigid, "good thing."

I roll my face toward his, loving the feel of his shirt against my cheek, but hating whatever emotion suddenly has his face in a choke hold.

"What, you don't like my dad's pancakes?"

A muscle in his cheek twitches, but he says nothing. He pulls his beater onto our gravel driveway and parks it behind Dad's truck. I sit up, preparing myself for whatever's bubbling behind the silence.

"What's going on, Jake?"

It's another minute before he says anything, his fingers deathly still on my leg.

"Your dad hates me."

The words are flat. There's no anger in them, but I don't need the halo on my head to see the storm brewing in Jake's eyes. Dad's really gotten to him.

"I'm sorry about this morning. He can be a jerk sometimes. He doesn't like change, and having his Sundays interrupted is like the—"

"It's not just this morning. It's . . . Canaan's seen fear on your dad. He's seen it multiply when he looks at me."

Dad afraid of Jake? The thought is ludicrous. "Jake, this—"

"Have you seen it? The fear—have you seen it on your dad?" There's something of an accusation in his tone, and it irritates me.

"I see fear on *everyone*, Jake, all the time. I've seen fear on Kaylee when she's scrubbing a table at Jelly's, for crying out loud. I see fear on the pizza delivery guy and the mailman. I've seen it on Miss Macy. Jake, I've seen fear on you."

He blanches, but I press a hand to his chest, doing my best to still his thundering heart.

"*Everyone's* afraid of something. But I swear to you, I've never seen anything excessive on Dad. Nothing that he hasn't just shrugged off. If Canaan's seen it—"

"He has."

"It's not you," I say, squeezing his hand. "It's not you at all. It's . . . when he looks at you he sees . . ."

"God," Jake says, his voice quiet. "And your dad hates God. He hates that your mom put her trust in God and then she died."

I shift, moving away from him, from words that wedge into my ribs. I've come to grips with the reality that I may never understand my mom's death, but it still hurts when it's put out there like that. That for whatever reason God chose not to heal my mom.

"He thinks you trust your mom's God because I do. He can't see me without thinking of your mom. Without thinking of her death."

The car feels smaller. All this talk of death and hate, suffocating.

"I think you're overstating things a bit," I say, finding a shaky version of my voice. "I'm his daughter—the only one he has. He's jealous of my time and overprotective."

"No, it's more than that." Jake shakes his head. Fear is invisible to me without the halo in place, but I hear it in his words, see it in the heaviness of his shoulders. "Canaan's overprotective. Your dad's got a vendetta or . . ."

He looks at me, really looks at me. I'm not sure what it is he's seeing, but the hard shell of frustration that so quickly encased him begins to melt away. The rigidity leaves his arms and neck, and he hangs his head.

"I'm sorry," he says. "It's not you."

"Of course it's me. Dad's a part of me, of who I am." I run a finger from his ear down his jawline, wishing I could make this better for him. He closes his eyes at my touch, tiny bead-like tears pressing through his lashes. My heart breaks, and I press my lips to his. "I'm sorry this is so hard. I'm sure he'll . . ."

"Come around?" Jake finishes. "But what if he doesn't?"

Jake and I both know I could never walk away from Dad. I'm all he has. And I can't even contemplate the other alternative.

"He will," I say. I try to be adamant, but my words quaver.

Jake strokes my hand, his head bowed, wet lashes curling gently against his cheek. So warm, so close. But there's something between us now. The beginnings of a wall, and I don't know how to tear it down.

"I don't want you to have to choose between me and your dad, Elle. We have enough battles to fight." There's something strange in his tone. Something that sounds like surrender.

But that can't be right. Jake's a fighter.

"There's room in my life for both of you, and if the Throne Room's right, I won't have to choose."

Jake goes pale, his hands clammy against mine. He pulls them away and wipes them on his pants. There are mere inches between us, but fear put them there. And I hate fear. It's my hatred that fights back.

"You have my engagement ring next door, hand-delivered to you by the Throne Room of God Himself." My voice is all high and squeaky. But I need him to hear me. I need him to fight the fear. "Why are we even talking about this?"

Jake licks his lips. "Because your dad—"

"That's not it. It can't be. You knew my dad had issues with God. You've known for half a year, Jake." My throat is tight, sucking on the emotion of the moment. "You never said it was a deal breaker."

Something shifts then. I feel it in my chest, in the fear dissolving around us. Jake leans across the seat, conviction in the russet flames that burn deep in his eyes. Their fire tugs at my skin, at my heart, pulling me closer, reducing the distance between us. He's fighting it.

"There is no deal breaker, Elle. One day I *will* ask you to marry me whether your dad likes it or not."

I lean my forehead against his, relieved. "Then why all the angst?"

I breathe him in. He smells like he always does, like coffee laced with sugar. Like adventure. Like safety.

Like the rest of my life.

I inhale it all.

And then an elephant lands on the roof of the car.

5

Brielle

I think your dad's going to eat my car."

Jake's face has lost all of its color. He's looking over my shoulder and out the passenger-side window.

"It's not your car he's glaring at," I say.

The pounding stops, but Dad is just standing there, his face all irritation and bristling whiskers. He's . . . off. Something's wrong with him. Against the yellow house a shimmer of red catches my attention. Olivia Holt drops gracefully down our porch steps. Her long legs bare, the hint of khaki shorts peeking out beneath her silky red blouse.

"If you're done with my daughter," Dad says, "could you move this piece of junk?"

I can do nothing but stare gape-mouthed. Dad's always been protective, always been uncomfortable around Jake, but this isn't like him. Dad can be a roughneck, but he's not rude. At least not usually. It's hard to imagine him treating anyone this way, especially someone I care about. Especially Jake.

"What?" Dad asks. "I'm just trying to back my truck out here."

"See. Hate," Jake whispers.

"Something's wrong with him," I say, my eyes falling on Olivia once again. I'm straining, trying to figure out how she messed Dad up so badly in two short hours. "I'd better go."

"Yeah. I'll call you later," Jake says, his face a mess of sad and awkward. I want to fix it, make him feel better, but I can't do anything with Dad's fist hovering over the car. "You better go. He's not getting any happier."

No, he's not.

I step from the car with every intention of throwing a massive tantrum, but as Jake backs down the driveway, I catch sight of his face. His lips are moving furiously. He's praying. For me. For Dad. Probably for himself a little too.

So instead of rising to the occasion, I hook my finger through the halo on my wrist and say a silent prayer myself. I can't think of anything nice to say to Dad, so like a good girl I won't say anything at all. But when I try to step past him, I catch a whiff that stops me cold.

"Have you been drinking?"

"We had a couple beers," Dad says. "Why?"

Olivia loops her arm through Dad's. The sun streaks her hair; a world of bright color lies in those dark strands. It's only then that I realize how young she is. She has the appearance of maturity, looks like she's lived some, but she's closer to my age than Dad's. I turn my attention back to him.

"Because it's noon," I say.

I refuse to hide my disgust. He's had drinking issues before, back when I was in junior high. It almost cost him the company, but he swore he'd taken care of that.

"It's noon on a Sunday, love." Olivia breaks away from Dad and moves closer. "Your dad's all right. Just enjoying his weekend."

I step away, sliding my hands into the wide pockets of my skirt. It's a gesture her dark eyes don't miss.

"That's a beautiful bracelet," she says. "Where'd you get it?"

"Why?"

"Elle," Dad says, his voice a warning.

Olivia laughs, all teeth and throat. "Because it's lovely. I think I'd like one."

"Her boyfriend gave it to her," Dad says, his eyes hard. "Can you believe that?"

Olivia taps her teeth with a crimson nail. "Boys don't give their girlfriends trinkets like that, love."

"That's what I told her," Dad says.

"Not unless they want something in return," she finishes.

I look to Dad, hoping he'll jump in, defend my honor, but he just raises his eyebrows, a stupid drunken grin on his face.

"I have to go," I say. "I'm meeting Kay."

"Tell her I'll call tomorrow, will you? So many ideas to chat about. Can't wait to really dig my hands into Stratus, you know?"

I don't know, actually, but something about the gleam in her eye tells me I should. I should want to know exactly what she's planning to do with Stratus. But right now I need to get away. From her. From Dad.

I run up the driveway, my sandals sending gravel flying like shrapnel. It peppers my bare legs, but I don't slow. I stomp up the porch stairs and fling open the kitchen door. When I've slammed it behind me, I sink to the floor and yank my sandals off. One at a time, I dig out the rocks that have wedged themselves between my toes.

And I cry. I do. I'm a crier. I wish I wasn't, but I am.

And that's when I hear it.

The music.

Every note pitch-perfect. The arrangement unearthly. So unearthly I tug the halo off my wrist and wait as it transforms into the crown. "Come on, come on."

Finally!

I jump to my feet, the halo on my head. With a slow build of heat and color, the Celestial comes into view, and with heavenly eyes I see the worship. My house is full of it. Ice-blue tendrils curl through the blazing air around me, filling my kitchen. They press against the walls, lifting higher and higher, slipping through the ceiling and into the sky above. I spin, looking for the source of the song, but I can't find it.

I run through the house, holding the halo tight to my head, looking for the rogue worshiper, looking for the maker of such beautiful music. I run through the archway and into the living room, down the hallway that takes me past the bathroom and the laundry room. I step into Dad's room, but there's nothing. Just the incense of worship tangling together as the music continues on, note after breathtaking note.

A door slams.

"Brielle?"

It's Dad.

Shoot. I'm standing in the doorway of my own room, my hands still on the halo. I yank it from my head, wincing at the hair I've torn away. It starts transforming immediately, but it's not moving nearly fast enough, so I toss it onto my bed and pull my door shut before ducking back into the kitchen.

"Dad? What are you doing? Where's Olivia?" I'm talking too fast, my body reeling from the abrupt transfer back to all things Terrestrial, but Dad doesn't seem to notice.

"She's in the truck. You seen my wallet?"

I pluck it from the counter and hand it to him.

"Thanks, kiddo."

And then I watch as his face turns pale.

"Dad, what's wrong?"

His legs buckle and he stumbles, grabbing a barstool for support. I run to his side and duck under his arm, putting mine around his waist. "Are you going to be sick?"

My dad is not a small man, so when he swoons on his feet my knees buckle at the added weight.

"Let's sit, Dad. I'm going to lower you to the floor, okay?"

But then he straightens up. "No, I just . . . I thought I heard . . ."

My heart stutters, and I strain my ears, listening for the music, but it's gone.

"You thought you heard what?"

"Nothing," he says. "I didn't hear anything." He grabs a dish towel from the counter and swipes it across his face, barking a hollow laugh. "Maybe you're right. Noon might be too early to start drinking."

"You think?"

"I'm sorry about before. With your boyfriend." He smiles, but it's plastic and the corners tremble. "I'm all right, baby. Don't worry about me. I'll just . . . I'll have Olivia drive."

"Dad, I don't think you should go. You need to lie down."

He leans into me and presses his lips to my temple. The alcohol on his breath turns my stomach, but I stand still, let him kiss me.

"I'm fine."

He turns his back on me, every dish in the cupboards ringing with the slamming of the door.

6

Jake

It's late. Work was rough. Another crew member laid off and double the pictures to process. Jake doesn't mind the extra work, but watching a friend and coworker plead with their boss not to let him go, to let him stay on—just a few hours a week—was heartrending. The guy's meager wages are the only thing putting him through college.

It's been like this all summer—his boss, Phil, laying off one crew member at a time. "Tightening the belt," he said. Understandable with the economy the way it is, but any hiccup in the schedule means Jake gets called in to cover a shift. The pay sucks, but he doesn't mind the Photo Depot. He likes Phil, likes the quaint feel of downtown Stratus. Truth be told, he's never really felt at home like he does here.

But he's got that feeling again, the one he gets whenever Canaan's assignment requires a new zip code. It's a nervous itch that tells him change is coming. And for the first time, he can actually imagine telling Canaan he'd rather not go. That he'd like to stay here, start a life in Stratus. With Brielle.

Canaan would be fine with it—they've talked about this

day. But for it to work Jake would have to find a place of his own and a job that paid substantially better than the Photo Depot. But instead of applying to colleges or looking for a better job, Jake spent the last semester of senior year waiting.

And waiting.

And tonight he'd like nothing better than to crawl under the pile of laundry on his bed and sleep, but the fear inside his gut compels him to do just one last thing before turning in. He climbs the steps to the old Miller place—the farmhouse he and Canaan share—and opens the door. Unlocked as always. Shadows swim on the walls and carpet, but the house is mostly dark. He drops his car keys on the kitchen table as he passes and swipes an apple from the bowl. Then he thinks better of it and puts it back. Checking the chest always turns his stomach. Even now he can feel a tight ball of anxiety growing behind his ribs. He's fairly certain Canaan's not home, but habit has him knocking on Canaan's bedroom door. When there's no answer, he pushes it open and steps inside.

The white bed and black side table, the wrought iron bed frame that twists to the ceiling, the photo of the dove. It's all there, but Jake sees only the onyx chest at the foot of the bed. He moves toward it, anxious. Hoping.

Canaan's blinds are open and starlight slips through, painting the room in shades of gray. Beneath the hazy light the chest ebbs, its darkness alive. Jake opens the chest every day, every morning before leaving the house, but tonight he could use a little good news. After the disastrous run-in with Brielle's dad and a heartsick night at work, he needs something of hope to cling to.

Jake drops to his knees, running a tired hand down his face.

In one swift motion, he leans forward and lifts the lid. And the fear burrows deeper.

Damien's dagger is still there.

Brielle's ring is still missing.

He cracks his neck and mutters a desperate, rambling kind of prayer.

He's so tired of waiting.

He stares at the seven-inch blade, crusted with Brielle's blood, wishing he could change what he sees.

But he can't.

He can only wait. And pray.

And hope the Throne Room won't take away the one person in the world he actually needs. But waiting and praying, hoping even, were much easier to do seven months ago. As the months passed, fear set in. He's ashamed of it. Of the fear. Because it's not a fear of demons or death. It's not a fear of disease or pain.

He fears the Throne Room.

He fears the path his heavenly Father has placed before him.

It's a fear that he shouldn't feed. But he does. Every day he opens the chest, looking for the ring, for the hope that there will be a tomorrow for him and Brielle.

But all he finds is death—her death—and the fear digs a little deeper, costs him a little more.

It's a fear that Brielle can see. And it mortifies him that his cowardice is displayed so openly before her. He lifts the lid back in place and stands.

"Anything?" It's Canaan, returned from wherever the Throne Room had him today. He's been leaving Jake behind more often, allowing him to put down roots in Stratus. Jake understands and he's grateful. One day their time together may cease entirely, and it's only right that Jake prepare for that day. But with the silence of the Throne Room and Canaan's frequent absences, it's lonelier in this house than it used to be.

"Just the dagger," Jake says.

He feels his jaw tighten at the word, wishes he could maintain the calm self-control Canaan has mastered. Even now, his Shield's face is devoid of strain or stress, his brow free of lines. Jake misses the comfort of before, the calm of not worrying about the future. But would he trade that peace for Brielle?

No, he wouldn't.

He couldn't.

"The rumors still have Damien suffering the pit," Canaan says. "He and Javan both."

Jake turns. It's been awhile since he's heard anything about the fallen ones who targeted him last year. "And the others? Maka and the Twins?"

Canaan loosens the tie at his neck and leans against the door frame. In a suit and tie, he could be any one of a million other corporate employees home from a hard day at the office.

"I wish I knew. They're higher in the Prince's esteem. Information is harder to come by."

The air conditioner shuts off, and a new level of quiet falls around them.

"The Throne Room is cryptic, Jake. Rarely do things signify exactly what they seem to."

"A diamond engagement ring isn't at all cryptic."

Canaan steps toward him, his silver eyes holding nothing but concern for Jake. "The ring helped us understand Brielle's role and your future affections for her. It allowed us to act in faith, knowing that one day you two would be one. It served a purpose."

"And its absence. What purpose does that serve?"

Canaan puts a hand on his shoulder. "Maybe nothing."

Jake steps past him into the hall. He's tired. He doesn't want to argue.

"Jake," Canaan calls after him. "Keep an eye on Olivia Holt."

Jake turns back. "Yeah?"

"I asked around today, at the foundation, at her offices downtown. The reactions ranged from bewitched awe to terrified silence. She has a reputation for getting what she wants."

Jake thinks back to this afternoon, to the look on Brielle's face when Olivia materialized on her porch. And he remembers something she told him on the way to church, something he wasn't sure how to process.

"Brielle said the halo responded strangely to Olivia. That it flashed hot all of a sudden. Is that—is that normal?"

"The halo is a mysterious thing, Jake. I don't understand how or why it does any of the things it does. She said it flashed hot?"

"Her exact words."

Canaan is quiet. Thinking.

"Olivia was next door today," Jake says. "With Keith. The halo spooked Brielle pretty bad. I don't think she likes Olivia much, but Mr. Matthews seems to enjoy her company."

Canaan chuckles, but there's no humor in it.

"Sounds about right. Eyes open, Jake. She wants something, and I don't imagine it's Keith Matthews."

7

Brielle

aylee's waiting for me on Tuesday when I wrap up my tap class. I'm working to detangle one of my teeny tiny dancers from the stereo cord when I see Kay standing in the doorway. I have to laugh. She's on the carpeted side staring at the hardwood dance floor like a first-time swimmer about to launch into the deep.

"You can come in, Kay. The water's fine."

"This place terrifies me," she says, watching my students file past her and into the arms of their parents waiting out front.

"Why?"

"Everyone here's all coordinated and stuff." *Coordinated* gets air quotes.

"Not everyone," I say, winking at the little dancer I've finally freed from the stereo.

Kay and I leave the studio, crossing the street and heading up Main. We pass The Donut Factory and the Photo Depot. Jake's inside, his head bent over his work. I'm tempted to feign some sort of dramatic predicament just to pull him away—we've done nothing but text since Sunday—but I settle for knocking on the window and waving. Of course, Kay's not content with that. She presses her face to the glass, leaving a smear of lip gloss that someone will have to clean up later. Probably Jake. But he laughs at her and smiles at me. His eyes linger, making me reconsider that dramatic predicament idea. But I'll see him tonight. We have plans. And according to the text he sent me at 3:14 this afternoon, he has that surprise all ready for me.

Kaylee tugs me on. We pass a real estate office and the Auto Body before turning down a side street that will take us up to the community center. I heft my duffel bag higher on my shoulder and let her step in front of me as we approach the center. I love Kaylee dearly, but she hasn't shut up about the wonderment that is Olivia Holt. I just nod and blink, a realization setting in as we climb the steps to the front door.

Getting rid of Olivia isn't going to be an easy thing. Her money's found a home here, the city council is practically falling all over themselves for her time, and closer to home, Kaylee is madly in love with anything and everything the woman touches.

"I have to show you what Liv got donated for your dance classes, but first things first." Kaylee makes a big sweeping gesture with her arms, and I look up. "Meet Teddy."

We're in a foyer of sorts. To the right is Kaylee's office. To the left are the bathrooms, and there above the entrance to the multipurpose room is what appears to be the head of a dead animal.

I squint into his marble eyes. "What is it, exactly?"

"I don't really know," she says. "It's like a deer or a moose. Maybe a yak. I really have no idea. I bet your dad would know."

"I bet he would," I say, tilting my head. "His nose is too wide or something."

"I know. And the antler thingys are gigantic."

Our laughter echoes off the walls, and a scissor-wielding scrapbooker pokes her head out of a room to our right.

"Sorry, ladies," Kaylee says, lowering her voice. "So, Teddy. The mayor had him installed yesterday. Some kind of tribute to the history of the center. I guess he used to hang in the Elks Club that was here before us."

"He's an elk!" I say.

She gasps, "He is!"

This time our laughter is silenced by a man in an apron. "Sorry, sorry. How are the muffins turning out, Mr. Hamilton?"

Kaylee pulls me across the basketball court and onto the stage, the same stage I danced on Saturday afternoon.

She makes another mad gesture with her hands. "Aren't they awesome?" She's talking about the portable ballet barres lined up in the wings. "I don't have a clue what to do with them, but Liv says they'll be helpful for your class."

I frown at them, at just how much easier they'll make our volunteer efforts here at the center.

"Oh gosh, Elle. They'll be helpful, right? Are they all wrong? I should have asked you first."

I put a hand on her arm, stilling her, stopping the panic. "They're perfect. They're just perfect. Tell Olivia thank you."

That last sentence cost me. I smile bravely for Kay.

"You can tell her yourself. Tomorrow."

"What's tomorrow?"

"Fourth of July, crazy. We're doing a picnic thing out at the lake. Liv said you and your dad were coming."

Liv said? Why is she speaking for my family? I scratch at my nose, irritated. But I'd forgotten tomorrow was the Fourth, and there are no plans to fall back on. "I didn't know anything about it," I say.

"Oh, please say you'll come! I already talked Delia into closing Jelly's for the day. And I bought her a bathing suit."

"Oh my. I've never even seen Delia's legs."

"Right. It's time she unleashed them upon the world. So see, I'm invested in this thing—fifty-four dollars—and if you don't come it's going to be me and a bunch of old people."

"Olivia's not that old, Kay."

"Please, please, please."

"Okay. Sure. Of course. I mean, Dad and I usually spend the Fourth together, so if he wants to set off fireworks at the lake, I guess I'm in. I'm just . . . I'm not a huge fan of Olivia."

"Because she's canoodling your dad? I totally get that, but I swear you'll love her. You just have to get to know her. She's got these ideas on how to secure donations and raise money. She's a mad scientist, you know? She knows how to push buttons and get folks to cough up cash. And her ideas . . ."

"I get it, Kay. She's got ideas."

"Yes! Ideas!"

8

Brielle

Jake's sitting on the porch swing when I pull into the drive in Mom's old bug. I slide Slugger into Park and climb out wondering how many more trips down Main she can handle. She's a 1967 Volkswagon Beetle with a rusted rack on top. Dad's done everything he can to keep in her shape, but she's starting to sound a little tired. I pat her hood gently and make my way toward Jake.

His hair's damp and he's changed out of his work clothes. He looks relaxed, much more relaxed than the last time I saw him. The swing moves slowly as he thumbs through his old Bible. I love that thing. It's old—really, really old. The paper has yellowed and the leather has cracked, but he continues to cram the margins with words I can't decipher, his handwriting's so bad.

We still haven't talked about the thing with my dad— just cryptic text messages conveying our undying devotion in the face of adversity. I hate texting. It's all so melodramatic in tone and underwhelming in content. Nothing like seeing him face-to-face.

"Hey," Jake says, smiling at me, closing the Bible.

"Hey." I drop my dance bag at the foot of the stairs and climb toward him. I'm still wearing my dance clothes, but Jake doesn't seem at all offended by that. "Whatcha reading?"

"A story from the book of Acts. Philip and the Ethiopian. Have you read it?"

"Haven't gotten there yet," I say, climbing onto the swing.

"One of my favorites. Angel fingerprints all over it."

"Do angels leave fingerprints?"

"I don't think so, no."

"So you were being histrionic."

"I don't know what that means," he says, smirking. "But I was being figurative."

"Ah."

"Speaking of histrionic," I say. "I really am sorry about my dad."

Jake kicks off the ground, swinging us back and forth. He takes my hand in his, running his index finger down each one of mine. I let him, relishing the butterflies dancing like idiots in my tummy. I wonder if we'll have a porch swing one day. If we'll do this every night till we're a hundred.

"You heard me, right? I was apologizing for my dad."

"I heard you," he says, turning toward me. I love the darkness of his brows juxtaposed with the brightness of his eyes. A brilliant green iris with a tawny starburst exploding at the center. "And you don't have to apologize for him. Look, Elle, I don't have many good things about my dad to cling to. In fact, I don't even know his last name. My real last name."

I feel the shock on my face. "I never realized. I thought you took Shield to avoid questions."

"It helped, but if I ever knew it, I forgot. It's been a pain lately because I've been looking into possible connections between Marco and myself, but it's near impossible without a last name."

"I'm so sorry, Jake. That's hard."

"It's fine, and I didn't mean to change the subject. What I'm trying to say is that I envy what you and your dad have. You're close, and that's rare. I don't want to mess that up. I don't want you to have to choose between us, between family and me."

"You *are* family," I say, wishing he'd relax again. Wishing he'd smile. "At least you will be soon enough."

"Right," he says, his eyes searching my face. "Soon enough."

"Tell me you won't worry about my dad, please."

"Okay," he says. "I won't worry about your dad. Not tonight."

"Good. Thank you."

He stops the swing. "I, um, meant to tell you. Marco's home . . . er, here."

"Is that my surprise?" I ask. "I had no idea he was coming home today."

"No, Marco's not your surprise. I didn't know either. He was crashed out on the couch when I got back from work today."

"You really should lock your door."

"If I had, Marco would have been sleeping on my doorstep."

"Where is he now?" I ask.

"Ran into town to pick up a few things. Canaan's making dinner, and I wanted to invite you."

"I'd love to. Let me change, okay?"

"You don't have to," he says, a sly smile tugging at his lips. "I like tutus, remember?"

"This," I say, standing, twirling, "is not a tutu. It's a skirt."

"There's a difference?"

"Yes. Tutus aren't soft."

I lean in for a kiss, but he makes me wait for it.

"You don't like soft?" I ask, brushing my lips against his.

He closes his eyes, a sound deep in his chest answering for him.

"I like soft," I say, our exhales mingling. But he remains still, his self-control far too refined for my taste. So I stand and turn toward the door.

He grabs my wrist and pulls me against him. The porch swing squeals in protest, but I get my kiss. Or two.

Or twelve.

Canaan goes all out at dinner. Grilling up prime rib and corn on the cob, sprucing up potatoes and concocting a fruity iced tea drink.

"These things must be celebrated," he says.

For his part, Marco is fairly subdued. Quiet and calm. His dragon-green eyes clear, clearer than I've ever seen them, actually. His hair is shorter, and he's gained back some of the weight he lost during his imprisonment.

"Why didn't you tell us you were coming home?" I ask.

The four of us are at the kitchen table, reaching across one another for second helpings.

"It happened pretty quick. Last week the doc said he'd submitted a good report to the authorities, and this morning I woke to the news that the state was satisfied and now considered the matter closed."

"Wow, just like that?" I ask.

"Yeah, just like that."

"You weren't guilty of the charges," Jake says. "There's no reason for the state to insist you stay any longer if the doctor's satisfied."

"That, and they finally got that Eddie punk talking. His parents had him lawyered up, I guess. Took the DA forever to unravel all the details, but once Eddie started talking, the state was able to put the pieces together. They found Horacio's body in a separate warehouse, along with evidence that people had been held there against their will. They're trying to gather enough information on Damien to start an official manhunt."

I swallow the corn that's been sitting on my tongue, refusing to make eye contact with anyone but Marco.

"Well, I wish them luck," Canaan says. "I imagine catching someone like Damien would be a difficult task."

After dinner, Canaan steps out. Says he needs to check in at work, whatever that means. I imagine he's circling the skies over Stratus. I imagine he does that a lot.

Jake clears the table, leaving Marco and me to talk.

"I wanted to show you something, Elle," he says, standing and moving to the living room. "You have a sec?"

"Sure." I follow, watching as he pulls a blue-and-gray backpack up next to him on the couch and unzips it.

"Jake's got a bag just like that," I say.

"Not surprised. There were only three options at the sports store on Main, and one of them had a purple kitty cat on it. Anyway"—he pulls out a small leather journal, Ali's journal—"Ali's mom contacted me at the psych hospital."

"Did she? That's awesome."

"Well, don't get too excited. They haven't agreed to see me, but she sent a card telling me they finally had the gravestone placed." He opens the journal, flipping to the last quarter of the book, to empty pages Ali hadn't gotten to.

Just the sight of all the days she'll never have, all the journal entries she'll never make, has my chest tight.

"What happened here?" I ask, running my finger along a half-inch strip of frayed paper near the seam. Several pages have been torn out.

"I don't know," he says. "Blank pages on either side. I never could figure it out." He keeps flipping. "Here. I didn't have my camera with me, but I did the best I could."

It's the sketch of a cemetery, of gravestones and trees. Of flowers and benches. It's a place I've only been to once, but I can easily spot it in the lines of Marco's sketch. I touch my finger to the place I stood at her funeral, under an umbrella, alone in my guilt and misery. He turns the page once more, showing me a sketch of Ali's grave marker.

A ridiculous sort of laugh erupts from my throat. "Oh man, she'd hate that."

A half smile emerges on Marco's face. "That's what I thought too. Rich people," he says, shaking his head. The gravestone is huge. A gigantic stone tower formed into a triangular point at the tip top. "But look, I thought you'd like to see the engraving."

I lean toward the page, reading the words Marco penned on the bottom of the monument.

ALISON MARIE BENI

OCTOBER 18, 1993 – NOVEMBER 5, 2011

THERE IS SPECIAL PROVIDENCE IN THE FALL OF A SPARROW.

I run my finger over the words. "It's Hamlet," I say, my voice quiet.

Marco's lips twist, his cheeks wet with tears. "Yeah. I know you two used to run Shakespeare quotes. Thought maybe you had something to do with this."

I shake my head. "I didn't. I haven't spoken to Serena in a long time. Not since the day after the warehouse."

Marco closes the journal, wrapping the long leather strands around it and tying Ali's memories away. He looks at me, swiping away the tears that have made it all the way to his chin.

"Providence, I guess."

9

Pearla

The Cherub can't help it. Questions ravage her mind, but her soul longs to sing. So she does. Pearla's childlike voice is soft, effortless. The frenzy of her wings masks the sound, but she knows He hears and that's all that matters.

She flies low, the sea churning beneath her. Blues of every shade sparkle in the light of the Celestial, illuminated by the Creator of all things. His glory bursts from within the waves and without, reflecting, bouncing off the water and bending across the sky in an enchanting show of color. Her dark skin grabs onto the light, pulling it with her in a dazzling shimmer across the Atlantic.

In the distance she sees land. Sandy shores and tall leaning trees. Palms waving in the wind. She presses high into the sky and flies on. The coastal villages give way to expansive plains of undulating yellow grasses spotted by the occasional acacia. Migrating creatures, great and small, move in chunky swathes, crossing the Serengeti. Abruptly, the glory of the savannah vanishes, swallowed by a thick, emerald rainforest. Thunder shakes the sky, and a twisting river of deepest bronze cuts through it all, disappearing beneath the lush canopy of the Congo.

And then she stops, her tiny wings skittering like a hummingbird's, keeping her in place. Before her, emerging from the horizon, is the Army of Light. Not all of it, of course, but the host who travel always with Michael, their commander.

Michael rides out front, his steed a blaze of red and gold. The Commander lifts his javelin, and in turn the flag bearers leading the troops raise their banners high. Three thousand angelic horses halt, their riders' obedience instantaneous.

A legion of angelic Warriors stare at the Cherub. From this distance there's not much to distinguish her from the black enemy of darkness.

Pearla moves forward cautiously, her eyes wide open on approach. She carries no weapon—her speed and her size are all the protection she needs. But it's the white light of her eyes that will identify her as an ally. She knows the moment the Commander sees them. Knows the very second her features can be discerned. She knows it because Michael too becomes clearer in her sight. The creases around his eyes and mouth melt into the luminescence of his skin. His shoulders, armored in thick battle gear, relax and his spear comes down. He kicks lightly with his heels, pushing the faithful creature forward. The steed snorts and gallops ahead, his hooves lost in the atmosphere that birthed him.

Humans rarely think of the spiritual realm as a physical thing, with streets and buildings and beings who can touch and be touched. But the Celestial is every bit as physical as the Terrestrial—if anything, its physicality is even more demanding than the realm they see.

The skyscrapers and bridges of earth, her mountains and lakes—they do not cease to exist in the heavenly realm. It's true anything without a soul can be passed through, but to angelic fingers it can all be grasped, held on to, and thrown. The angelic mind works quickly, the decision to pass through a wall or to lean against it second nature. It's subconscious, instinctual, like a chameleon changing colors. But even here, in the realm for which they were created, there are things they can't do.

The Cavalry, for instance, is gifted with a single set of wings. Rarely abandoning the deep trenches of battle, they have no need to cloak themselves or others. The sinewy inner wings held by the ranks of the Shield and the Herald are not necessary. Instead, they are armed with a pair of large arching wings that tower several feet above their heads. Strong, powerful wings to carry strong, powerful angels. But even formidable wings tire. So the Creator gifted his army with a race of noble steeds. They are an extension of the Warriors themselves—a band of horses born of light, emerging from it when needed and diving beneath the surface, like creatures of the deep, when their presence becomes unnecessary. Never has a warhorse known the minds and needs of its riders like these. Never far from their rider. Ever as near as the Warrior's next breath of celestial air.

Certain Michael has identified her, Pearla speeds her wings, meeting him halfway. He stows his javelin in the scabbard at his back and swings off his mount. His wings snap wide, catching a gust of light and wind. He moves them softly, keeping him in place. Slivers of wheat-colored hair jut from beneath his helmet, mingling with a downy beard cut close to his chin.

"You are fast, little one."

"Not nearly as fast as I'd hoped. I thought to join you for the coronation."

"All went as planned. The malevolent Dominion of Uganda

has been uprooted, replaced by one of our own. We've left a small contingent behind, and the Shield are receiving orders now."

Testimonies like this are why she exists. Why she flies to and fro. Success on such an expansive level fills her with adoration.

"Holy, holy," Pearla begins. Her commander finishes with her: "Holy is the Lord of hosts."

"Indeed," he says. Michael's steed bumps his nose against Pearla's small shoulder.

"Hello, Loyal." She reaches out a small hand and scratches his nose.

"He's missed you. But tell me, Cherub, how fares Abaddon?"

"There's movement, Commander."

"The Palatine?"

"Yes. They make for the skies over Stratus, Oregon."

The wrinkles return to Michael's brow. "Of the American Northwest?"

"Yes."

"Reports have their general suffering the pit for his loss here. Whose command are they under now?"

"General Maka."

Michael's face and neck flash red and then fade quickly. "The assembly wasn't just a diversion, then. If the dragon's sent Maka, he sees Stratus as a threat. Did he allude—"

"Yes, sir," she interrupts. "One of the Fallen has made contact with a boy who heals."

This news doesn't surprise the Commander as much as Pearla assumed it would.

"He's not the first."

"He's not," she agrees. "But according to the fallen one— Damien by name—the boy's hands share the same grace as ours. Healing is given with a touch. With speed. With fire."

Michael smiles. Not only with his lips, but with his eyes and his arms. With the joy spreading his chest, hefting his breast-plate. "In the Americas, then," he says. "It's about time."

"Then you've seen this before?"

Michael's hand runs the length of his steed's back. "Many can heal, little one. The how and why is up to the King. What happened to the demon, this Damien?"

"The boy's Shield engaged him, and he was cast down."

Michael stretches his arms and legs, shaking them out, preparing to ride again.

"There's more, Commander."

"Go on."

"Damien claims the boy's companion—a girl named Brielle—saw through the veil."

Michael's mind laughs. Loud and strong. He leaps into the air, dropping onto Loyal's back. "This *is* interesting."

"One more thing."

"Your trip was fruitful, it seems. Tell me, Pearla, what else do you know?"

"The Prince has received word from an impish spy that the Sabres have been released—that they've been spotted in the skies above Stratus."

The Commander goes still—something he's not known for.

"If they are allowed to worship, if the veil is torn . . . ?" Pearla inquires, twisting her fingers into Loyal's mane.

"The Father has made provision for their worship, Pearla. And He's torn the veil before. A handful of times. The very day our Lord was crucified, the Sabres destroyed not only the temple curtain but the Terrestrial veil over Jerusalem."

Pearla's hands knot into tiny fists. She'd known about the curtain, but not the veil.

"Why?"

The Commander lifts high his spear, and the legion of light behind him engages, marching toward them. As they close in, Michael leans toward her, his white eyes sharp against the glowing red of Loyal's mane. "Only He who created the veil can demand it be torn asunder, Cherub. There is only One, and His mind is His own."

"What happened? In Jerusalem?"

"Tombs opened, dead men walked again, healings, miracles."

Pearla knew such things occurred just after the death of Christ, but she'd not connected them to the work of the Sabres.

Michael continues, "But it wasn't to last long. As men stitched away at the temple's curtain, repairing it, the Fallen unleashed their own forces, resealing the Terrestrial veil."

Pearla contains her surprise. "The Creator tore the veil and allowed the Prince's minions to repair the damage?"

"We all have a role to play, little one. Even darkness. The Father wasn't done with humanity that day, and He allowed darkness to think they'd won. But not before giving them a glimpse of His power—of His earthshaking, life-giving power."

Michael spreads his wings wide, opens his mouth, and releases a song of war. The sound rushes through Pearla's small body, and she clutches the steed's mane more tightly. Beyond the Commander, three thousand Warriors raise their voices.

"My forces cannot travel nearly as fast as you, and we're sure to encounter opposition as we approach the Americas. So, go. I'd like to know more about our fallen brother and his plans for the gifted ones. We'll rendezvous in the skies over Stratus."

Micheal's word is law to Pearla, and she waits for no further instruction. Turning back the way she came, she flies west, the Commander and his forces falling farther and farther behind.

10

Brielle

The nightmare grabs hold before I realize I've fallen asleep. Jake's hand is on my knee, he and Marco discussing cameras and video editing equipment. I'm thinking how great it is that they have things to talk about when a sea of color pulls me under.

The colors pop and fade until all that's left is a marble hallway stretched with a red Venetian rug. At the far end, pressed against the wall and shrouded in shadow, sits a girl. The shadow makes her appearance hard to discern, but I see wide, dark eyes above two trembling lips. It's clear she's not a child. Not exactly. Ten years old, eleven maybe.

I hear footsteps making their way up the hall. From above I search for their source, but I've turned my head too quickly, and with a sickening sensation I'm tumbling, falling toward the girl.

I blink. And blink again. Now I look out through her eyes, seeing what she sees. Feeling what she feels. And she's afraid. Looking out through her eyes, I can tell they're swollen, the tears chilling her face. A man walks toward her. A man I know. I'm sure I know him. I just . . . Who is he?

I can't place him here in another's mind.

"You're safe," he says.

He's handsome. Tall, lanky. Like a basketball player. His hair is light and it looks soft—even his mustache. But the girl is embarrassed. I feel the shame as if it were my own. Her shirt is burnt through; charred holes gape open, exposing her back and stomach. She crosses her arms over her chest and stares up at the man.

"My mom's dead, isn't she?" The words strike a melancholy chord in my heart. I know what it's like to be motherless, and if it's true, I don't envy this girl.

The man crouches before her and takes her face in his long, thin hand. He moves his fingers lightly over her forehead and cheeks, brushing away the ash and dirt that remain. He's gentle, and she needs gentle.

"I believe she is, yes." I feel the sob swelling in her stomach, expanding her ribs. "But you're not," he says, cupping her chin. "You were lucky."

She doesn't want to cry in front of this man, but she can't help it and the sob rips free. "She pulled me out. I can't believe she pulled me out."

"Yes," he says, his words silk. "And I'm so very glad. Your grandfather would never recover if he lost you both tonight."

Her eyes turn to the room at the end of the hall. The door is open a crack, tipping a sliver of light onto the Venetian rug. Whatever's in that room scares her. Every second that door holds her attention, her fear grows, her legs catching the tremors that have already claimed her arms. She leans closer to the man before her.

"Is he bad, my grandfather?"

The man looks affronted, his blond brows raised, his eyes wide. "Why would you ask such a question?"

"Mama told me never to be alone with him. She hates him," the girl says, another sob snagging her voice. "Hated him, I mean."

The man's face relaxes, and now he looks almost curious. It's this curiosity that worries me. "Do *you* think he's bad?"

"I don't know. I don't know anything about him. After Daddy died, Mama kept me away. I haven't seen him in years."

The man tilts his head, the chandelier above throwing triangles of dimmed light onto his face. For the briefest of seconds, she considers just how reptilian the shadows make this handsome man look. She's not wrong. With that long, thin neck and those dark eyes, he looks very snake-like. But he leans closer and the light shifts, and the thought flees the girl's mind.

"Your grandfather loves you," he says. "You needn't worry."

But I catch something in the words he's not spoken, something evasive that the girl notices too. His answer's not good enough for her, so she asks again.

"But does he . . . does he hurt kids?"

The man rolls back on his heels, and the reptilian triangles return. He says nothing, his face passive under the lights.

"He does, doesn't he?" She sobs again.

It's a sob I didn't feel coming, and it jars me. It must have taken the girl by surprise as well, because she bites her lip and the bawling stops.

"I don't have anyone else," she says. "There's nowhere else to go."

The man runs his thumb over his mustache, one side at a time.

"What if I told you that I could protect you from him?"

There's a hardness in his dark eyes, but it doesn't scare the girl. She sees strength in it. My eyes follow hers as she considers how muscled this tall, lean man is. He could be her protector, she thinks. She hasn't had one since her daddy died. He could be her knight in shining armor.

Warning bells sound in my mind, but my silent cautions do not reach the girl.

"Could you?" she asks. "Could you protect me?"

He takes her chin between his crooked forefinger and thumb, sending a thrill through her ten-year-old body. A thrill like she's never felt before. It's strange and confusing amidst the grief.

"Would you like that?" he asks.

"Yes," she says, her voice reduced to a murmur. "Please."

"You really are very pretty," he says. "Do you know that?"

Her heart flips at the flattery. "The boys at school think so."

I want to scream and shake her. I want to force her away from this man and his charming words.

"I'll bet they do."

He releases her face and pulls her up as he stands. "What would you say to a partnership?"

"You want me to be your partner?"

"I'd like that very much." His voice is lower now. Seductive. Enticing. "I can protect you from your grandfather easily enough. But I bet there are things you can help me with."

"Like with grandfather's company?"

He rubs his thumb against her hand, the dirt there chafing. "Something like that."

For the first time I can feel the anxiety brewing in her gut. She doesn't understand what she's agreeing to, and she's anxious to have her hand back.

"Okay," she says, discreetly trying to tug her arm from his grip.

"Okay." Before she can free her hand, he flips it palm up and drags three fingers along the soft, milky skin of her forearm. It's cold. So very cold, and she cries out. His other hand is quick, covering her mouth and pressing her head against the wall. I feel the pain shoot through her crown and down her neck. His dark eyes are as hard as ever, and for the first time she shares my terror.

And then it's done. The pain fades and she stops struggling, stops screaming into his palm.

"I'm sorry I had to do that," he says, pulling his hand away. "But I don't want you to forget."

Tears and snot run down her face. "To forget what?"

"Our partnership." The smile he'd been liberal with before is gone, his lips a tight line. "You won't forget, will you?"

Before she can answer, the door to her grandfather's study opens. The man before her steps to the side, giving her a view of her grandfather. He follows two police officers into the hall, a cane draped over his right arm.

"I am so very sorry about your mother, child," her grandfather says. His face is shadow, the light behind him catching the flyaway strands on his balding head. "I know you'll miss her terribly, but you'll be safe here. I promise. Come, let us find you a room."

Turmoil sloshes around in her stomach, making both of us ill. She thinks about what her mama said. That her grandfather hurts little children. That he's the worst of the worst.

Three gray scars sit side by side on her forearm, like rivers of ice under her skin. They don't hurt anymore, not like the burns she has on her calf and ankle, and she makes a decision. She clasps a hand over her forearm.

"I won't forget," she whispers to the man next to her.

He slides a long arm around her shoulders, pressing her tight to his chest.

"I'll find her a room," he says.

Her grandfather waves a hand. "Yes, that'd be fine. Put her on my floor, will you?"

The girl's knees lose their strength, but the man steadies her, keeping her close. "The room next to mine will suit her better, I think. Closer to the restroom, closer to the stairs. Has a balcony. What do you say, sweetheart, would you like a balcony?"

Her mouth is dry, her lips cracked from the flames. "Yes, I—I think I'd like that, Javan."

Javan!

Through the girl's eyes, I sneak a look at the old man once again. At the cane trembling on his arm. My glance is brief before her eyes are slammed shut, but I've seen enough to know the girl's fear is not in vain. I've watched this man try to buy children. I've watched him laugh at the terror leaking from their tiny frames.

Henry Madison.

I'm flailing, I know I am. Trying to get out of this girl's head, out of this nightmare. I finally succeed in opening my eyes, but it's Javan's ghastly celestial form that stares back at me. The gaunt face, blackened skin stretched over it, dead black eyes. They swallow me whole and I scream out, finally wrenching myself upright.

The warm light of the old Miller place greets my frantic form. Jake's just inches from my face, his arms around mine, holding me still. Marco's sitting in the arm chair across from me, his eyes wide, his face white.

"Hey, hey. You're all right."

I'm slick with sweat, my hands shaking. Like the girl's. The girl in Javan's care. We have to do something. I will my eyes to focus and turn them on Jake. He has a scratch on his neck, and his eye is red and swelling fast.

"Did I do that?" I say, reaching for his face.

"It's fine," he says, taking my hands and pressing them between his. "What *was* that?"

His touch brings me back to the now, to the reality of where I am.

"Nightmare," I say. "I had a nightmare."

Jake's eyes are asking all kinds of questions, but it's the statement that escapes Marco's lips that demands attention.

"You said Henry."

I roll my neck, leaning back against the couch. "Did I? I don't . . . He was there. In my dream, my nightmare."

"Does he always visit your nightmares?" Marco asks, leaning forward in the chair, his hands clenching the cushion.

I glance at Jake, but he looks as confused as I feel. "No. Never before. Why?"

"Because I dream about that monster every night."

11

Jake

The chest is still empty. Well, not empty. The dagger's still there, inscrutable, taunting. Jake closes it away, careful not to wake Marco. He's out, snoring softly on Canaan's bed, his shag of black hair hanging over the side. Jake leaves him there and retreats to the kitchen where he takes refuge at the table. He sits, his hands in fists, his body unable to relax. He tries praying, but his mind won't still.

Brielle's nightmare was far too detailed to be just a nightmare. Too specific. Too terrible.

Jake has very little experience with visions and prophetic dreams. He's heard stories, of course, read accounts in Scripture, but such things are less prolific now, it seems, less common than they used to be. He needs to talk to Canaan, but he's been gone all night. So Jake sits up, hoping to catch him before the barbecue, hoping they have some time to discuss Brielle's dream.

And Marco. Jake didn't realize just how much Marco remembered about the night at the warehouse. It seems doubt didn't shroud everything.

"I see him every night," Marco said. "I see him laughing and clapping. Mocking the children he came to purchase. And then, right before I have the chance to show him what it's like to be victimized, he disappears. Just like he did that night. You remember that, don't you? Him disappearing. You remember that?"

He and Brielle sat in silence while Marco ranted. They dodged questions. They didn't dare look at one another. But Jake's certain Marco won't let this go. As yet, he hasn't been able to locate a last name for Henry, but it's not for lack of trying. Jake stares into the darkness and wonders just how big a mission this has become.

If Brielle's dream holds any truth, Javan's out there somewhere. In Portland, most likely. Just hours away, reunited with Henry and terrorizing a young girl. Which means Canaan's intel is faulty. And if his intel on Javan is faulty, who's to say Damien is still suffering the pit?

Suddenly the dagger is so much more significant than the missing ring.

12

Brielle

I have mixed feelings about the Fourth of July. Both Dad and Olivia are going to be there, and that can't mean good things for Jake and me, but I don't want to deal with them alone, so I drag Jake along.

And Canaan.

And since Olivia is going, Helene decides she'll get some sun as well. The first time I met Helene, she was yanking me out of a warehouse full of abducted children and tucking me beneath her wings. Like Canaan, she's assigned to Stratus. Assigned to me.

Marco's also a reluctant participant in the Independence Day festivities.

"I'm not really a sunshine kind of guy," he says.

Cue every vampire joke I can come up with—and I've read all the books, seen all the movies. Eventually I shame Marco into getting some sun.

Jake hauls him down to Main Street to grab some sunblock and a pair of shorts—something that takes them far longer than is reasonable in any city, big or small. I wait outside, sitting on Slugger's hood in a pair of shorts and a Bohemian-looking

84

swimsuit cover-up. I've also got the halo on my wrist. It's a ridiculous-looking thing to wear to the lake, and I fully expect Dad to give me grief, but I'm determined to nap in the sun today, and I'll do whatever it takes to stave off those nightmares.

It's another fifteen minutes before Jake and Marco make their way to the car. I'm tempted to make fun of them—call them girls or something—but they look like they're bonding, and Marco needs that. I huddle them into the car and drive up a block to Jelly's to meet the rest of our party.

Jelly's is an old diner of the greasy spoon variety. A giant grape jelly jar sitting atop its stainless steel structure is the first thing you see when driving onto Main Street. Neon purple lights spell out Jelly's on the jar and run like racing stripes around the center of the building. When Kaylee's not at the community center, she's here helping her Aunt Delia, who owns the place.

I pull Slugger up to the curb, just feet away from Canaan and Helene. The two Shields sit side by side on a weathered wooden bench outside the diner. Canaan, with his broad shoulders and chiseled jaw, one leg crossed over the other; Helene, a lovely heart-shaped face framed by auburn hair, her hands resting gently on her knees. So different, but with so much in common. There's the obvious, those striking silver eyes, but it's more than that. It's the look on their faces as they converse. It's that incorrigible interest they have in every single interaction. I watch as they talk, their heads bent close, their lips moving intently. It's like they understand the gravity of the present. That every moment has meaning.

Jake opens my door and offers his hand. "You all right there?"

"Just daydreaming."

Our flip-flops smack the pavement, pulling the angels from their counsel.

"Marco, this is Helene," Jake says. "She and Canaan go way back."

"Yeah, we've met, haven't we?" Marco steps onto the curb and takes her hand, his eyes lingering on the connection. "When I was here before? Or wait. No . . ."

Helene slides her dainty hand away, tucking a strand of hair behind her ear. "You're from Portland, right?"

"Born and raised," Marco says.

"I've spent some time there. We could have run into one another."

"Huh." Marco tilts his head, blinking at her like she's too bright, or like he's got something stuck in his eye.

She turns to me, unfazed by the awkwardness. "Where's your dad?"

"Picking up Olivia." I don't make a face or growl when I say her name. In fact, I do my very best to keep my irritation to myself. "They'll meet us there."

"And you know where we're going?" Canaan asks.

"Not the foggiest. We're following these guys," I say, gesturing to the comedy act making their way onto Main.

Kaylee has tugged Delia out of the diner and locked the door behind her. "Don't even think about it!"

"This might be one of them times when waving a white flag is your best option," Delia says, screwing her sunhat in place.

"Not a chance," Kaylee says. "You're going."

"Humph. You think I'm a difficult boss, you just wait. I'm going to make one needy sunbather."

"Fine. Be needy, but you're coming." Kaylee gets behind her and pushes Delia toward our circle.

"Oh, you unleashed it now, girl. I'm talking little umbrella drinks and foot rubs and . . ."

Jake makes the introductions.

"I know who this boy is," Delia says, tugging Marco toward her large chest and squeezing him tight. "I watch the news. I've been praying for you, boy."

"She doesn't pray," Kaylee whispers.

"I do. Sometimes."

"Well, thank you," Marco says, pulling away and straightening his shirt. "I've done some praying myself of late."

"You're riding with us," Delia says, grabbing his elbow. "He's riding with us, Jake-y boy. You just follow. Kaylee knows where we're going. Right? You know where we're going? Yes. She does. We'll get you there."

Marco is hauled away, looking amused and slightly panicked. We should have helped him, or at least prepared him for the cataclysmic event that is Delia.

"Think he'll survive?" I ask.

Helene pulls her hair into a ponytail. "He's survived worse."

Dad and Olivia are already at the lake when we arrive. They've managed to avoid the crowds gathered for the annual fireworks display and still found a picnic area not far from the water. A couple tables positioned on the hard-packed dirt and flanked on three sides by a shaded wood. It's kind of perfect.

Canaan and Helene duck into the trees. "Just checking things out," Canaan says. "Be back in a sec."

I throw a towel over my shoulder. "He's been 'checking things out' a lot lately."

"You just used air quotes," Jake says, closing my door.

"Kaylee doesn't own them."

Marco joins us. "That is one heck of a woman," he says.

"Sorry, we should have—"

"Let me sulk away the holiday in a darkened room? Na. Delia—that's her name, right?—Delia, she's crazy, but she's a good audience. I got this."

Dad's already grilling, a plate of hot dogs at his elbow, tongs in one hand and a beer in the other. I can't help but notice the three empty bottles at his feet. I resist the urge to check my phone for the time, but I know it's not yet noon.

"Hey, Dad," I say, kissing his cheek.

Jake steers clear. He and Marco walk down to the water while Kaylee does whatever she can to make Delia comfortable, which apparently includes some sort of plastic pool float positioned precariously close to the water on the lava rock that surrounds the lake.

I can't imagine that ending well.

I step away from the barbecue, shielding my eyes from the sun. The lake is smooth, like glass, like a mirror reflecting the periwinkle sky. It's strange to see Marco out of place. He's so at ease in the city, surrounded by cement and brick and grungy coffeehouses. But the lake seems to truly freak him out. He places a foot in the water and then yanks it out. With all the snow runoff, I know it's freezing, but Jake's having none of that. He wraps his arms around Marco's chest and hauls him out into the water. Marco's a few inches taller, but there's no doubt who'd dominate a wrestling match. With a testosterone-fueled grunt, Jake throws him. Marco lands with a water explosion that has Delia protesting. She waves her arms, demanding Kaylee move her farther from the water. Marco comes up sputtering and laughing and promising revenge.

I spent last Independence Day on a bus traveling from St. Tropez to Paris. It was hot and crowded and smelled like armpits. This beats that by miles and miles. I inhale the spicy woods and the musk of water deep into my chest. Today has potential.

And then I catch Dad glaring over my shoulder at the splashing, laughing boys, his face murderous. I wrap my arms around his waist, and he breathes a little easier, patting my back, splattering beer down my shirt.

"Dad!"

"Sorry, baby," he says, mopping me with his apron.

I hate when he drinks like this. Hate it. He gets forgetful and clumsy and—his eyes are back on Jake—he gets vicious.

"It's fine, Dad." I push him away and back toward the barbecue. The back of my swimsuit cover-up is drenched, so I pull it off and readjust the suit underneath. "Where's Olivia?"

"Round here somewhere," he says, flipping a dog blistering on the grill. "Looking for cell reception."

"Ah."

I grab a soda from the ice chest and climb up on the picnic table.

"I wish you liked her," Dad says, bringing me a hot dog.

I could say *I'll try*, but I'm not going to lie to him.

Still, I'm not going to start a fight either.

"I do too, Dad."

When Canaan and Helene return, I'm stretched out in a perfect patch of sunlight. Helene lays her towel next to mine. She's humming. Always humming. Canaan splashes into the water, rescuing Marco. He sweeps Jake from his feet and throws him farther, much farther than any human I've ever met is capable of throwing a person.

Dad steps into my sun, shading my face. "Holy . . . Did you see that?"

Kaylee and Delia clap and cheer. Marco's eyes are huge, like perfectly round, perfectly green planets. Jake emerges, shaking his head and paddling in.

"Yeah. Um."

"He's a circus freak, isn't he?" Helene says, perched on her elbows. "I've always thought so."

Dad stumbles back, dropping to his bum on the dirt. "Yeah. Circus freak."

Olivia doesn't return until Delia's slicing up her famous apple pie. By then Dad's so sloshed, sprawled across a lounge chair, he hardly notices her presence. Still, she sits next to him, her pretty face tense.

"You all right, Liv?" Kay asks, dishing up the pie.

"Oh sure," she says, tucking her phone into her pocket. "People are a disappointment sometimes, but it's nothing a little sun can't cure."

"Liv?" Marco's sitting in a beach chair under a covering of trees on the opposite side of the picnic area from Dad and Olivia. Clothed in a dry shirt, he's been reading, lost in Ali's journal for the last half hour, but now he stands and crosses the picnic area. "Liv? Olivia Holt?"

She sits up, startled. "I'm sorry, do I know you?"

"It's Marco. Marco James. Benson Elementary."

Her face softens, and she looks almost childlike. "Marco? Oh my gosh!" She jumps from her chair and embraces him, laughing and . . . Is she crying?

"How long has it been?" she asks.

"A lifetime, I think."

She squeals again, and suddenly it's not hard to believe she's younger than she looks.

"I didn't see that coming," Jake whispers. Dad's started to snore, so he's brave and takes a seat next to me. "Did you?"

"Not in a million billion years," Kaylee answers, gape-mouthed, apple pie stuck to her cheek.

Kicking up a cloud of dirt, Marco drags his chair over to Olivia's and they talk. And talk. Somehow Marco doesn't look so out of place next to her, and she looks substantially less like Cruella de Vil. Engaged in conversation with an old friend, her plastic smile's been replaced with something genuine, something wholesome. I run a finger over the halo on my wrist, unsure how to reconcile my bipolar impressions of her and the halo's strange warning.

I lose track of them after that. We eat pie and play cards. Delia is remarkably good at rummy and Canaan is not, which is kind of hilarious. Jake's not any better. Tired of losing, he takes my hand and drags me down to the water.

I don't complain.

13

Brielle

The sun's low in the sky now. It's cut a yellow boulevard across the lake. So beautiful, so clear. I can imagine stepping out onto it. I can imagine walking on water.

But when my toes touch the rippling current, my feet sink into mud.

"Let's walk," Jake says.

I've still got my ratty jean shorts on over my suit, and the smell of sunblock is everywhere. Jake's chest is golden in the evening sun, his hair ruffled and loose. It's like a vacation being with him like this.

"You're staring at me," he says.

I'd blush, but we're so far past that. "I am."

"That could make a lesser man feel uncomfortable."

I laugh. "But not you?"

"Definitely not me. Please stare away. In fact"—he stops and steps in front of me—"let me return the favor."

An impromptu stare-off. Awesome. I am so not going to lose.

Jake keeps his gaze on me, but he moves it from my eyes to my lips and then to the hair tucked behind my ear. It isn't until he bites his lip and waggles his eyebrows that I realize just how hard he's flirting, how hard he's trying to win. A laugh bubbles in my stomach, but I shut it down and set to examining his face further. Not at all an unpleasant task.

Sweat curls the hair around his face. Some of it catches in his sideburns, in the scruff he's not shaven. Other strands tangle in his long black lashes—lashes that send shadows spilling across his cheekbones. His lips are wet, that lower one still stuck between his teeth. I let my eyes trail to the hollow at his throat. And that's when he grabs my shoulders and pulls me to him. That's when his lips crush mine. Electrified little bugs crawl from my bare toes to the crown of my head. I close my eyes and press closer, the luckiest girl on the planet.

It's a solid minute before I realize my mistake.

"I win," Jake says, his lips still touching mine.

My eyes snap open. Triumph gleams back at me from his.

"Cheater."

My feet are still in the lake, the moon joining the sun overhead, a dock materializing out of the water in the distance. We head toward it, three hundred and thirteen steps without talking. I like that we can do that. I like that we don't have to fill every silence. But the farther we walk, the heavier the silence seems to be.

"It bothers you that I know when you're scared, doesn't it? Bothers you that I can see your fear."

The dock is before us now and Jake steps onto it, pulling me up after him. "It's not that I didn't know you could see it, Elle. I just thought . . . I thought I was managing it better than I am, I guess."

"You mean hiding it."

We're at the end of the dock now, the water sloshing gently against the wooden beams below. Crickets fill the air, but Jake is quiet.

"I wish you wouldn't. Hide them, I mean. Your fears are the only ones I feel remotely equipped to handle."

"See, that concerns me."

"What?"

Jake drops to the dock and I sit with him, our feet dangling over.

"The other day you were talking about fear being everywhere and I just . . . I realized how little I've done to help you. To prepare you."

"Jake . . ."

"You can do more than handle fear, Elle. You can destroy it."

I almost laugh. Sitting here in my bathing suit, perched next to the water like a cattail, I couldn't feel less like a warrior. But Jake continues.

"Think about the warehouse. Think about the child, Ali."

His change of subject takes me by surprise.

"I think about her all the time," I say. Of all the children locked away in Damien's warehouse, she's the one I find myself wondering about the most. Her name is a ghostly reminder of *my* Ali, my friend, killed by the same man who took her hostage. Something inside me warms at the thought of her, free and mending somewhere.

But when we first met the child, there was no guarantee. She was terrified, shaking, her dirty face smeared with fear. And then Jake spoke hope. He promised her a way out, and the fear dissolved, evaporating into the heat and light of the Celestial.

"It takes a word. A touch. A prayer. You were created to be

a light. So be that to the scared and broken. Be that, and watch what happens to fear."

Starlight appears in the water below. I watch as, one light at a time, the darkness of the glassy lake reflects the beauty overhead. "It's overwhelming sometimes."

"I know," he says, staring at his own hands. "I feel like such a hypocrite telling you what to do with your gift."

He's been skittish with the healing in his hands. In the seven months since the warehouse, he's not used it once.

"Does it scare you?" I ask. "Healing?"

"It's not the act of healing that scares me. It's the consequences. A demon thought he could corrupt the gift, and it almost got you killed."

"Technically, it did get me killed."

I'm joking, of course, making light of a memory that terrifies both of us, but I've underestimated Jake's tone.

"Put the halo on," he says.

"Now?" I glance around, but we're alone.

"Yes," Jake says, removing the halo from my wrist. "I want to show you something."

As always, the halo shifts and remolds, melting and transforming into the crown that was given to Canaan as a reward for his loyalty. The liquid gold sheen catches the stars tonight and throws their light back at us brighter than they appear above.

When the change is complete, I place the halo on my head and watch as shards of white light pierce the hazel of Jake's eyes. The lake follows, and the sky, the moon a vibrant ball of blue and yellow against the orange expanse. I see the Celestial.

And I see fear.

Black and thick, it sits on Jake's shoulders. My heart aches at the sight. It's heavier than anything I've seen on him.

"You see it, then?"

I nod, my insides knotted.

"You're afraid. Very afraid. But why?"

"Destroy it," he says.

My inadequacies curdle in my stomach, but it's Jake, and I'd do anything to take this burden from him. Even carry it myself. I reach out a hand, sliding it across his shoulder and into the fear. The malevolent substance leaps at the heat of my body, climbing onto my hand. It twists and turns, inching up my arm. Cold. So very, very cold.

"Now pray," he says.

But my hand trembles and my mind slows. "I don't . . . I don't . . ."

So Jake prays in my place. Words of faith. Words of fire. He speaks promises from Scripture. That God won't leave us or forsake us. That He's conquered fear and we, His children, aren't subject to its bondage. He prays the words I can't find, brave words. I watch, riveted as the light, the celestial air around us, sparks like the striking of a match. Sizzling stars assault the black sludge on Jake's shoulders, setting it ablaze. My eyes water at the stink of burning rubber, but I watch until every last clot of fear turns to smoke.

His words did that.

His faith set fear on fire.

"That's . . . that's new."

Jake sits taller now, the weight of terror lifted. "I haven't been trying to hide my fears, Elle. I've been trying to destroy them before they attack both of us. We've spent this last seven months getting to know one another, but I haven't done enough to teach you how to fight. I haven't done enough to show you that the fear you see—every fear you see—can be destroyed. I'm sorry about that."

"I . . . I forgive you?"

"Good." He laughs. "Thank you."

"So it's prayer, then. Prayer is how I fight."

"And Scripture. Scripture is like acid to fear if it's wielded correctly. But I can't always see the fear, Elle. Not like you can. It's far too easy for me to forget the burden it must be to you."

"It's not a burden if . . . I don't see the fear if I'm not wearing the halo like this."

"But you will. It's your gift, Elle. One day you'll see it all the time. You won't be able to close your eyes to it, and you have to know how to fight."

Jake's eyes are on mine, the purity of love's greatest expression gently caressing my face. But it's not long before the tiniest drop of fear blossoms in his chest. Canaan told me once that the tragedy of fear isn't that it can be used as a weapon by the Fallen, but that humans hold it inside their very being and can unleash it upon themselves unwittingly. Even now it worms its way to his shoulders where it multiplies, settling once again like armor he need not wear.

It seems something's captured Jake's heart. Something that keeps the fear tucked deep inside.

"What is it, Jake? What has you so afraid?"

His smile is a sad one. "Back so soon."

"It's not just my dad, is it?"

His mouth opens. It's soft, there's an answer there, but with the frenzy of wings, we're pulled from the ground and airborne before he can say a thing.

14

Brielle

The dock falls away below us.

We're flying.

And I hate flying.

Canaan's voice sounds in my head. Loud. Excited. "There's something you have to see."

I can't move much, his sinewy inner wings holding us tight. But Jake's shoulder is pressed against mine, his grin wide, the fear gone.

"You good?" I ask over the beating of Canaan's wings.

"Best part of being raised by an angel," he says. "You?"

I twist my hand around and grab his, willing my gut to unclench as Mount Bachelor grows in front of us: a fat triangular mound with emerald green trees climbing up its sides. Dwindling patches of snow gleam like dollops of diamond frosting near the peak.

Bachelor's an everyday sight for me. On a clear day, I can see it from almost anywhere in Stratus. At its tallest, the mountain stands just over nine thousand feet, and with the extended winters we court here in central Oregon, the ski area stays open longer than most resorts in the country. It's one of the few legitimate reasons for visiting.

I've photographed it, skied it, even hiked the summit a few times, but seeing it like this—flying toward Bachelor with the eyes of an angel—the familiar suddenly becomes extraordinary.

"I wish I could photograph it like this," I say, my voice raised. "Frame it. Hang it on the wall."

"It'd be one heck of a conversation piece," Jake says, his boyish scratch louder as well. "It wouldn't be the same, though, would it?"

"No, it wouldn't."

The wind steals my reply, but I don't repeat it. Instead, I close my eyes and let my imagination run wild. I imagine Dad staring at a picture of Mount Bachelor—of what it looks like in the Celestial. I imagine explaining it to him: *This, Dad . . . this is what it really looks like.*

But Jake's right. It would take more than a picture to convince Dad.

But why? Why can't we just snap a picture, hang it over the sofa, and stand our loved ones before it? Why can't we let a picture convince them of a realm beyond our own?

I know firsthand that it takes more than a single glimpse to persuade a soul. Still, something in my chest aches for the ease of an explanation without words.

Why can't it be that easy?

My question borders on the ridiculous, but an answer comes nonetheless. It's quiet—a whisper riding the breath of Canaan's wing.

Creation, it says, *without belief in the Creator, will never be anything more than a pretty picture.*

Canaan opens his inner wings, releasing us onto the mountain. My bare feet catch rock and I stumble, the halo tumbling from my brow. Jake catches it and steadies me. Behind us, Canaan stands in his Terrestrial form wearing his swim trunks and nothing more.

"Watch," he says, his eyes shining with excitement. "Watch."

So we do.

There's little that amazes like the top of a mountain. From here we can see the Sisters—Faith, Hope, and Charity—three volcanic peaks sitting to the north, the moon lighting the snow still glistening on top. There's also Broken Top and a few other peaks whose names I can't remember. Bowls of snow nestle into the mountain here and there. There are a handful of lakes that surround the mountain as well, but the night has cast many of them in darkness and I catch only glimmers of moonlight winking back at me from their surfaces.

Jake's hand cups my elbow. He moves his fingers down my forearm, sliding them into mine.

"Look," he says, his hazel eyes dancing like Canaan's.

It takes a considerable amount of self-control to look away from those eyes, but when I do I nearly forget myself and take a step forward. Jake pulls me against him, preventing a fall.

"What *is* that?" I ask.

He shakes his head. "What is it, Canaan?"

"It's the veil," he says. "The Terrestrial veil."

It *is* a veil. I see it now. It's as though a sheer curtain hangs in front of the mountain, blowing in the wind.

So delicate. So fine.

And then it starts to glow. The gray-and-white mountain brightens, its snow shimmering. The stone is no longer a flat gray but has the look of precious stones stacked one on top of the other. Their shades vary from a deep chocolate to a glossy silver, light springing from their craggy facets.

I'd panic, but I'm fairly certain I know what I'm seeing.

"It's the Celestial," I say. "But how?"

"Come," Canaan says, transferring, pulling us with him, the Celestial swallowing us once again.

"What are they?" I yell.

Standing, flying, hovering about the summit of the closest mountain—Charity—are several angels. I'm not close enough to make out their features, but they're definitely angels. Something about the way they move, though, something about the color of their wings is unfamiliar. They're different from Canaan. Different from Helene, but I can't quite see how.

"They're Sabres."

"Sabres," I say, savoring the sound of the word.

Our flight is not so much a flight but a glorified jump toward Charity. My stomach is sick with the roller-coaster-like phenomenon, but now that we're closer, I look more carefully at the angels before us. They're larger than any I've seen before, and brighter. I count them on approach—a dozen—and then I watch them, trying to understand their movements. Light curls around them, tendrils of incense rising into the sky.

"What are they doing?" Jake asks.

"They're worshiping," I say, awestruck.

Is there a rhyme or reason to where they've positioned themselves? Some of them kneel, some of them stand staggered across the rock, but the one thing they all seem to have in common is their wings. They're metallic. Not just in color, but in their very construction, it seems. I have an inexplicable need to reach out and touch them, to run my fingers over a single feather.

"They're huge," Jake says. "How tall are they, Canaan?"

"Eight, nine feet." There's no mistaking the amusement in his voice.

Canaan leans forward and tucks his wings close, throwing us into a fall. I'd scream, but I think my stomach might tumble into the sky. A moment later he pulls us right side up, my lunch somersaulting back into place.

We're close now, so close that I can see that touching a Sabre's wing may be the fastest way to lose an arm. I set to examining the nearest one. He's gigantic, like Jake said. And his eyes are pure white, trademark white. Like Canaan's. Like Helene's. He has the celestial gaze of one who'd lay down his life for another. His skin, too, is white, so white it looks almost silver. His muscled arms and chest make Canaan look trim. But as much as I can find things to admire about his physique, it's his wings that so separate him from any other angel I've seen.

Their beauty is staggering, their design inexplicable. Where I expect to see rows and rows of snowy white feathers, one blade lies on top of another—thousands of them—sharp and glistening silver. I can't help but compare each and every one of them to the dagger that pierced my chest this past December. To the instrument of death that bled me dry on a rooftop.

Yet these blades are pristine, polished, organic even. The Sabre adjusts them and they ripple, a trilling tune making its way to my ears. His kinsmen do the same, and the skies fill with music. Loud, warlike, with a tremor of delicate strings woven through it. It's unlike anything I've ever heard. My throat tightens with emotion, and I gasp again and again.

Canaan's voice sounds in my mind: "These are the twelve who originally reported to Lucifer himself."

I remember now that Lucifer was created to be the Chief Worshiper, and yet I find it hard to believe that the Prince of Darkness could be as beautiful as these.

"Leaders of song," Canaan continues. "Their wings are instrumental wonders, their vocal prowess unmatched. At the Prince's command, these twelve were responsible for leading all of the heavens into worship of the Creator."

Canaan sets us down near their crude circle, but he doesn't release us from his embrace. There's a Sabre kneeling ten yards to our left, his hands cupped before him. Another stands just in front of us. His wings tower high above his head and scrape the rock at his feet, hundreds and hundreds of daggers making up his wingspan. They rub one against the other, trembling, sending music far and wide.

He doesn't acknowledge us in any way. None of them do. They're lost in worship.

Their song fills the air, and with my feet so close to the earth, it's all I can do not to fight against Canaan's hold, so deep is my desire to dance.

I think of Moses on the mountaintop, a story I read in my mother's Bible. I remember the burning bush and the voice speaking out of it, telling Moses to take off his shoes. Telling him he was on holy ground. It makes sense to me now.

The Sabres open their mouths and lift up a song, and tears pour down my face at the sound. I sniff, trying to keep another round at bay, and that's when the fragrance catches my nose.

It's the smell of worship.

Sweet like honey and smoky like a campfire. Deep and thick like the ocean's waters and fresh like their spray all in one inhalation.

I turn to Jake. Tears dampen his face, and his eyes are riveted on the sky above us. I tilt my head to see. Tendrils of smoke waft into the sky, bright colorful incense. It curls from the chests of the Sabres as they sing and lingers above us.

Canaan's voice seeps softly into my mind. "It's time to go," he says.

I want to plead with him for just a minute more, but his outer wings are already moving, pushing us away from the Sabres and back toward Mount Bachelor.

Jake says, "That was . . . it was . . ." But he can't seem to finish the thought. I understand entirely.

"Keep your eyes on the sky," Canaan says.

The gentle tenor of his voice stills me, calms my hurried heart. In the distance the Sabres continue to worship, their wings sending mirror-like reflections bouncing across the sky. Tendrils of incense twist from their mouths, from their wings, climbing higher and higher, tangling with the scent of worship pouring from the others.

One final ice-blue tendril curls toward those of his kin. Up and around it loops, twisting like a ribbon around the bundle, lifting the sweet smell of their worship ever skyward.

The sky sparks. I grab Jake's hand as it hisses, spitting light and color in every direction. The Sabres' song grows louder, more insistent. Their wings continue to play, whirling faster and faster, eventually lifting each one into the sky.

"Canaan?" I yell, his wings whipping hot air against us. "What's happening?"

"Watch," he says, his mind as calm as ever. "Just watch."

Our hands clenched, our breathing fast, Jake and I watch as the wings of the Sabres tear through the Terrestrial veil.

15

Brielle

Helene meets us in the skies, the lake a golden mirror below us. Her auburn hair flies about, red leaves blown on a warm celestial breeze.

"You saw them, then?" Canaan's mind asks.

"I did," she answers. "Did you know they were here?"

"No, I've heard nothing from the Throne Room. You?"

"Nothing. I'd very much like to see Virtue. Is he among them?"

"He is."

Her white gaze travels beyond Canaan's wings. I've never seen her so eager. "Will you join me?"

"I shouldn't. It isn't safe for Jake and Brielle."

"Yes, and they're needed back at the picnic area. I should have told you. The others are ready to go."

"It's not far, Canaan," I say. I can tell they'd like to see their brothers.

"Yeah, we can see the campground now," Jake says. "Drop us here. We'll walk."

"Well, don't actually drop us," I say.

Canaan laughs. "Never."

Jake's right. The walk is short, and we've very little time to discuss the Sabres or their song. But it consumes me. Their precisely crafted wings, violent in their beauty. Their worship—their stunning, sweet-smelling, harmonious worship—fills my mind. The air around me feels generic without it. Manufactured, unrefined. I'm struggling to explain my impressions to Jake when we emerge from the trees and the Terrestrial becomes far more real than I'm ready to deal with.

Olivia's guiding Dad to his truck. The food's been packed away; Delia and Kaylee are nowhere in sight. Our festive picnic area looks forlorn, and my face falls. Seeing the Sabres was an experience I'd never trade, but I suddenly feel bad for abandoning the party.

There's not much time to dwell on that, though.

Dad's further gone than I realized. He stumbles, nearly taking Olivia down with him. Marco catches her and they laugh, but there's nothing funny about it. Marco grabs Dad's other arm, and together they coax his foot up and onto the running board. The sight of their two slight figures hefting my father into his pickup drains the life and light that had blossomed in my chest. My feet are heavy, frozen to the dirt.

But Jake jumps in, taking Olivia's spot and hoisting Dad up and in. With a hand to his chest, Jake holds Dad against the seat while Marco stretches the seat belt across Dad's lap.

Olivia stands with her hands on her hips, her long, dark hair hanging loose.

I hate her.

She did this. Dad was fine until he met her.

I step to her side. "You should have cut him off."

"Me?" She doesn't look nearly as offended as she should. "I hardly know him. But you—where *were* you?"

I want to slap her. I'd like to say I'm above that, but I'm not. She broke my dad.

I hold out my hand. "Keys."

"I can take him."

"No. You can't." I feel her gaze on me, sharp, like a knife. But I've been stabbed before, and I can handle the threat in her eyes.

"And just how am I getting home?"

"Jake," I ask, walking toward the truck, "will you drive my car, take Marco and Olivia?"

He looks over his shoulder, his expression tender. "Whatever you need."

And he means it. He'll do anything to make this easier for me. There was a time, not long ago, when Dad was that person—the one who made it all better.

Olivia isn't done talking. "What if I don't want to ride with—"

"Then walk." There's a shrill edge to my words, and Dad rouses. His eyes swim in his head, but he's aware enough to notice Jake's hand on his chest. He swats at it.

"Dad!"

He leans past Marco and throws up. Jake sees it coming and tugs me out of the way, his arms the only thing tethering me to sanity.

"I'm so sorry," I tell him.

"Hey," Jake whispers, holding me tight. "It's not a problem."

Tears roll down my face as I look at the wreck Dad has become. When he's done emptying his stomach, I dig a beach towel out of my bag and mop his face, the others looking silently on. I'm ashamed. Of my dad. Of the little amber bottles that have turned him into an idiot. Of the fact that he's turned me—his nineteen-year-old daughter—into his babysitter.

Jake walks me to the driver's side and opens the door for me. "I'll call you tomorrow," he says, lifting me into the cab and closing me in. Dad's snoring surrounds me, loud and obnoxious. My hands shake, but I turn the key in the ignition and leave the lake behind. Dad wakes only once on the drive home. His head rolls toward me; his face is impossible to discern in the darkness, but his hand finds my knee.

"You missed the fireworks," he says.

I rest my hand on top of his, forcing the anger from my voice. "Sorry about that."

But he's snoring again.

It's better that way, actually. I've nothing to say. Nothing kind, anyway. And we did miss the fireworks, Jake and I. A stitch of sadness pierces my heart. It's been two years since I've seen fireworks with Dad. Two years since I've seen fireworks, period.

Then I think of the Sabres and their wings of blade. I think of their song, twisting bright and fragrant, surrounding me. I think of the mountain shining in the darkness, and the Terrestrial veil hanging like a ravaged curtain, the Celestial bleeding into the night.

I didn't miss the fireworks after all.

16

Jake

Jake's window is open. The scent of sweltering evergreens invades his room, clings to the bedsheets. He's cleared his bed of the books and clothes and sits cross-legged facing the window. The Scriptures lie open on the sill next to a sweating glass of ice water. A secondhand lamp casts an amber glow over the book of Daniel, and Jake's calloused hand thumbs the thick corner of the leather tome as he reads.

Parts of this great book feel intensely personal. A boy separated from his home, from his family. A boy with gifts and integrity. A boy who has something the powers that ruled wanted. A boy thrown to the lions.

But above all, a boy who is a dreamer. Something he has in common with Brielle, which is why Jake is searching the pages tonight.

He's started marking things down so he won't forget, so he can piece this thing together. It's been six days since the first nightmare, three since Independence Day when the Sabres tore through the veil, and Brielle's nightmares have done nothing but grow in intensity. It doesn't matter if she has the halo with her or not, the dream visits every night. The girl in the hallway. Javan and Henry. Three scars marking the girl's arm.

The more Jake thinks about it, the less probable it seems that the Sabres and Brielle's dreams are disconnected. The timing is just too close.

He plays July Fourth over and over again in his mind. The Sabres—the gigantic Sabres—and their killer wings. And then the veil. Torn. It's a thing Jake never thought he'd see, and it was over before he'd had time to really consider the significance.

After the Sabres had broken through, Canaan set him and Brielle down on Bachelor's summit, and they saw with their very human, very Terrestrial eyes just what anyone else would see if they were watching.

The sky was torn. Like a tattered curtain, the veil did very little to hide the Celestial behind it. They saw jagged patches of orange sky where it should have been night. Wings of sharpened daggers flashed through the tear, widening the gap, as the Sabres' worship rose to the Throne Room.

"It's their presence that thins the veil," Canaan said.

But it was their worship that tore it.

Canaan used to tell him stories about the Sabres. Jake's favorite was the one about the great rebellion.

When the Prince of Darkness attempted to overthrow the Creator, it was the Sabres who stood staunchest against him. Canaan said it was the first time their instrumental wings were used as weapons. He'd love to have been there—to have seen the twelve of them unfurling their dagger-like feathers, locking blade into blade, keeping the Prince from the throne he so desired. While most of the ranks lost a third of their own that day, of the twelve, not a single Sabre fell.

But the Prince's rebellion changed their role. Before, their worship of the Creator was a thing never contested, never questioned; now, with thousands and thousands of angels standing in opposition to the light, the Sabres' song became a weapon against the Fallen, their adoration a swift blade that kept the celestial skies free of the rebels. Free of demonic attack against the angels of light.

Their song tore at anything that stood between the Creator and His creation.

They were the sword of God Himself.

But then mankind rebelled too. Darkness blossomed in the one place the Sabres could not fight—in the hearts of the woman and her husband. And the pure light of the Creator's glory became a danger to Adam and Eve. Without the Terrestrial veil, without something to dim the light of the Creator, God's holiness would eventually destroy them.

And God wept at the tragedy of it.

The Sabres were pulled from the surrounding skies. If left to worship freely, their song could tear through the veil, leaving humanity vulnerable to the unfiltered light of the Creator.

This part of the story always saddened Jake. That the veil separated humankind from their heavenly Father. When he was young, it made him cry. But Canaan would take him on his knee and tell him the end—the part of the story that hasn't happened yet.

"One day," he'd say, "a new heaven and a new earth will be established. One day the Sabres will be allowed to worship where they wish, but until the veil is no longer necessary, the Sabres worship only within the safety of the Father's Throne Room or on the mountaintops, far from creatures who could be damaged by their song."

It's a beautiful ending to a tragic story, but it doesn't explain why they're here now.

In Stratus.

Canaan told Jake he didn't know. But as Jake sifts through the pages of Scripture, he's more certain than ever that their presence has something to do with Brielle's dreams. And if he can just figure it out, maybe it'll shed light on the missing ring and the dagger that's replaced it.

Maybe solving one mystery will lead to solving another.

A yellow rectangle spreads across the field outside, catching his eye. Brielle's living room light has been flipped on, and the glow spills through the window. At first Jake thinks it's Brielle, but she never uses the front door. The one leading from the kitchen to the porch is closer to her room.

The door opens, and Keith stumbles into the field wearing what looks like a bathrobe. He trips over something and sprawls face-first into the grass. His booming laugh makes its way across the field, and he pushes awkwardly to his feet. He's drunk. Something else Jake's been keeping track of. The first time Brielle noticed his uptick in drinking was Sunday, six days ago. Too many coincidences to ignore.

Jake climbs out the window and drops to the ground. He resists the urge to holler across the yard. Brielle doesn't need to see her dad like this, blundering around in the middle of the night.

Jake darts across the grass, his feet catching stones and dropped pine needles, but that's nothing to the devastation he knows Brielle will feel if he doesn't get her dad back inside. He ducks a series of branches and emerges to see Keith standing, staring into the apple orchard behind his house. Jake draws closer, slowing his footsteps, not wanting to scare the guy. The blood runs fast in his ears now, but he swears he hears music.

Is Keith singing?

The long grass brushes against his shorts, a rustle that seems loud in the silence of the night, but Keith doesn't turn around. He stands at the edge of the abandoned orchard, the grass dropping away to hardened dirt and weeds. The sound seems to be coming from within the grove.

And it's familiar.

Not nearly so loud as the worship of the twelve Sabres, but similar.

Jake steps closer. He rubs the sleep from his eyes and looks again. The trees are gnarled and the weeds growing around them tall and knotted, but there's no sign the veil is thinning here, no sign it's torn.

He looks back toward Brielle's house, wishing for her eyes. Should he wake her?

He swivels toward the orchard once again and finds himself face-to-face with Keith. He's tempted to take a small step back, but something in Keith's eyes keeps him close.

"Sir," Jake says. Keith wobbles, and Jake reaches out a hand to steady him.

"Hands off." He swats at Jake with a heavy hand, but he's slow and sloppy and he doesn't connect.

"Sorry, sir," Jake says, but he doesn't release Keith's arm. He can't. Keith's leaned into him now, and Jake supports a hefty portion of the large man's weight. Keith's other arm swings around, pointing into the orchard. Jake's bare feet dig into the grass and his thighs tense, keeping the two of them standing.

"You know what it is?" Keith says. "That music?"

Jake doesn't answer. He's too busy holding the man upright. But his hands and arms are damp with nervous sweat, and Keith slips free, stumbling into Jake, who steadies him.

"I do," Keith says, regaining his balance and standing taller. "I know who's singing."

Jake doesn't have a response to that.

"It's them," Keith says, his gray eyes moist. "The ones that took her."

Jake turns his eyes back to the orchard. "Who? I don't see anyone, sir."

"I don't see them either. But I hear them." He laughs, but there's no hilarity there. It's sad, defeated. "You don't believe me, I know, but I heard them. Heard them that day like I hear them now." Keith's swollen eyes leak tears as they scrutinize Jake—as they dare him to contradict his assessment. And then he blows out a puff of air in disgust. The sour smell of yeast and vomit lingers between them. "Who cares what you think? Who are *you* anyway?"

Jake knows it's the alcohol talking, but still this man's hatred of him tears at his chest. Scratches at the hope there.

"It's Jake. I'm Jake."

Keith pushes him off and turns back to the orchard. "I know who you are, kid. You and your dad." Keith sinks to the ground, crosses his legs like he's a first grader and it's magic circle time. "And now you're taking my little girl. Taking her away. Like them. Like they took Hannah."

Jake can't help it. Compassion is who he is; it's who he was raised to be. He knows he risks further rejection, but he sinks down next to his girlfriend's dad anyway.

"She'd never let that happen, sir. She loves you. More than anything."

Keith folds in on himself, curling into a ball of terry cloth. He rolls to his side, his knees drawn up, his arms wrapping his body.

"Not more than anything," he says.

17

Brielle

Saturday's turning into a day of double duty for me. Between classes at Miss Macy's and our new program at the community center, I'm exhausted. The nightmares don't help. I find myself scanning all my students' faces to see if anyone resembles the girl from the marble hallway. I look for her on the street and at the supermarket. Yesterday I terrified a poor old man having lunch with his granddaughter. I'd do anything for a really good, dreamless nap.

Since that doesn't seem possible, I've been trying to pay attention to the scene that captures me when I sleep. I try to let my eyes wander, try to pick up anything that tells me what to do with what I'm seeing. So far I've not been able to see anything beyond the girl's own gaze, but I'm determined. If figuring this dream out is the only way to get rid of it, I have to keep trying. Canaan did check Henry's place for me. He's been there several times now, to the city, to the townhouse Henry owns. The old man's there, he says, but he swears Javan's nowhere to be found.

"Dad, I'm home." The cool linoleum of the kitchen floor soothes my tired toes. I tug open the fridge and feel unexpectedly violent. A wall of amber-colored beer bottles separate me from the pitcher of filtered water behind. I shove them aside and free the pitcher.

"Seriously, Dad. This is ridiculous. You stocking up for the apocalypse?"

When I kick the door shut with my sweaty foot, I see my father. He's leaning against the archway separating the kitchen from the living room.

"Am I out of beer? Can you pick me up a six-pack?" Each word carries the hint of a slur, and sick runs down his shirt. Speckles of it fleck his beard.

"Really, Dad?" I say, shaking the pitcher at him. "Really?"

He just stares at me, his eyes on my wrist. I plop the pitcher down and yank the halo off, shoving it into my back pocket. Dad pushes past me and grabs a half-empty beer from the counter.

"You really think you need another one?"

"It's Saturday, all right?" he says, swatting at the air like a petulant child.

"Saturday is not synonymous with 'drink yourself stupid,' Dad. Neither is Tuesday or Wednesday or—"

"Independence Day."

"Exactly."

"I *am* sorry about that, Elle." He takes a few wobbly steps into the kitchen and pulls a glass from the cupboard next to the sink. He presses two hands flat on the counter, steadying himself, before he picks up the pitcher. He fills the glass, sloshing water onto the counter, and hands it to me.

"And yet here you are, drinking yourself stupid again. What is going on with you?"

The fur lining his lip trembles. His eyes slide back and forth behind red-rimmed lids, veins blossoming like roses against the yellowing whites of his eyes.

"I just miss you, Hannah."

There are moments when looking like my mom royally sucks.

"Dad . . ."

My phone beeps. Dad and I both turn our eyes to my pocket, where the light of my screen penetrates my jeans. It beeps again.

"That your boyfriend?"

"It's probably Kaylee. We're supposed to—"

"Bet it's your boyfriend."

I yank the phone from my pocket intending to prove him wrong, but when I look up again, he's trundling away. He falls into his La-Z-Boy, his eyes unfocused. My phone beeps again—the call going to voice mail—but I power off the phone, watching instead as the strongest man I've ever known opens another bottle of beer.

It's still light, but the sky is streaked with pink and orange, the sun finally going down on this long summer day. So I slide into an old tank top and a pair of boxers and give myself permission to call it a night.

Turns out it *was* Jake on the phone earlier. I text him, promising to see him tomorrow, and crawl into bed far too aware that a nightmare is waiting for me. It doesn't matter. I can't keep my eyes open any longer.

The halo won't prevent the nightmare, but I slide it under my pillow anyway. I think it eases the transition, and it certainly makes drifting off more pleasant. Warm, soft. I close my eyes as the celestial heat of the halo spreads down my back, my hamstrings, my calves, even my heels. Color assaults my mind, and I surrender to it. How pleasant this used to be before the nightmares. As sleep takes me, I pray for a reprieve.

Instead, the nightmare changes.

It's the girl again, her face emerging from the colors. But I'm closer and I get a better look this time. She has large, dark eyes and raven hair that frames her face. She's young, younger than she was the last time I saw her. I ponder the impossibility of that as my ears prick at a sound.

She's talking to me. "Are you sick?"

I blink, looking around. It's bright here. Much brighter than the marble hallway. We're in a waiting room. At a hospital, I think.

"You look sick."

"Do I?"

She nods, scribbling away at the coloring book in her lap. I feel my face stretch as I offer her a smile.

"Daddy looked like you before he died."

My smile falls away. I feel that too. My stomach is sick, but I don't know if it's the child's words that have done that or if it's part of my illness.

"The doctors think the medicine will make me better," I say.

"I hope so."

"Me too." My voice is weak and crackles with phlegm. I want to clear my throat, but I don't seem to have any control over my body. "Are you here to see the doctor too?"

She shakes her head and points her red crayon at the woman in scrubs manning the reception counter. "Mama has to work. She helps people."

"That's nice. Maybe she'll help me."

"Maybe."

I watch her coloring the picture of a unicorn. A red unicorn. "I have a little girl," I say.

Her eyes light up. "Is she here?"

"No, she's home with a friend. Sleeping, I hope."

"Will you bring her next time?" she asks. "It'd be nice to have someone to play with."

"Maybe," I say, trying and failing to produce a smile. "She's younger than you. Would that be okay?"

"Sure," she tells me, coloring the unicorn's tail blue. "I can be her babysitter. Like Amy. That would be okay."

I'm tired. My arms are heavy and my neck is weak. "Do you always come to work with your mom?"

"Not always. Just when Amy can't watch me. She's pretty. She has a boyfriend with a motorcycle."

I let my head fall sideways on my shoulder. "My husband has a motorcycle."

Her large eyes get even bigger. "Does he let you ride it?"

"Sometimes." My eyelids are heavy. The girl's face swims before me. Her eyes. Her necklace, so pretty with the beaded rope and the charm. Is it . . . is it a flower?

I'm going to be sick. I'm going to be sick and it's so very, very dark.

"Mama! Mama! The lady's dying. She's dying like daddy."

Her voice bounces around the darkness, tugging at my consciousness. It's not me, not my body that's dying. I know that, but the fear of death is suffocating.

I don't want to die.

I don't want to die.

I don't want to die!

"You're not dying, Brielle. Sit up. You're not dying. You're dreaming."

I blink my room into view. It's still dark. The clock on my side table says it's three a.m. Helene stands next to me, her hair braided back, her face tense.

"I'm sorry," I tell her. "I had another nightmare."

She runs her hand under my pillow. "And with the halo too."

"I don't understand why it keeps happening."

"That's not why I'm here," she tells me. "Are you presentable?"

"Yes, of course."

Without another word, she lifts me from my bed and pulls me into the Celestial, the fear of death melting within her wings.

18

Brielle

elene's wings push against the air, pulling us through the roof and over the old Miller place toward the outskirts of town.

Something's wrong. I see fear crawling down the street. A sludge of blackness, a mist fogging the air above it, makes its way down the highway. It moves quickly, speeding over the pavement toward us. I see fear daily, but this . . . this is a lot.

Helene dips low, and my stomach lurches. We're just inches off the road now, Helene's thin arms extended. We approach the fear with the crazed speed of a drag racer, but as soon as Helene's fingers make contact with the gloppy stuff, it hisses and dissolves, leaving behind only a foggy residue. Her hands have a different effect than Jake's prayers, but at her touch the fear glubs and glops to a stop. It actually retreats. Or tries to.

We're flying too fast for it to succeed, and Helene doesn't seem to be keen on letting a single gurgle of the stuff escape. I'm mesmerized.

"Where is the fear coming from?" I ask.

I hear Helene's voice in my head. "From the crowd."

The crowd?

I lift my eyes from the highway and look ahead, but the scenery's flying by so fast and it's all so bright.

"There," she says.

My eyes stream tears, but I force myself to focus. Just ahead, lining the gate to the Stratus Cemetery, are nearly a dozen people, their focus arrested by whatever's going on inside.

And there is *something* going on.

Strange flashes of light split the night. They're not yellow streaks, or orange, or even red like I've seen in the celestial sky, but silver, electric flashes. Not unlike lightning, but less chaotic, more focused.

Both of Stratus's patrol cars are parked haphazardly at the entrance to the graveyard. Deputy Wimby stands guard at the gate, though by the fear pooling from the onlookers, I don't imagine a single one of them is too eager to enter.

"What's going on?"

Helene doesn't answer, but her wings pick up speed, lifting us off the highway and over the crowd. Over Wimby. We fly over headstones and statues, over placards and grass wilting in the summer heat. I can't help but notice how calm it's gotten in the past few seconds, and then I realize we're approaching the eastern boundary of the cemetery, near my mother's grave.

My heart couldn't beat any faster—not after that nightmare and Helene's unexpected visit—but it's trying its hardest.

And then I hear it. High pitched and eerie, like the sound of a missile falling. Every half second brings it closer and closer. I see nothing, but I sense it, hear it, the sound of something large dropping from above.

"Here it comes again!"

The cry comes from below us, where the sheriff squats behind a crumbling gravestone. His hat is askew, his orange hair almost neon in the celestial light. His walkie-talkie is pressed to his mouth.

"Everybody down!"

There's authority in his voice, and even within the safety of Helene's wings, I flinch.

And then destruction. A crash like I've never heard or imagined. The world shudders as that strange silver lightning explodes everywhere. So bright it cows the buttery yellows of the celestial sky.

Helene doesn't slow, doesn't wince. She moves forward, faster, if anything, and I see the willow tree come into view. Like the spattering of a strobe, the umbrella-like canopy of its branches spits shades of silver light into the sky.

Whatever's happening is happening beneath that tree.

Where my mother's been laid to rest.

Helene rises above it, giving us a bird's-eye view. I look down in awe—terrible, horrible awe.

Mounds of dirt encircle my mother's grave. Upturned soil and grass mingle in violated bedlam. Tree roots protrude like skeletal fingers from the soil, and the cement bench I've sat on so many times is nothing but a pile of concrete crumbles.

Nothing about this image makes sense. It's like a sick kaleidoscope—the original image twisted and twisted beyond recognition.

And then I see the stone angel. The one who's been weeping over my mother for a decade and a half. I watch as she is shattered by a shard of silver light ricocheting from within my mother's grave.

Helene darts sideways to avoid the shard, and I suddenly understand that my mother's grave has been desecrated.

That it's *being* desecrated.

That I'm watching it happen.

The stone angel falls sideways from her rectangular platform. With a heavy *thud* she hits the ground, her head and shoulders, the top of her wings, separated from the rest of her sculpted figure. They topple away several feet and sink inches deep into the upturned mud.

"Why?" The word forms in my mind. I've no idea if I actually say it, but it's the only thing I can think. Over and over it hums in my chest. *Why? Why? Why?*

Dirt flies from the grave en masse, and then a face appears, rising from the mud.

Glowing. Radiant.

Angelic.

He rises from the gaping hole, wings of blade lifting and then holding him in place before us. I can do nothing but stare.

Helene speaks to him, leaving her mind open, allowing me to hear the conversation.

"Virtue," she says.

Her mind is quiet but sure.

"Helene," he says, giving me the same courtesy. "I am sorry to arrive with the sound of destruction."

"If it's necessary . . ."

"It is, and I am not yet finished."

Helene pushes back with her wings, deferring to him, giving him room, but the angel doesn't move. The tilt of his head makes me think he's looking at me, and indeed his words seem to be for me alone.

"I am sorry for your pain," he says, pressing closer to us.

Which pain? Which one?

"But you've chosen truth. It is best that you have it all."

And then he opens his mouth, worship pouring forth as he rises into the sky again and plummets to the earth, his dagger-like wings tearing through the gigantic hole he's created and into my mother's casket. It's a violent, forceful thing that pulls my stomach into my mouth. It's sick. Whatever this is, this is a desecration of something . . . sacred?

Is my mother's grave sacred? I don't know. But it's special. It's where her body was laid to rest, and while I know deep down that it's her soul that's most important, her body surely has some value.

Surely it doesn't deserve to be unearthed like this, exposed in its decay.

I lash out. Or try to. My legs squirm in an attempt to kick against the sinewy wings holding me tight; my elbows and fists press against them too, but I'm useless against Helene's embrace. Exhausted, I give up, sinking deeper and deeper into confusion and hating the beautiful creature clawing away at my mother's resting place.

"There's a reason, Brielle," Helene tells me. "There has to be."

I can't see it. The possibility that this senseless, frenzied devastation can have reason.

And then Helene is singing. Something about the kindness of God. About His holiness and truth. They're words I've heard before, words I've mouthed at the little church in town, words I've learned much from. But now, in the midst of the flying mud and the shivering lightning, they anger me.

Holy? Kind? Just?

Canaan arrives, Jake tucked to his chest. I stare through his inner wings and into Jake's face, into eyes that burn with compassion, and then I pinch my eyes shut. I close him out and let fear take me. I let it shake me. I let it consume every part of me, because it's better than the disappointment that comes with watching God destroy the tiniest shred of something I never had. Of something I always wanted.

Of the thing I lost before I knew I needed it.

My mother.

And then it's quiet. Even Helene's voice is gone. I open my eyes. Before me is nothing but a silver sheen. I squint at it, beginning to make out the silhouette of a man-like head and shoulders.

Virtue.

He's close, so close to my face.

I burrow back into Helene.

"Finding truth is hard. But yesterday's knowledge is a lie. The grave is empty, child of God. See. Understand."

The grave is empty? Isn't that what the angel said at Christ's tomb? What is he talking about?

The sheen before me increases, brighter and brighter until I have to close my eyes to be rid of it. When at last the shimmer beyond my lids fades, I open them to find that Helene has set me down and released me from her inner wings. I stand in the mud before my mother's grave, the silver angel and his wings of destruction gone. And then Jake is next to me, his hand in mine.

Sirens wail. Radios beep and sputter words that are garbled and meaningless. In the distance, the sheriff's voice crackles through a megaphone.

I pull away from Jake and step toward the rift cut into the ground, to the place where my mom's casket was buried.

"Brielle," Jake says, all concern and kindness. "Why don't you let me look first?"

I don't even spare him a glance. Protecting me can only go so far. And what that angel unearthed was unearthed for me. I drag shaky fingers through my hair. I don't know why I have to see, but I do. I know that black hole holds nothing but bones and dirt, but I need to see. I need to know why it was dug up.

Still my breath comes quick and shallow, and I don't refuse Jake when he takes my hand. The debris is everywhere and makes it hard to walk in a straight line. Jake kicks aside a large hunk of root and grass. I sidestep several shards of cement from the fallen angel and wood slivers from . . . the casket.

The thought makes me light-headed, and I grip Jake's hand more fiercely.

When I reach the lip of the grave, Helene is already there. Without a word she drops into the hole, a flash of her auburn hair the last thing I see.

I kneel, intending to follow her. My bare knees press into the upturned soil, and I find relief in the earthy feel of it. The dirt is cool and damp and my hands sift it, knead it, looking for answers I don't expect to find.

Jake's next to me, the muscles in his arms tense, his face staid. At last I summon the courage to peer over the edge of the grave, and I see . . .

Nothing.

The darkness presses close, and I can't see past it.

"What do you see?" I ask Jake.

"Nothing," he says quietly. "Not even Helene."

I shift my feet and drop to my backside, using my heels to pull me closer to the edge.

"Here," Jake says, wrapping my forearm with his hand. "I'll lower you down."

Now I do spare a glance for him, for a look into his eyes. It's too dark for their color to show through, but there's understanding there. He knows I need to do this.

I need to know.

I think he needs to know too.

I wrap my fingers around his forearm and let him lower me. Helene finds my waist in the dark and guides me down. It's not far—I guess they really do bury you six feet under.

The great silver angel has carved out an area much larger than my mother's casket. Helene and I stand on a flattened plane of dirt just next to it, but my sight is still limited. I can see that the lid of the casket has been shattered, and I kneel to pull the wood away. My hands tremble at the task.

"What will I find?" I ask Helene.

It's a minute before she responds. "Stand and I'll show you."

I do, allowing her to step behind me. With a tic of her inner wings, Helene pulls me once again into the Celestial. She kicks her feet sideways, so that we hover over the casket.

Light floods my eyes and heat assaults me. My heart hammers, blood rushes loud in my ears, and I finally release the scream that's been building inside my chest.

My mother's casket is empty.

19

Brielle

*N*o bones. No clothing fragments. The inside of Mom's casket is pristine, the satin lining marked only with today's mud splatter. The ruched pillow at the head of the box has flattened over time, but it's never been lain upon.

I don't know that, I suppose. But I do. Deep in my gut, the emptiness of my mom's grave confirms so much of what I've never felt. Of what I've needed.

How many times have I sat here, on a stone bench that's now nothing more than rubble? The willow tree, the angel, the quiet surroundings offered simple condolences, but instead of completing something in me, instead of being a place to mourn and remember, Mom's grave has never felt anything but vacuous. This place sucked my emotions away, leaving me as empty as the coffin below.

At my request, Helene releases me. We're still belowground, the wooden box shattered, the moist dirt falling in small avalanches around us. Without Helene's wings wrapped around me, without the halo, it's all so dark, and it takes a minute for my eyes to adjust. The moon is wonky tonight—a balloon that's

lost some of its air—but it's bright, and after a few moments I
have to acknowledge that I've seen all there is to see.

There's nothing here. No sign my mother was ever laid to
rest. I sink to the ground, press into the mud wall behind me,
and stare at the hollow coffin.

"I'll give you a minute," Helene says, "but that's all we can
afford. The sheriff is gathering his resources now. They won't
be long."

If by "resources" she means Deputy Wimby, we might have
more time than she knows.

Out of the corner of my eye I see her throw Jake a glance,
and then she's gone. His face, however, hovers above, but it's
only there for a moment more. His feet swing over—bare—and
he drops next to me—shirtless. He was dragged from bed as
well, it seems. From his dream to my nightmare.

He doesn't say anything. He just sits and takes my hand.

I'm grateful.

"The first time you kissed me was here," I say.

"And the second."

I turn and press my face into the hollow at his neck, wanting to be anywhere but here, wanting to relive that moment. I've
done it so many times. Eyes closed, quietly remembering. But
I'll save it for later, when the sirens are silenced, when I'm lost in
my own sheets and blankets. When my surroundings are more
dream and less nightmare.

But even my dreams aren't safe anymore.

I force my thoughts back to now, as dreadful as now seems
to be.

"When we visited Ali's grave last month, and the month before,
and the month before that," I say, "I felt a peace. It was like my own

feelings, but what I was experiencing were hers. Her body was at rest. At peace." I shift, something sticky pulling at my knee. "But here? The only time I've ever felt anything here has been with you."

Jake doesn't say anything, but we've had similar discussions before. He's always kind, but I know he's not as dependent on feelings as I am. And I do *feel* now. Confused. Lost. And from somewhere deep within a sense of betrayal starts to form.

"Dad must've known—when he buried her. He must've known the casket was empty."

"Why do you say that?"

I have to think about the question. Have to reason my way to an answer, because Jake's implication—that it happened unbeknownst to Dad—is entirely plausible. It could have been an error by the funeral home or something else equally unlikely. But something about Virtue's words, about his showing up while Dad is all misery and alcohol—something makes me certain.

Dad knew.

"Give him the benefit of the doubt, okay?" Jake says. "This is going to be hard enough on the guy."

After all my dad has put Jake through, it's strange for him to be all Bill O'Reilly about it. Fair and balanced or whatever they claim. But he's right, and I know it.

Still, I'd rather he just take my side.

"There aren't sides here," he says, reading my mind again. "Just"—he fingers a shard of a wood protruding from the casket—"man, just devastation. And there's more than enough of it to go around."

Something skitters across my foot, small with lots of legs. I jerk, trying to be rid of it, but the thing is stubborn and clings to my ankle. I knock it away with my hand.

And then Helene is here.

"The sheriff's heading this way," she says. "He's gathered a crew to assess the damage. If you'd like to stay we can, but we should at least take to the Celestial."

I can hear them, their voices, their feet on the cobbled path. The sheriff shouts instructions; several men interrupt, asking questions. Their voices are gruff, demanding.

Angry.

In my mind's eye I imagine them carrying pitchforks, and I don't want to be here when they arrive.

I turn back to Helene. Her hands are on her hips, her legs straddling the casket. It's casual, almost haphazard, and my stomach twists at the near disregard for . . .

For what?

It's nothing but an empty box.

And it's never been anything more than that.

"I'm ready," I say. "Let's get out of here."

We land in my living room to the sound of a ringing phone. The answering machine picks up as we transfer to the Terrestrial. The three of us stand in a triangle—Helene, Jake, and I—staring at the end table where the phone and the small machine sit side by side. Our outgoing message is old, recorded nearly a decade ago—Dad and I singing some stupid jingle and then bursting into laughter. It's a relic of older, kinder days, and it makes me ill to hear it.

Especially now.

With a click, the machine starts recording.

"Keith. Mike here." I recognize the voice. It's Sheriff Cahill. The one we saw cowering behind the crumbling tombstone just minutes ago. He and Dad are friends, played high school football together back in the day.

"We've had some . . . vandalism out here at the cemetery." It's quiet for a second or two. "It's going to be on the news, buddy, there's no way around that, and I'd rather you get the details from me. I'm going to be stuck here for some time, but as soon as I can get away I'll stop by your place. Just do me a favor, Keith. If you get this, give me a call on my cell before you even think about snapping on the television."

I drop onto the couch and curl into a ball. My legs and arms are grimy, my shorts brown with muck. I need a shower, but all I really want to do is curl up and watch reruns of *I Love Lucy*.

I don't want to deal with Dad. He's either drunk or hungover. Maybe both.

And it's late.

Or early.

Whatever.

"Go to bed, Brielle," Helene says. "Let the police assume the responsibility of informing your dad, and let me talk to Virtue."

Her instructions are tempting, but I can't help feeling like I'm shirking some sort of daughterly responsibility. Do I really want Dad to hear this from someone else? From the sheriff?

"I don't know."

"She's right," Jake says, kneeling before me. "Unless you want to explain to your dad what you saw and how you saw it, you'd better let Sheriff Cahill talk to him."

I count the stitches on the couch cushion, picking at them as I go. I've torn eight of them free when I lose it.

"This is . . . ahhh! It's just ridiculous," I say. I'm tired and angry and confused. "What was he thinking, burying an empty box? Visiting it every week. Taking flowers and cards and . . . and me to a mound of dirt with . . . nothing underneath it."

Jake rubs my knees. "Benefit of the doubt, remember?"

He's gorgeous—that soft hair, those eyes both dark and light, a tall, muscled build—but sometimes I want to punch him.

"Let's not jump to any conclusions just yet, okay?" Helene sits next to me on the couch. "Virtue's words—his presence here—shouldn't be taken lightly. Whatever happened to your mother's body holds some relevance. If it didn't, I doubt he'd have unearthed the absence of it."

My throat dries at the mention of the Sabre. "Why are they here?"

She smiles. "He's no threat to you, Elle. He's a Sabre. A very powerful, very gifted angel."

"But my mother's grave? Why?"

"I can't begin to guess why he destroyed your mother's grave," Helene says. "But all twelve of them have left the Throne Room, Elle. Only the Father Himself could make such a request."

"I don't understand, though. They could all see him—the crowd—and they could hear him."

"They get brighter as they fight," Helene says, her face seeming brighter itself. "It's beautiful, isn't it?"

I think of him plummeting to earth, of the sheriff screaming a warning. "Surely he could have accomplished . . . all that . . . in secret."

Helene brushes away a tear I never intended to release. Her hands are warm, sisterly, almost motherly, and for the first time tonight grief replaces anger and fear at center stage, and I mourn the loss of the thing I never had. I mourn the one thing that would fill the emptiness.

I mourn my absent mother.

"Some things," Helene says, "were never meant to be secret."

I let Jake walk me to my room. My thigh brushes the rumpled comforter on my bed, and for a moment I crave the deep escape of sleep. My pillow's warm, the sheets inviting, but memories of my last nightmare chase the desire away. The last time I let warm and inviting take over, I dreamed about red unicorns with blue tails and little girls I didn't know.

And death.

"It's going to be okay, Brielle," Jake tells me. "We'll figure it out."

I stare at my wall, at the child Cosette. I stare at her broom and her bondage and I wonder if there are puzzles that can't be solved. Jake would never think that way. He can't. He's a healer. He thinks everything can be fixed, but what if it's more complicated than that? What if someone doesn't want to be fixed? What if there isn't a body to heal?

I don't have the wherewithal to argue with him. I'm hollow. There's nothing left to expend, just dents and dings where I've been scraped empty.

I run a hand over Cosette's face. "Okay."

"No, I mean it," he says. "We will."

He's on a mission. I feel it. He's going to make me feel better or die trying. But the idea of rehashing today is overwhelming.

"Okay."

"Elle . . ." There's an ache in his voice as he gathers me to his chest, holding me. Like a bandage, like one of those butterfly bandages that hold everything together. But as a wound I'm bled dry, and his arms make it hard to breathe. I pull away.

"I believe you, Jake, I do. But can we figure it all out tomorrow? I'm just . . . I'm . . ."

His arms are still open, still hanging there, waiting for me to crawl into them. "You're tired," he says. "Of course you are."

"I'm . . . yes, I'm tired."

He's hurt. I know he is, but there's that emptiness in me, that inability to carry his hurt alongside mine.

"Okay," he says, dropping his arms. "I'll go."

The door closes behind him, and still I feel nothing. I'm not scared. I'm not angry. I'm just nothing. I fall into my desk chair and roll it to the window. The blinds are up, and I press my cheek to the glass, wanting to feel the cold on my face, wanting it to wake me. It's not enough, and my eyes close. Forcing them open, I yank the window open, feeling the cold night air on my face. But the night can't last forever, and when the sun crests over the horizon my face is warmed by its rays and my eyes close. I've no energy left to fight it.

And the nightmare takes hold.

20

Brielle

I wake screaming.

My rolling chair has slid away from the window and tipped me onto the floor. I clamp a hand over my mouth, mortified, hoping I haven't roused Dad. If there's anyone I want to avoid this morning, it's him.

But he's gone. His bed unmade, his room empty.

I wander his room, looking for the old Dad, I guess. It's a man's room. A stinky room. On his side table is the oldest Harley Davidson key ring in the world, seven keys hanging off it. Wherever he's gone, he didn't do the driving. Someone's picked him up. I'm guessing the sheriff, but I don't let myself think about where they went or what they're doing.

His dresser is cluttered with pictures, but at the front is a picture of Mom, her loose curls lying perfectly on her shoulders, the same shade as mine. The picture's faded, so her blue eyes look gray here, but they sparkle. Like she's madly in love with the guy taking the picture. I wonder what she was like back then.

I'm up early courtesy of that dreadful nightmare, but Jake's still here to pick me up before I've even brushed my teeth. He's looking all handsome, dressed in black, a pair of slacks and a suit shirt. He's even wearing a thin gray tie today, and it's hard to remember just why I needed him to leave last night.

"I'm sorry about last night," I say.

"You needed space. You're entitled."

He busies himself in the kitchen, nuking me a Pop-Tart and whistling the *Transformers* theme song. The whistling is a habit he picked up from Canaan, and if there's any habit of his that drives me crazy, it's that.

Especially when I haven't slept.

I shush him twice, warning him not to wake up Dad before I remember that Dad's not even home.

He's out.

With the sheriff.

All ready, I find Jake in the living room watching the morning news. Sheriff Cahill was right. Mom's desecrated grave has made headlines. In fact, it seems to be *the* headline. It's terrifying and far too familiar seeing my last name on the television screen.

I watch the big city reporter with her big city hair, but all I really see is my dad in the background standing over a mound of dirt, Sheriff Cahill's arm around his shoulders. The sheriff's not a tall man, so he has to actually reach up to accomplish the feat, but it's a sentimental shot.

A rip-out-your-heart kind of shot.

And it kills me that my family's given the media another one of those shots to splash about.

I walk to the television and snap it off.

I turn away, toward Jake. Toward the one person I know would never mess with my emotions. He's staring at me, his eyes soft.

"I'm so sorry, Elle."

"Let's just get outta here, okay? Before we have reporters camped out on the doorstep."

"Good call," Jake says. "You still up for a stop at Jelly's? We don't have to, if you'd rather not."

"No, let's. I haven't had a single cup of bad coffee today. I'm due."

Jake and I have this Sunday morning tradition. It's silly, really, and it started as kind of a joke. When Kaylee realized that Jake was a churchgoer and that he'd "dragged me into the Jesus stuff"—please note the air quotes—she gave him a hard time. Nothing awful, just Kaylee being Kaylee in her awkward, clumsy, goofing-on-everybody kind of way.

But Jake wasn't fazed by her good-natured contempt. Instead, he went out of his way to invite her to church. Almost daily. Slipping it into conversations. Texting her. Sending her Evites. He even signed her yearbook, "See you at church!"

Her excuse, as always, was that she works on Sundays.

So we stop by Jelly's.

Every Sunday.

And Jake comes up with new ways to torment her. And even though Delia's tried to shove her out the door with us a few times, we still haven't gotten Kaylee into a pew.

But it's a lot of fun trying.

I shake my hair out. This morning I could use a little fun.

"So what's the plan today?" I ask, forcing my mind away from Dad, away from what he's probably seeing right now—or not seeing, as the case may be.

"Doughnuts."

"No, I mean for Kaylee."

"So do I."

Jake waggles his eyebrows but says nothing more.

I squint at him, but this is a secret I can let him keep. For now.

Jelly's is packed. We park across the street in front of the theatre, and I start toward the diner.

"The Donut Factory first," Jake says, taking my hand and leading me across the street. "You look gorgeous today, by the way."

I'm wearing a pale green slip dress and three-inch heels that make me nearly as tall as he is. But the real stunner, I'm sure, is that I've actually done my hair—I mean, beyond a simple braid or a knot on top of my head. I got the blow-dryer out and everything. It's silky and shiny because I feel a fraction better about the world when I'm all dressed up.

"Thought a good scrubbing was in order," I say. "I think I've rolled around in the mud enough for a while."

"You don't look half bad caked in mud either," he says.

"Yes, well. I'd rather not repeat last night if it can be avoided."

The back of his hand grazes my cheek. "Point taken."

The ever-present trio of old men are holding court in front of The Donut Factory as we approach. Custard-filled long johns and the upcoming elections seem to be on the agenda for today. Based on what I pick up as we close in, Bob's throwing his name into the ring for president.

Woody—short, square, hobbitish—whistles as I step onto the curb. I give him a slight curtsy.

"Donut, Jake?" Bob says.

Jake slaps Bob on the shoulder, throwing his aviator cap forward.

"Thanks, but I've got an order waiting for me inside. Rain check?"

"Depends. Who you voting for?"

"You're kidding, right? I've got my Bob Cobb for President T-shirt on order, and take a look at my bumper."

We all turn. Sure enough, the Karmann Ghia's dented bumper sports a red, white, and blue sticker with the words *Bobb Cobb for President* printed on it.

How did I not notice that before?

"Does Bobb really have two Bs?"

Jake shushes me.

I bite my lip to keep from laughing, but Bob's oblivious—to both my question and the typo.

"Good man," he says. "You can share my table anytime."

Woody whistles once again, and I give him a little wink. We leave them to their politics and step into The Donut Factory where you don't breathe oxygen—you breathe coffee and sugar. Two things that will forever remind me of Jake.

"You have doughnuts on order?" I ask.

Another eyebrow waggle.

"Thanks, Lizzie," Jake says, bypassing the line of customers and taking a pink box from the girl behind the counter.

"Sure, Jake."

"Don't you have to pay her?" I ask as we step back onto the sidewalk.

"Nah. She'll just put it on my tab."

"You have an open tab at The Donut Factory?"

"Better than having one at Beers and Bikes, right?"

I cringe, pretty sure that Dad has a tab there.

"So, you gonna show me?" I ask.

"Show you what?"

"The doughnuts!"

"I don't think so," he says, opening the door to Jelly's. "Let's just say I've been doing some research."

Kaylee's sitting in a booth. Alone. Which is funny, because the place is crammed with people, shoulder to shoulder, waiting for a table. She sits, with only a glass of OJ and a book called *The Idiot's Guide to Peru*.

I drop into the seat next to her. "Hey."

"You're here! I so did not expect to see you guys this morning." She closes her book, looking strange and sympathetic.

My stomach twists. I hate that look. The one that says she feels sorry for me. That she wishes there was something she could do to help, when clearly there's not.

I had enough of that after Ali.

"Delia said she saw on the news—your mom's grave? I'm so sorry, Elle."

I look away, tuck my hair behind my ear, straighten my dress—anything to avoid the pity on her face.

"What's up with—"

"My dad burying an empty casket?" I shrug. "Really couldn't tell ya."

Her mouth drops open. I hear it pop and look up.

"The casket was empty?" She grabs my hand. "What does that . . . I don't think that was on the news, Elle. Delia would have said something."

"Yeah, well. Let's talk about you, okay? I'm kinda done talking about me for a while."

"Sure," she says. "Sure."

We all go silent, allowing the *clink* and *clank* of the diner to invade our booth. I can't think of a thing to say.

"So what's this?" Jake says, thumbing her book. "Elle says

you've been studying Peru since freshmen year. What don't you know?"

"I don't know," she says. "That's the point. I don't know what I don't know, and if I'm going to be assigned there . . ."

"You got your Peace Corps assignment?"

"I wish. It's taking forever. But if I'm going to live there for a year, I need to know everything. Anyway," she says, yanking the book from Jake's hands, "don't try to be all interested in my book. I know why you're here."

"I don't think you do," Jake says, opening the pink box.

Kaylee's face wrinkles like a squished pear. I really can't blame her. The contents of the box are unexpected, to say the least. We're looking at a dozen or so of these onion-ring-looking things.

"What are they?" I ask.

"Picarones," Kay says, her face brightening.

"That's right!" Jake says. "I can't believe you know what they are."

"I've had them before," she says, hooking one with her finger. "At a cultural seminar I took in Portland." She breaks off a piece and slides it into her mouth. "Oh my gosh. I forgot how good they are. How did you . . . Where did you . . ."

"There was this lady who worked for Canaan at the orphanage in Chicago—one of the kitchen staff. She was from Peru, and she made these picarones for the kids from time to time. I hold her solely responsible for my doughnut preoccupation, by the way. Anyway, I got Lizzie at The Donut Factory to give the recipe a shot. This is her first batch, but she loved them so much she's going to get her dad to add them to the menu."

"Jaaaaake. You really are the nicest guy in the whole wide world." She leans across the table, squishing half the donuts and pulling Jake in for a hug. When she settles back down, her shirt

145

is covered with crumbs and her eyes are full of tears. "Thank you. Really. I mean, holy cow, is it weird to say that a box of Peruvian doughnuts is the best gift I've ever gotten?"

I beam at Jake. Talk about knocking this one out of the park.

"What about the Furby Delia got you for Christmas that one year? She tackled Liam Hanson's dad to get you that thing."

"Forgot about that," she says, giggling and shoving another bite into her mouth. "I won't tell Delia, then, but, Jake, seriously. Best. Gift. Ever."

"You won't tell me what?" Delia asks from a couple booths away.

"Nothing," we all say.

Delia sets down a couple plates and shoves past a slew of diners to get to our table.

"You're taking this girl to church, aren't ya?"

"Auntie, I can't, remember?" She looks to Jake. "But I really, truly have a good excuse this time."

"Let's hear it, then," Jake says, feigning frustration.

"My mom and dad are stopping by."

"We'll see," Delia huffs, her stomach moving up and down, bumping the table.

"Well, anyway, that's why I'm not working today. They don't know about my Peace Corps plans yet, and I thought I should at least let them know."

"You should," Jake says. "Tell your parents. Share your doughnuts. We'll leave you to them, actually. We don't want to be late."

I kiss her cheek and slip out of the booth and past Delia.

"Thanks again, Jake," Kaylee says. "Really. Better than a Furby."

Delia steals a doughnut from the box and heads back to the kitchen.

"We'll see."

21

Brielle

Sunday revelation: an astounding percentage of church-goers watch the news before heading off to worship. I'm squeezed and patted, my cheeks smeared with various shades of lipstick. It's overwhelming, all these ladies in their Sunday best, their hairspray and perfume and soft sweaters pressed against me. Their promises to keep Dad and me in their prayers.

My lips tremble, but I force them into a smile and grip Jake's hand.

They're all so kind. But I'm angry and lost, and their kindness just might break me today.

The sanctuary fills with voices, human and flawed, singing about our Savior. Some sounding like skilled musicians, some pitchy and flat all at once. I mouth the words but let the others do the singing. I notice Pastor Noah's not here today, but his wife, Becky, leads the congregation from the piano. Stephanie stands at her side, harmonizing. The two of them are lovely, angelic even. Next to me Jake sings, his eyes closed, the tender rasp of his voice most appealing here, in worship.

And though our elbows brush, I've never felt so far from where he is.

The song is a favorite here, and I know each word before it's sung. They're beautiful words. Words that lift up Christ, thank Him for His sacrifice, declare that all things work together for the good of those who love Him.

But today it's hard.

I close my eyes tighter and tighter. Try as I may, I just can't see it.

Jake's working again today, so I plan to grab my camera and disappear for a while. Far from Dad and whatever explanation he's cooking up. But the second I step through the front door, I know I've walked into an ambush.

Pastor Noah is here. He sits on a barstool at the counter, eating a hefty serving of chocolate chip pancakes. I happen to know Dad hates this guy. Hates. More than he hates the Red Sox. Seeing him in my kitchen is bizarre—weirder than finding Dad flipping flapjacks for a koala bear. Next to him is my boss, Miss Macy. She's pancake-free but stands there in a pair of jeans, nursing a cup of steaming coffee.

It's always strange to see her wearing anything but a leotard.

"Elle, sweetheart." Her lips are tipped down, her chin puckering. More sympathy. Yeah. But she squeezes me tight, smelling like fruit and sunshine, and I can't help the tears that spring to my eyes.

"What are you doing here?"

"Your dad asked us to stop by," she says, rubbing my arms

like I've caught a chill. I turn my eyes to Dad, but he's flipping a pancake, patently avoiding eye contact.

He's a chicken.

A big, fat chicken.

The kitchen door opens then, and the sheriff walks in.

"Sorry I'm late," he says, removing his hat. "Cemetery's a mess. We're going to have to—" He sees me and stops.

Miss Macy and Pastor Noah are strange additions to the kitchen this afternoon, but Sheriff Cahill? Pretty sure I know exactly what that's about. I can only assume Dad invited Miss Macy and Pastor Noah for moral support.

And suddenly I'm out of place here. In my own house. I know things I shouldn't know. Things they have to tell me but would rather not.

"I'm just going to change."

"Go ahead, Elle," Dad says, his eyes lingering on Mom's Bible clenched in my fist. "Get changed. We'll be here when you're through."

I kick off my heels as soon as I enter my room. They skitter across the carpet, disappearing under my bed. I swap out my slip dress for jeans and a yellow T-shirt, all the while considering just why Dad included Pastor Noah in this terrifying little gathering.

Of all the people in the known universe, Canaan included, Noah is the last person I'd have expected Dad to invite into our house. Noah and Becky were old friends of Mom's, churchy friends, and Dad's not keen on churchy folk. Out of ideas, but still hoping to stall, I run a brush through my hair and stare at myself in the mirror over my dresser.

I catch sight of the halo on my wrist. It's grabbing hold of the sunlight spitting through my blinds and sending it back brighter and more beautiful than ever. I wonder what they'd all think if I put it on my head and wore it out there.

I wonder what I'd see.

I grab the white sweater hanging on my desk chair and slide it on over the halo. No point provoking Dad right now.

I leave my room, lingering in the hallway outside the kitchen. I listen, but the words are all whispers. I consider hiding in my room and calling Jake, telling him to call in sick, get over here, help me face this. Instead, I press my head against the wall and I pray. A good one. A long one. And then, sliding on my sneakers, I step into the kitchen.

But it's empty.

Answered prayer?

"In here," Dad calls, deflating my happy thought. "Thought we'd be more comfortable this way."

Maybe it's not an answered prayer, but it's progress. I can't remember the last time Dad thought of anyone's comfort but his own.

I walk across the kitchen, grabbing a lukewarm pancake from the stack. I tear off a piece and shove it into my mouth as I step through the archway leading to the living room. Dad's given his chair to Noah, which might be the weirdest thing yet. Miss Macy sits on the couch, her legs crossed, coffee cup still glued to her hand. Sheriff Cahill sits in my favorite reading chair. He's thumbing through a magazine and puts it down as I enter.

Dad stands by the television, like he's going to be doing magic for us or something. I expect him to produce a large, flimsy saw and a box for me to climb into.

"Sit, baby," he says, gesturing to the couch.

Miss Macy pats the spot next to her and I sit, glad I'll at least have a hand to hold through this whole thing.

Dad clears his throat. "Elle, last night, there was some . . . trouble out at the cemetery." He rubs a sleeve across his brow and looks around. The cool he seems to have manufactured for this little meeting has fled, and panic takes control of his face. "I don't . . . umm . . . Mike, you wanna?"

"Sure," the sheriff says, leaning forward in his chair. But the pity on his face is too much, and I decide. I don't care what I have to tell this room of people, I'm not pretending my way through this conversation.

"I know about Mom's grave," I say. My words are delivered to Dad, but he's the only one in the room not looking at me.

Miss Macy rubs my arm all the harder, and Noah prays under his breath. The sheriff rolls onto his heels and pushes back so he's sitting on the ottoman of the reading chair.

"How?" Dad says, his voice strangely gruff. "How do you know?"

This right here, this is why I should have listened to Helene.

"It was all over the news," Noah says. "All over the papers, Keith."

But Dad shrugs Noah off. "She doesn't read the paper. Doesn't watch the news. Your boyfriend told you, didn't he?"

I shake my head, but the hatred in his eyes keeps my mouth shut.

Miss Macy saves me.

"It's been everywhere, Keith. Knock it off."

The room goes quiet. It seems Dad is still waiting for an answer. He wants to know how I knew, but I'm not going to lie to him.

"Why?" I say, my voice dry. "Why was the casket empty?"

Dad's eyes snap to Mike's.

"I swear," Mike says, "that part wasn't released to the press . . . to anyone, Keith. No one knows about that. It's just like I told you."

"You're still trying to hide stuff? I *know*, Dad. Does it really matter how?"

"It's a small town," Noah says. "Word gets around."

"I want to know how," Dad says stubbornly.

I'm mad now. Really, really mad. "Yeah, well, I want to know why, Dad. Why was her casket empty?"

The sheriff is embarrassed, yanking at his collar, his face slick. "There are several scenarios that fit the evidence, Miss Matthews."

"No, no, no," Dad says. "If we're gonna do this, let me do it right."

"Good man," Pastor Noah says.

Dad glares at him, forcing Noah farther back into his seat. Then he laces his fingers and turns to me. For the first time in forever he looks clear. Determined.

I'm hopeful. And then he starts talking.

"Your mother was terminal," Dad says. "She was incredibly ill and you were very, very small. I needed help. Miss Macy was the logical choice. She was a friend of Hannah's. In fact, when your mom made up her will, she insisted on listing Miss Macy as your godmother."

I turn to her, surprised. "You're my godmother?"

Miss Macy's eyes are full of tears, her voice soft. "I can't magic you a ball gown or anything, but yes. It's what your mother wanted."

"Why didn't you tell me?"

"I wanted to," she says, stroking my hair.

"Then why didn't you? All these years . . ."

"I asked her not to say anything about that stuff, about your mom," Dad says, gruff. Irritated. "I'm not ashamed of it, Elle. I was doing my best to protect you. I'm still trying, if you haven't noticed, but I'm not the voice you listen to these days."

He's cheating. It's not fair to make me feel guilty now. But it works, and my voice wobbles.

"Dad . . ."

"It doesn't matter, kid, I'm fine. Just let me get through this." He takes a haggard breath, his shirt stretched tight across his chest. "Miss Macy helped. To tell the truth, I couldn't convince her not to."

"I loved your mom, Elle."

Dad soldiers on, brushing Miss Macy's words aside. "So Miss Macy helped. She'd sit with your mom when I couldn't, and she'd keep you when Grams was too tired. It was a hard time, kiddo. Impossibly hard. When we knew your mom had only days to live, that there was nothing more to be done, I brought her home. She wanted to be here. With you."

Tears pour down my face, but I'm silent. Her pain, the cancer, these are things I've known or assumed. Dad's response to it all, his own agony, is something he's never discussed. But I see it on him now. Even without the halo on my head, without celestial eyes, his pain is all I see.

"Miss Macy and I were both here that last night," Dad continues, producing a handkerchief and blowing his nose. "And you. You were here. You were with your mother."

"You were brushing her hair," Miss Macy says. "Painting her

nails with that Hello Kitty nail polish you loved so much. They were the most precious moments I've ever witnessed."

I pinch my eyes shut, trying to remember, willing my mind to paint the picture. But there's nothing. Only blackness. Only fear.

"And then she was just gone," Dad says.

My eyes snap open.

"What do you mean, gone?"

"Miss Macy was cooking dinner," Dad says, looking at my teacher fully for the first time. There's tenderness there—a memory shared. Miss Macy nods, tears pooling in the corners of her eyes. "And I'd just stepped out to grab a book. She liked it when I read. There was this . . ." He shakes his head. Whatever he was going to say, he's changed his mind. "It was quiet. Very, very quiet."

"Keith," Miss Macy says. Her voice is soft, but there's something of a reprimand there.

Dad ignores it, his eyes back on me. "And then your mom's machines went haywire. The alarms beeping. We'd been expecting it, knew it was coming. Her breathing had been so weak. We both dropped what we were doing and ran to the room."

He stops, unable to go on.

"You were there," Miss Macy says. "Asleep on your mama's bed. A Cinderella crown on your head and ballet slippers on your feet."

How I wish I could remember that. "And Mom?"

"She was gone," Dad says.

Gone?

Miss Macy turns me toward her, her soft, wrinkled hands firm on my forearms. "The bed was empty, honey. She must've walked out, walked past us when we weren't looking."

"How? You said yourself she was weak, her breathing frail."

"We don't know," she says, shaking her head. "We've never known."

"Could someone have taken her?" Noah says.

I'm still not sure why he's here. This information seems new to him as well.

"Perhaps," Sheriff Cahill said. "It's a theory we considered. I was just a deputy back then, but we combed the county. Had help from other agencies. Never found a thing."

"Several weeks passed with no sign of her, no leads. And with some . . . help," Dad says, looking at Miss Macy, "I finally realized that even if she was out there somewhere, she was surely gone. Her body had so little life left in it, baby, she couldn't have made it far, even with medical attention."

My head spins. My stomach aches, and I just want to go back to wondering what happened. To come up with my own unlikely scenarios. "But why the grave? Why bury an empty casket?"

"For you. For Grams," Dad says. "She begged me. Said you needed a place to go, to visit. Weeks before your mother . . . passed," he says, flinching at the outright lie, "Grams had already picked out the plot, paid for it, and selected the grave marker."

"The weeping angel."

"She was convinced it had to be done right," Dad says with a stiff shrug. "She convinced me."

"Many people have a memorial for a lost loved one," Miss Macy says. "It gives us a place to pay our respects, Elle. To mourn."

They're all so . . . nice. So benevolent about this deception. *They did it for me. For Grams.*

Whatever.

"That grave wasn't a memorial to Mom. It was . . . a lie."

"Elle . . . ," Dad says.

"I had a right to know," I say, slamming my fist into the couch. "Maybe not when I was three. I understand that. Fine. But when I was old enough to know, you could have told me, and you didn't." I let my eyes rest on Dad. "You lied to me."

He yanks at his collar. "I planned to tell you. One day. I always said I'd do it when you were older. And then you were in high school and it was easy not to. There were reasons, decent reasons not to get into it. And then you went away to Portland, to Austen. And when you came back, Elle, you had more than enough tragedy to deal with."

I'm trying to see this from his point of view. From Miss Macy's even. From the point of view of everyone who let me sit and stare at a stone statue for years and years and years.

But I can't.

I want to yell now, but Miss Macy's here, and Noah. Pastor Noah, who's the most soft-spoken man in the world. I bet he's never yelled. Ever.

Maybe that's why Dad asked him here. Anything to keep me quiet. To keep me from losing my mind. I pull away from Miss Macy and stand. "You did what you thought was best, but it sucks. A lot."

It's an awful way to exit, but they don't seem to have anything else to say and I'm through with the sympathetic stares, so I walk from the room, through the kitchen, my sneakers squeaking against the linoleum floor.

Dad's pancakes are all soggy now. The entire stack stares at me, begging me to forgive him for a lie that's stretched my entire lifetime. I'm tempted to take the plate and slam it against the floor, against the wall. I'm tempted to make a statement, to show him how mad I really am.

But I don't do mad well. I'm a crier and I know it.

I do slam the door on my way out. That's about all the violence I have in me.

22

Pearla

Pearla crouches atop a roof on Main Street. Below her, in the recessed entryway, is her mark.

Damien.

She's been following him for hours, waiting for him to do something, anything worth reporting to Michael. He's taken his human form now. Tall, olive skin, dark eyes. He leans against the wall, staring at the empty street.

It took her some days to locate him. His new eyes spotted her at once and she had to lie low for a time, but today she's managed to stay hidden, discreet. Still, he's done little to merit report.

His first stop was a farmhouse skirting the highway. He circled once and dropped through the roof. She watched as he strolled the house, his black wings brushing everything with fear. Down the hall he went and into a bedroom.

She knew right away that a Shield had made his home here. She could tell that by the onyx chest in the dwelling place. That Damien would enter a Shield's residence showed a reckless disregard, and Pearla wondered then just how much stock he was putting in those new eyes.

At first Damien ignored the chest. He walked the house,

sniffing each room, leaking fear onto the furniture. But before departing, he re-entered the Shield's room and glared at the chest. He hacked at it with his talons, beat it with his wings. He attempted to pick it up, but the chest would not move.

Finally he crouched before it, and with taloned fingers he lifted the lid.

Pearla clung to the roof, out of sight, amazed that the Throne Room would give up its secrets to one of the Fallen. She watched as he lifted a dagger from its depths. Watched as he opened his mouth and howled with delight. And then watched as his face turned hard. He tried to take the dagger, tried to slide it next to the curved sword at his waist, but the moment he sheathed it, the dagger vanished. Damien cursed as, with a heavy *clunk*, it rematerialized in the chest below. He tried again to retrieve the dagger. And once more the weapon would not be removed. In a fit of rage he left the house, flying past her, his mouth screaming hate.

Pearla doesn't understand the demon's actions, doesn't understand the significance of the dagger, but it's the one piece of information she has to report, so she tucks it away for her rendezvous with the Commander.

Soft footsteps pull her attention back to her mark. A woman approaches, crossing the street and stepping into the entryway next to Damien.

His human voice is low, threatening. "You came highly recommended."

Fear presses through the woman's satin shirt, but her voice is steady when she speaks. "So you said."

Damien steps closer. "I'm reminding you because I've yet to see progress, and my fingers are just itching to send that e-mail."

"Oh, stop. I'll get it. Things take time." She turns to go.

"You're stalling," he growls, yanking her back into the doorway.

The fear multiplies, but Pearla's impressed by the woman's ability to sound unmoved. "And why would I do that?"

"I don't know." Damien's eyes rove her face. He really doesn't know, and Pearla can see that bothers him. "But you being here, in Stratus, now, seems far too convenient."

She pokes at his chest with a long fingernail. "You didn't care where I was when you found me. You just wanted that bracelet. And I'll get it."

He pushes her back against the wall, a massive forearm to her throat. "Why Stratus?"

"The bracelet is here, right?" she says, her throat scratching for air. "Why does it matter?"

He releases her, but not before pressing her into the wall once more. "You had ties here before. Your work predates our arrangement."

"You're blackmailing me. That's not really an arrangement."

His hands curl into meaty fists. "You're not answering me."

"Look, the foundation has to do actual work from time to time. We can't just continue to funnel money into Henry's addictions. When Javan disappeared, that became possible again. And the girl . . ."

"Brielle?"

"Oh, please. Kaylee. She intrigued me. She's smart. A fast learner. We could use someone like that at the foundation."

Damien scowls. "That's it? Your interest in Stratus is a gangly teenager?"

"Yes. Like you, I'm looking for a protégé." Her words are delivered with precision. "Why would I lie to you?"

"You wouldn't, because one rogue e-mail to the authorities and you'll spend the rest of your life rotting in a jail cell."

"You've made that perfectly clear. What you haven't made clear is exactly why you want the girl's bracelet."

"Collateral."

She steps into him, running her fingernail along his chin. "That's a big word for a bad man. Are you sure you know what it means?"

Again he pushes her back. "Watch your tongue. We're running out of time, and I need time to test it before . . ."

"Before what?" Her almond-shaped eyes narrow. "What else do you have planned?"

"Just get it. And keep your phone on. I don't like having to find you."

"We done?" she asks.

Damien shoos the woman away. Fear covers her body, but she moves as if she's used to the substance, worn it often, made friends with it. With hardly a tremble in her step, she leaves the entryway and turns right, her high-heeled shoes taking her away from Damien.

He watches her go and then steps from the curb and strolls down the center of Main Street. His swagger says Stratus is his for the taking. But Pearla can't stop thinking about the bracelet that seems to have captured his imagination.

What does he want with it?

And why didn't he tell the Prince he had other plans?

23

Brielle

ad is cursing when I step out of the shower Monday morning. I hear his voice through the bathroom door, hear the hurt in his words, the anger, the hangover.

I wrap a towel around myself and slide down the wall, listening. Sheriff Cahill's trying to calm him. "We don't know. We just don't know, Keith."

Dad curses. Again. "What do you mean you don't know? It's been a day now, you should know something."

"Well, we do know there were . . . explosives involved."

"Explosives? Like firecrackers, that sort of thing?"

There's a long pause, and I press closer to the door, imagine the sheriff taking off his hat, scratching his head. "Maybe," he says. "I guess it coulda been firecrackers."

He can't believe that. I *know* what he saw, and it wasn't a souped-up Roman candle.

But I wonder how his mind assimilated the Sabre, how much it shrouded what he saw in doubt. Virtue was more light than anything else that night. Still . . .

I put my ear to the door. I'd like to get dressed, but after

162

my dramatic exit yesterday, I really don't want to talk to these two again. They can't talk long anyway. Dad's got work, and the sheriff's obviously got an investigation to conduct. But I hear nothing to suggest they're leaving. I dry my hair, and still I hear only their low voices and their feet bumping across the linoleum floor.

And then I realize they're waiting on me.

They want to talk.

What else could they possibly have to say?

I yank my pajamas on, one leg at a time, and then I climb into the shower and pop the window out with my elbow. A trick Kaylee taught me freshman year. Squeezing through is considerably more difficult than it was back then, but I pull myself through the tiny window and onto the row of trash cans Dad keeps on the side of the house. I knock the recyclables over and scratch my knee on the stucco, but I make it out.

I round the house and grab my own window, still cracked. I shove it all the way open and half climb, half tumble inside.

"Brielle?" Dad's muffled voice carries through the door. "You 'bout done in there?"

I freeze, a weird bundle on the floor, and I listen.

"Brielle?" He's knocking, but he's still at the bathroom. I strip off my pajamas and rifle through my drawer for a pair of underwear. There's a red sundress draped over my hamper. I pull it on over the underwear, grab my sandals, and cram the wretched halo onto my wrist before jumping out my window and running across the field that separates my house from Jake's.

If running away from your problems is ever acceptable, it's right now. It's this moment.

The fact that I've become an imposter in my own house—that

I'll do anything to avoid talking to my dad—hits me. The halo sends waves of heat up my arm, but it's not enough to end the battle tearing my insides apart. Still, I don't really lose it until I'm at Jake's, standing in his empty living room.

"Hello?" I yell. "Jake? Canaan?"

But no one answers.

Hating the darkness, I march through the house turning on every light. My fist slams into the switches down the hall and in the office. The walls rattle, and I release a laughing sob at the stupid sense of power it gives me. When I reach Canaan's room, I pause. It's empty. Marco's bag is tipped haphazardly on the bed, but I don't waste much time staring at the bed. It's the chest at the end of it that seems to always have half my attention these days.

Really it's the ring inside.

The hope of a happily-ever-after.

And I want to feel better right now.

But I want to be mad too.

I don't want to hurt, but I want to nurse the anger a little longer.

I can feel the halo doing its thing, thawing me, calming me.

I'm half-tempted to yank it off. To give in to the frustration. Just for a while. Because this warring sensation in my gut sucks.

The wanting to be angry.

The needing to know what happened to my mom. The wanting to forget. The desire for it all to go away.

And the whole time the halo reminds me that there's something else going on. What I see isn't always what is. It's certainly not all of it.

I tip my hand and shake the halo off my wrist. It reforms into the crown—the crown given to Canaan by God the Father.

For refusing to join Lucifer's rebellion. For staying when so many left.

The risk of sleep is nil, so I place it on my head.

Canaan's room gives off rays of light here and there, the transition slow. And then the light swallows me. So bright, so real. And as much as I hate to admit it, the sadness wanes and my anger at Dad dims. But I still don't want to see him, so I'm careful at what I look at, at how much focus I give the walls.

I like walls right now. I need them to keep unwanted sights from my eyes.

And yet it's been months since I've looked inside the chest. Months since I've seen the ring that's to be mine.

I turn my gaze on the chest and focus.

But nothing.

The sides don't thin out, they don't become transparent like every other surface when focused upon. I try harder, stepping closer to the chest.

Zip.

Zilch.

Strange.

I move toward the chest, slowly, very aware that this is not my room. But I'm trying to understand. The chest was given to Canaan by the Throne Room. Does that mean it's impenetrable?

I kneel and place my hands on the lid, lifting and shoving at the same time. The smell of wet grass and spicy evergreens wafts from within, and for the first time in forever I look forward to the autumn. To cooler weather.

"Hey!" a voice calls from the living room. "Anybody here?"

It's Marco.

Shoot.

I slide the lid shut and yank the halo from my head. I stare at it, willing it to move faster.

Come on!

As soon as it's reformed, I jam it onto my wrist and head for the door.

"Yo, intruder?" Marco calls again. "You left the door open, and I'm a paranoid ex-con. I'd answer if I were you. You don't want me going psycho on your—"

"Yeah, Marco," I yell. "It's just me. I'm here."

"Brielle?" he says, his voice closer.

We meet in the hallway near the office door.

"It's me," I say. "And you're not an ex-con."

"Tell that to the talking heads."

"Yeah, well, it seems truth depends on who's holding all the facts these days."

He looks at me through waves of black hair. "Jake told me about your mom, er, her grave. I'm sorry."

"Me too." I step past Marco and into the kitchen.

"You really think your dad buried an empty casket?"

I open the fridge and pull out a bottle of water. "He did. Told me he did, anyway. You want?" I say, offering Marco the bottle in my hand.

He takes it and sits at the kitchen table. "Why would he do that?"

I shrug. I don't want to give Dad's excuses credence by bantering them about.

"You not talking to him?"

I take a swig. "Jumped out the window instead."

"Ah. Jail break." Marco removes the lid from his water bottle and spins it on the table. It spins, spins, spins—longer than I would have thought possible, his long fingers nudging it as it slows. "Been there. Done that."

"Any advice for a first-timer?"

He stops the lid with his palm.

"Nah. Well, just that sooner or later you have to face the music. But you know that. And your dad's a good guy. Can't hold his alcohol, but he's a good guy. I'm sure there's some kind of explanation."

It's different talking to Marco. He doesn't try to fix me.

He twists the lid again and I watch it spin, thinking about the barbecue, about Marco's first impression of my dad—that he's a good guy. How could he possibly have arrived at that conclusion after the drunkard Dad turned out to be?

"You and Olivia went to school together?"

"Yeah, Benson Elementary. I haven't seen her in years. She had it rough back then. Rougher than I did, at least, and that's saying something."

Despite my dislike for the woman, I'm curious. "Her parents split up?"

"Her dad died. But that was before I knew her. She and her mom moved into the neighborhood—sheesh, when was that— well, it was the summer before fifth grade, so . . ."

"A century ago?"

He laughs. "Something like that. But then her mom died, and that was worse. A lot worse."

"How so?"

"It was a fire. We were there when it happened. Burned hot, burned fast."

"*You* were there?"

"Yeah, gah, it was awful. A fire at the school, her mom was

inside, parent/teacher conference or something. Just, you know, one of those freak things, I guess."

"Freak thing? How did the fire start?"

"I couldn't say, really. I was a kid. Eleven maybe. Ten. There was an investigation, though, I remember that. I remember the police combing the neighborhood, so I bet we could find details online." He pulls a smart phone from his pocket and opens the browser.

"But what were *you* doing there?"

"Flirting."

"With Olivia?"

He sets the phone down. "Okay, I'll admit, it's weird to see her all over your dad, but back then, she was this gorgeous young thing in a neighborhood that was a little desperate for beautiful things."

It's strangely therapeutic to know I wasn't the only one with a fractured childhood. "I didn't realize you grew up poor. I thought your dad had money."

"Sometimes. He had these ideas. Always with the ideas. Half the time we were rolling in cash, the other half we were scrounging the couch cushions for change to pay rent." He slides his finger over his phone again. "Internet's slow here."

"It's Stratus."

"Right. Hey, can I ask you something?" he says. "I just . . . Hang on a sec."

"Sure," I say to his back. He's already halfway down the hall. I think of Olivia, of a story that feels familiar, like a book I've read in the distant past. I can't place the title and I can't remember the players, but the plot rings true. I take another sip and Marco's back in his chair, flipping through a leather journal.

Ali's journal.

I can't help but notice it's taken quite a beating since he was here last, creased down the middle like it spends a lot of time in his back pocket.

"I'm glad you keep it with you."

He keeps flipping. "I like to read it. It's her, you know? I mean, I know it's not, but she's in here somewhere, in these pages. It's stupid, because I always thought I knew her so well, but she was brilliant, you know? Like, really brilliant. Her words make me think."

Memories tackle me, tickle me, summon a smile. "I always loved that about her."

"Here," he says, turning the journal toward me. "This quote, it's not Shakespeare like everything else in here. Do you know it?"

A single sentence lines the top of the page: *Men loved darkness rather than light, because their deeds were evil.*

I know it. This quote. I know where it's from. But it's the drawing below it that splits my world in half. It's a pencil sketch of a woman's hand.

Rings adorn her index and middle fingers, manicured nails gently curving toward her palm. Her forearm is exposed, three jagged lines marking the skin.

"Elle?" Marco asks, his hand suddenly on my wrist. "You okay?"

I search the page for something, anything to put this in perspective. But all I see is the girl in the marble hallway, Javan digging invisible claws into her arm. Somehow this girl made it to adulthood, otherwise how could Ali have seen her arm? How could she have drawn it? And now the child in the hospital makes sense—Ali's journal putting it in perspective.

I haven't been dreaming recent events. I've been dreaming about things in days gone by.

But why?

"Are you all right?" Marco asks, his hand on mine.

"I'm sorry. The apostle John wrote those words," I say, my voice a hoarse whisper. "They're from the Bible."

At the word *Bible,* the halo thrums against my arm. It's not a soft, subtle thrumming. The thing is shifting. I let my arm fall to my lap, but the halo's unraveling, moving slowly, reforming into the crown. It rubs against the underside of the table, the gold rim sliding against my arm.

This is a different kind of terror. Different from a sketch that mirrors my nightmares, different from my mom's empty grave. What do I tell Marco if he sees the halo move? I'm neither qualified nor prepared for that conversation.

My brow breaks out in a sweat, and I swallow. I have nowhere to hide this thing. I'm wearing a sundress, for crying out loud.

"Brielle? Are you all right?" Marco leans forward, looking into my eyes. "You're pale."

I want to reassure him, but mostly I want him to back away. Far away from the halo warming my arm. I lean against the table and press it against my stomach, wrapping it in the material at my waist. Standing, I turn away from him.

"Brielle?"

My sandals sound like army boots banging away at the floor as I run down the hall and into Jake's room. I try to slam the door behind me, but it bounces off of something with a dull *thud.*

I hear it vibrate open and turn back to close it.

But Marco's there. Followed me down the hall, his face concerned.

Stupid chivalry.

"What's wrong?" he says, grabbing my shoulder.

That's all it takes. My dress shifts, and the halo slides down my arm, tumbling into the air. It's about halfway between the cuff and the crown when Marco catches it. But even his grip can't stop it from reforming, and he jerks his hand away. I'm not sure if it's the heat or the foreign feeling of metal moving under his touch, but the halo falls, landing on a pile of neatly mated socks.

Marco crouches, peering at the halo like a boy staring at a wriggling earthworm.

What is he thinking?

I want him to say something.

No, I don't, because it's sure to be a question.

A question I don't know how to answer.

"Please tell me this is a homing device," he says. "That it'll take us back to the *Enterprise* if we click our heels together and say sweet things about home?"

I sink to the floor, kneading my face with the heels of both palms as the halo finishes its transformation.

"You know, I—I haven't tried that."

His eyes are reflected in the burnished surface. They look bulbous, amplifying this ridiculous geek-out. "Where did you get it?"

I don't know what he'll do if I tell him, but I know this: I won't lie to Marco like my dad lied to me. Not even to make *this* conversation easier.

"Jake gave it to me," I say.

"Can I touch it?"

I nod. He's not looking at me, but I do it anyway. "It won't hurt you."

He presses his face closer and his fingers prod at it, like he plans to dissect it next. After a minute he slides his index finger around the rim. "It's so hot. It's like . . . like your hands," he says quietly, his emerald eyes finding mine. "The night we found the children."

He's talking about something that happened at the warehouse. I reached down to help Marco up, and after wearing the halo for several days, my hands had taken on its heat. At the time he looked . . . well, like he looks now. Confused and in awe all at once.

It's a feeling I understand.

"It does that," I say.

He finally plucks up the courage and lifts the halo in his hands. I nearly have a heart attack, but I let him.

"What *is* it?"

And there it is. The question I really don't want to answer.

"It's a halo."

I jump at the voice, but it's Jake, standing in the doorway. Suddenly the world weighs half as much.

"Halo? Like the game?" Marco's eyes haven't moved from the crown in his hands.

"It's nothing like the game," Jake says.

And then he does it. There isn't time to do anything but gasp before Marco has the thing on his head. It's that fast. My throat makes a strange sound, and Jake looks as stupefied as I do. But he holds his hands up, his eyes telling me to wait.

Waiting is hard.

"It's so hot," Marco says. His shoulders sag and his eyes flutter and I don't know what to do, what the halo will do. Jake must sense my discomfort, my need to act, because he signals again that I should wait.

Marco's cheeks flush red, and his eyes, though closed, move back and forth behind his lids. He takes one . . . two . . . three . . . four peaceful breaths and then his breathing accelerates, faster and faster. He groans and cries out, jerking upright and sending the halo tumbling to his lap.

His upper lip breaks out in beads of sweat and his face takes on a slick, white pallor.

"Marco?" I say, crawling closer. "Are you all right?"

His Adam's apple moves up and then down as his trembling hands push the halo off his leg, flinging it from him. It tumbles to a rest under Jake's bed, but Marco's standing already, holding every bit of my attention.

"Marco?" I ask again.

He shakes his head and turns away, toward the door. Toward Jake.

"Sit down, Marco. We'll explain."

His head turns left and right, and his hands continue to shake. I remember a time, in this very room, when mine did the same. I realize only half a breath before it happens that Marco is going to run, just like I did.

And then he does.

His shoulder connects with Jake's as he pushes past him and down the hall. I stand and lurch toward the door, Jake already pursuing him. Before I make it halfway down the hall, I hear the front door open and close.

Marco's gone.

As I round the corner into the kitchen, Jake flings open the door, his momentum propelling him onto the porch. I'm right behind, but when I fall into step next to him, his arm wraps my waist and I stop.

"Let him go," Jake says.

"What if he saw the Celestial, Jake? He won't understand that without help."

"Not now. If I know Marco, he needs to try to figure this out on his own. When he reaches the end of his understanding, he'll be back."

"Jake . . ."

"Waiting is a part of the process, Elle. His mind can't be forced."

Canaan's said those very words to me. On that same night. The night of the warehouse. The night Marco touched my hands and realized something was different. What did he tell himself about that? Did he reason it away?

What will he tell himself about the halo?

And how long will it take him to realize he needs help understanding?

I lean into Jake and watch as Marco disappears. He's headed toward town. Toward Main Street.

There's not much there, but I hope he finds what he's looking for.

24

Brielle

You have time for a drive?" Jake asks.

He's released my waist and stepped away. It's weird to have distance between us. I try to shake off the look on Marco's face and focus on Jake. On this moment. But he's walking away from me, down the stairs.

"I have something to show you. It's not far." He opens the passenger door to his car and holds it for me. I turn toward my house, toward the conversation waiting there for me. The sheriff's cruiser is still in the drive. Dad will be fine. He has company and I'm still not ready to see him, so I drop down the stairs and slide into the Karmann Ghia.

Jake wasn't kidding when he said we weren't going far. He pulls off the highway and parks as near to the Stratus Cemetery gate as he can. Yellow caution tape marks off several areas where dirt and rocks seem to have been displaced.

"Is this all from my mother's grave?"

"Yeah," Jake says. "Crazy, huh?"

Being back here is strange. It feels very disconnected to me, and yet if I'm to believe Virtue, all this turmoil was caused because the grave was empty. Because my dad hid emptiness below the ground.

All this because I wanted truth.

I expect to be sad or angry being here again, but I'm just numb. We duck under the caution tape, and I let Jake lead me through the gate and along the path. It's quiet. Birds zipping through the summer sky, chattering. Dragonflies escort us, unaware that this place has been violated. And still Jake says nothing until we're standing beneath the mangled branches of the willow tree.

"I found something," he says.

"Here? When?"

"Last night. This morning, actually. I came back," he says. "Waited till the police cleared the area, and then I searched."

"What were you looking for?"

"Anything," he says. "Just something to point us in the right direction."

Us.

"I really am sorry about that night. About sending you away like that."

"Stop," he says. "I'm not mad."

His face is tighter than I'm used to, but I'm not about to call him a liar.

"Okay." I squeeze his hand. "So you found something?"

"Look up," he says.

The leaves of the willow are singed in places, branches bent and broken. Amongst the wreckage, it takes my eyes a second to find it. But there, hanging from a splintered branch, is a necklace.

It hangs about twelve feet up, a circlet of beads with a single wooden ornament decorating it.

A flower.

I refuse to sink to the mud here again, so I grab Jake's arms. "I know that necklace. I've seen it."

"Where?"

"I had another . . . it was . . . in a nightmare."

"You had another nightmare? A different nightmare?"

"It started Saturday night, before the cemetery. You think that was buried with my mom?"

"Elle, we need to talk about the nightmare."

"I know, and we will, but—"

He growls, frustrated.

"Jake! Do you . . . do you think it was in her casket?"

He releases my hand with a little more gusto than absolutely necessary and moves to the tree. "The thought crossed my mind," he says. "I don't know any other way it could have gotten up there."

Jake grabs hold of a low-hanging limb. Hand over hand, he works his way up to the necklace and with deft fingers works it free.

"Catch."

The necklace falls straight down, the wooden ornament tugging it toward me. I catch it easily and set to examining it. The beads are multicolored and strung in no particular order. There's no clasp, just a knot holding it all together. The wooden ornament is circular and smooth, a white plumeria painted on it. Its yellow center is faded, the white petals scratched, but there's no mistaking it. This is the necklace from my nightmare.

Jake drops from the tree.

"This is it," I say. "The girl was wearing it in my dream."

"The girl in the hallway?"

"Yes and no. It was the same girl, but she was younger, happier. Until . . ."

I have a terrifying thought. "Jake, I think the nightmares are coming from the Throne Room. I think they're telling me something."

"Why do you think I'm freaking out?" A cold wind blows through the cemetery, too cold for July. The willow shivers and my hair whips about. I tie it back in a knot, my mind trying to place the puzzle pieces. And now there are just so many.

"Marco found a picture in Ali's journal. It's of a woman with three scars marking her arm."

"Like the girl?" Jake asks, his face distractingly close to mine. Still, I soldier on.

"Exactly like the girl. And Marco was telling me this story that seems—"

"We need to talk to Canaan," Jake says. "He's the best at reading the Throne Room's intentions. I just . . . why weren't these things delivered as clues? If we're supposed to do something with what we know, why isn't the Throne Room using the chest?"

It's a good question. Why isn't Canaan the one putting these pieces together?

"Maybe because we won't always have the chest," I tell him, the idea strange but sensible. "If Canaan's reassigned and you stay with me . . ." But there's the other possibility. That I'm the one having nightmares because they could both choose to leave and I'm supposed to piece this together myself. "You *are* staying with me?"

"I'm not leaving, Elle," he says, tipping my chin to his and speaking soft words into my mouth. "I've told you that. I'm not going anywhere."

"Okay."

There's something in his eyes that makes my stomach clench, makes it crave. It's longing, I realize, and that scares me a little. There are things we can't share just yet. Things we shouldn't share. Until Jake, I never realized how easy it'd be to give up something that isn't mine to part with.

I step back, Jake's eyes falling to the necklace in my hand.

"What do you think about the necklace?" he asks, his voice thick.

I breathe away some of the tension and turn the wood flower in my hands.

"It's beautiful, but there's nothing to indicate it came from Mom's grave."

"Except the debris, of course," Jake says, looking around.

"Yeah, there is that."

"You could ask your dad," he says.

"As if." I blow a strand of hair from my face. "Although . . ."

"Although?"

"Dad's not the only one who might able to tell me if this belonged to Mom."

"Who then?"

"Miss Macy," I say.

"Grandmother Tutu?"

I slide the necklace over my head. "She hates that nickname, by the way, but yeah. She's the one who introduced Mom and Dad. She and Mom were BFFs back in the day."

"Then let's ask her," Jake says.

"Don't you have to work?"

"Took the day off," he says, pulling a leaf from my hair. "My girlfriend needs me."

But Miss Macy's not home. We check the studio too, but it's dark inside. A sign on the door says she's sorry for the last-minute closure.

"That's weird," I say. "She never cancels class. Can I borrow your phone?"

But she's not answering her cell either.

Jake calls Canaan, but the call rolls to voice mail.

"Okay, let's just figure this out ourselves," I say. "We can do that, right? We're smart."

Jake pulls the car into the drive-thru at Burgerville. "I'm much smarter after I've eaten."

We pick up shakes and onion rings and drive out to Crooked Leg Bridge. The sky is clear and blue, Mount Bachelor rising in the distance, crowning a horizon of evergreens with a tipsy white dunce hat. We sit side by side on the bridge, our feet dangling, and I tell him about my nightmares. All of them. And because I can't shake the thought that it's related, I tell him about Olivia's mom dying in that fire.

With all the pieces laid before us, a story begins to take shape.

"It's Olivia," Jake says. "It has to be."

I gather a handful of pebbles and drop them one at a time off the bridge. I can't see them fall, can't see them hit the water, but the ripples they make—I can see those.

"I know you hate her, Elle, but think about it."

"Is it possible to want to save someone and knock someone's face in all at the same time?"

"You tell me," Jake says. "Is it possible?"

"Seems so. What does that mean about Javan? If what I saw took place years ago, it's possible he's still in the pit, right? We don't have to worry about him coming to Stratus?"

"Canaan's fairly certain he's in hell."

The next question makes my hands sweaty. I dust the remaining pebbles from my hands and watch as the river below is freckled with ripples. Uncountable.

"And the woman, then, that Olivia spoke to at the hospital, that was my mom. Olivia was with her when she died."

Jake tosses his own rock into the water. Big, round. It makes a splash.

"We don't have all the pieces yet. That might be too big a leap to make."

"But if you were guessing . . ."

His words are soft, but they still cut. "It's not a bad guess, Elle."

I stare at the skies over Bachelor, wondering just what the Sabres' role is in all this. Was it just to unearth the emptiness of Mom's grave? That's why they came all this way?

"You know, for a second I let myself believe Mom was out there somewhere. I conjured up this reality that she'd survived somehow, and we'd find her." I can't help fingering the necklace hanging against my chest. "But if that was my mom Olivia was talking to at the hospital, then I've looked out through her eyes. I've felt the sickness inside her."

Jake leans forward and presses his lips to my forehead. "I'm so sorry."

I lay my head on his shoulder. The bridge is warm beneath our legs and our breathing resolves into the same rhythm. We sit like that for a long time. Until the summer eve is wrapped around us, and the trees are stained pink with the rays of the setting sun. How easy it would be to ignore the ugly parts of this world. The broken parts.

"Jake?"

"Hmm?"

"If my mom's dead, what happened to her body?"

The sun dips below the horizon and the world turns to shadow.

"I don't know."

25

Brielle

Helene's sitting at the desk just beyond the small waiting area when I enter the dance studio on Tuesday. She's lovely in a pale-pink leotard and tights, her auburn hair pulled up like mine. She's been working alongside me for months, but it's still strange to see her here. So comfortable in the Terrestrial, so graceful and light on her feet.

I'll be sad when she's assigned elsewhere.

"Isn't your class this afternoon?" I ask.

"I got a call from Miss Macy this morning. She needed to switch. Dentist appointment or something."

"Ugh."

I drop my bag next to a white folding chair and slide out of my boots and into my ballet slippers.

"How are you holding up?" she asks.

I shrug. "Managed to avoid Dad again this morning, so that's a plus. Have you . . . been in touch with Virtue?"

We're alone, but I keep my voice quiet. Helene leans forward, her hands cupping her chin.

"I haven't," she says. "But he's near. I've heard him. Seen him. Elle, I'm fairly certain I know—"

We're interrupted by the Sadler twins. Four years old, fuzzy red hair, and more freckles than Pippi Longstocking.

"Hey, girls!" Helene says. "You're up early!"

"Do you mind if I drop them off now?" their mother says. "I got called into the office. I'll be back on time, I promise."

"Go ahead," I tell her. "I was just going to warm up. You girls wanna come?"

Tia and Pria squeal.

"Can we play with the wings?" Tia asks.

"Of course," I say, waving Mrs. Sadler away and shooing the twins into the studio.

"We'll talk later," Helene says.

I nod, my mind a mosaic of mismatched thoughts: Virtue, the absent Miss Macy, Jake, Kaylee and the community center, the Sadler twins and butterfly wings in purple and green.

And Dad. There was another curse-laden message on the answering machine this morning from Dad's second-in-command. His drinking has to be taking a toll on the business. His truck was gone when I left, so I can only hope he made it to work today.

The girls raid the dress-up clothes and I settle into first position. Helene already has music playing. It's our warm-up CD—all classical and soft. I take to the floor and lose myself for a bit. The halo seems to agree with my need to forget and warms me through as I lift and stretch, dancing across the floor.

At one point I catch Jake's eye across the street. He's chatting with Bob and the guys, chewing on a doughnut. He must be on a break. I stop and wave. They all wave back.

When the rest of my class arrives, I'm ready. Focused on them. Everything else will wait. It'll have to.

Kaylee arrives just as I'm shooing the last of my girls into the waiting area. She drops into a folding chair just outside the door looking serious, which is unlike her.

"Hey, Kay. You all right?"

"You get my text?"

"No, I've been doing *this* all morning," I say, gesturing to a floor full of sparkly material scraps, feathers, and straight pins on little cushions.

She squints at the mess. "Reupholstering peacocks?"

"Costume adjustments for the summer dance recital." I wad the turquoise and fuchsia scraps into a ball and drop cross-legged before her. "So what's up?"

"Marco Mysterioso crashed on my couch last night."

I'm suddenly awake. "Oh good. Oh yeah. We were worried. How did that . . . Did he call you or something?"

"Showed up at Jelly's last night all hot and bothered." I must've made a face, because Kaylee quickly rephrases. "All sweaty and rambling."

"Yeah, he, um, he had a shock."

"You wanna tell me about the bracelet?" she asks.

And like that, my leotard's too snug and my tights are itchy. The world has become entirely too uncomfortable. "Wh-What did Marco say?"

"Nothing coherent. He was rambling. Delia took pity on him—I think she's crushing on him, to be honest."

"Delia?"

"Yeah, well, in a platonic, he's-a-cute-kid kind of way. She's always liked the tall, thin ones. Anyway, she force-fed him coffee and gyros, but he was going on and on about darkness and evil deeds, so she bundled him into her car and took him away from the customers. When I got home last night, he was curled on the corner of the couch staring at that journal he's had surgically attached to his hand."

"It's Ali's," I say quietly.

"I figured. Look, he said something else when I got home."

"About the . . . about my . . . bracelet?"

"He said it made him see things."

My pulse pounds against my temples, against the skin of my throat. I feel it in my hands and feet.

"Did he say what he saw?" I ask, my voice rough and shaky.

"You. On fire."

Kay lives with her Aunt Delia. Her parents live in town, but they're, well, lost souls, I guess. When we were younger, elementary school age, they were in and out of jail so often Delia set up a room for Kay at her place. Eventually she just never moved out.

Her parents are around—always at birthday parties and family affairs, usually inappropriately clothed or looking for cash—but they can't seem to get it together enough to really be there in any permanent way.

So, Kay has Delia.

Delia's given her a home and stability.

And Kay . . . well, Kay's given Delia someone to mother and quite a lot of messes to clean up.

The two of them live in a little house off of Main on a grassy lot between the train station and the high school. Years and years ago the place was painted bright green. It's faded now, the paint peeling away from the wood siding. But instead of the house looking run-down, it has a homey, broken-in feel. The front door is my absolute favorite. The green walls chip and peel, the weather doing its thing, and Delia hardly notices, but every single year she repaints that front door. It's bright blue, sky blue really. Like all those pictures you see of houses in Greece. Whenever I stand on her front doorstep I feel like I'm traveling to far-off places. Exotic places. With Kaylee as my tour guide.

And then there are the wind chimes. Metal and wood, both extravagant and trite—they hang in droves from the eaves around the house. When I was little I had trouble falling asleep at Delia's. Between the trains shaking the house and the chimes responding with their exuberant jangle, I took to sleeping with earbuds jammed in my ears.

Once, though, when Delia noticed my struggle, she plopped down on Kaylee's bed and told us a story about pixies and their jingling songs. I didn't struggle so much after that.

Pixies.

I like that idea.

It gives the place an almost dream-like quality. Suitable for Kaylee, who's always dreamed of far-off places.

The disaster of her childhood brought her here. To a home far more ideal and suitable for her than the place she was born into. I ponder that now as I stand on the stoop, Jake's hand in mine. The wind is still, the chimes silent. I tap a metal ladybug hanging by the door. Her wings bump a butterfly's, which in turn knocks a neighboring chime full of ceramic tea cups. Soon I'm surrounded by the song of pixies.

I don't even have to knock. Delia opens the door, her face

somber. It feels like we're visiting a funeral home, and after my night at the cemetery, it's an image I'd rather not encourage.

"Hey, Delia," I say, stepping inside.

"Elle, Jake-y boy." She squeezes us both.

"Smells good in here," Jake says.

"Moussaka. See if you can get that boy to eat some. He's nothing but gloom and doom and gibberish to boot."

"You leaving?" I ask.

"That nitwit I hired to run the kitchen just called in sick," she says, throwing a bunch of stuff into her purse.

She knocks a makeup brush to the floor, and Jake stoops to pick it up. "I hate being sick when it's so nice outside," he says.

"He ain't sick. I'll be back just as soon as I drag his sunshine-loving behind into the diner."

She squeezes me again, her ample hips forcing me back onto the stoop.

"Is Kay inside?"

"Yeah, in her room. Heard her squawking something about a nail polish emergency."

Kaylee left me after her proclamation that I'd been swallowed in flames. She had to meet Olivia at the community center, something about donated photography supplies. On any other day I'd have followed her there to examine the bounty. Instead, I left the teeny tiny ballerinas to Helene and begged Jake's boss to give him the afternoon off. He agreed to give him an extended dinner break, but that meant waiting until dinner. So I leaned on the counter and stared, making Jake smirk while he processed orders. It made Phil nervous, I guess, so he finally gave in and sent Jake from the building.

Delia's climbing into her car. I wave and step back inside,

closing the door behind me. The lamps are unlit, the room dark. A sliding glass door at the back of the house lets cloudy sunlight through. It settles on top of the furniture, making me squint, but stubbornly refuses to brighten the room. Marco's on the couch, Ali's journal resting loosely between his fingers. He's sitting upright, his feet on the table. His head rests on his chest and he snores. Jake takes a seat at the opposite end of the couch and turns his eyes to me.

"Should we let him sleep?" he asks.

"Maybe," I say. "He's pretty gone."

He's still wearing yesterday's clothes, and his five o'clock shadow has darkened, but he looks mostly peaceful. I hate that we're going to make him relive something that had him running from the room.

"I'm gonna tell Kay we're here."

I'm still five steps from Kaylee's room when the smell of acetone hits me between the eyes.

"Holy cow, Kay," I say. "What did you do?"

"Just painting my nails."

"Oh my . . . you look part Avatar."

Her right foot is blue and sparkly—just like her eyelashes—and she's mopping at it with a wad of paper towels soaked in nail polish remover.

"How did you . . . never mind." Sometimes the how just isn't important. I grab a few paper towels and set to work alongside her.

"You here to talk to Marco?"

"Yeah. Kay, maybe you should stay in your room. I don't want Marco freaking you out."

"Not a chance," she says, standing.

"I just don't think . . ."

"Look, I've known something was weird about that bracelet for months now. Since the warehouse. And I've known my nightmares from that night were more than just post-traumatic stress. Though I've had a bit of that too. But as shocked as I was to hear Marco tell me you were the human torch, I'm not shocked at all to hear your self-warming arm cuff has sci-fi-channel-like powers."

"You're not shocked?"

"No," she says. "I'm irritated that you didn't tell me before. Frustrated that I've been hinting around about that thing for months and you just brushed me off. But no. Your bracelet's more than bling. I'm not shocked."

How can she accept the weird so easily? Why was it so hard for me?

"Kay, it's not a bracelet. Not really."

"I know," she says, throwing her hip into the end of her bed, moving it away from the wall, covering the blue stain on the floor. "It's a halo. Marco told me."

Kaylee and I find Jake and Marco on the back patio sitting at a small table under a green fiberglass awning. The afternoon sun presses against the awning, making it glow, coloring everything below it a sickly shade of lime. Delia's backyard is really just a thousand yards of dried dirt and scraggly grass. No fence, just train tracks that cut through the back of her property.

Jake's made coffee, and while he sips from his mug, Marco stares at the steam escaping from his.

"Why are you always making me coffee?" he asks.

"I didn't realize it had turned into a habit," Jake says.

"Whenever you want me to tear out my soul, you serve me black coffee."

"Would you prefer cream and sugar?"

"No."

A train pulls through, shaking both the ground and the chimes that surround the house. I pull a crate over next to Jake and sit. Kaylee sits on the stoop, her chin on her knees. I wait until the train passes, and then I move his untouched coffee aside and take Marco's hands.

"You're still warm," he says. "It's because of that thing, isn't it? The halo."

I look to Jake. His hazel eyes are anxious, but we've talked about this. Honesty—complete honesty—is the only way to move forward now. He encourages me with a nod.

"Yes," I say.

"Where is it?"

"In my duffel bag. In the car. I can't tell you how sorry I am about yesterday."

He pulls his hands from mine and off the table, pulling into himself. "I shouldn't have run off like that, but . . ." He dissolves into silent sobs, his shoulders shaking. "I can't watch someone else I care about die, you know? I can't."

"We're here to help, Marco. We'll do whatever we can to keep that from happening." Jake's voice cracks, and he takes a minute to gather himself. "Can you tell us . . . You saw Brielle dying?"

Marco avoids eye contact now, his gaze on the splintered table. "Remember that story I told you, Elle, about Olivia's mom dying in a fire. Remember how I said we were there—Olivia and I?"

"Yeah, I remember."

I've told Jake, but Kaylee's still in the dark. She's quiet, though, looking on, her green face and blue eyelashes turning her into an alien.

"It was a long time ago, and I'd forgotten things over the years. But when I put that thing on, it all came back to me. Intense. Detailed, you know, moments fragmented, captured in lingering snapshots."

I picture a graphic novel. A comic book. Squares of color that, when assembled, tell a story.

"What did you remember?" Jake asks. I'm so glad he's here. I get all captivated when Marco talks, and I forget to ask questions. Important ones. It's like watching him perform. Even now, his tears trickle away and his inner storyteller kicks in, taking over, helping him articulate whatever the halo showed him.

"Well, it wasn't just Olivia and me, for starters. A bunch of us guys were there. Guys from the neighborhood sitting on the benches in front of the school, hanging out, making fun of pedestrians. You know, stupid stuff boys do."

My private school in the city had benches like that. We girls used to sit there and wait for the all-boys school to let out.

"Olivia was there that night, at the benches, talking to us. Her mom was inside meeting with a teacher."

"At night? Don't most parent/teacher conferences happen during the day? That's when they did ours," Kaylee asks.

"Yeah," Marco says. "Probably. I don't know. That's just, that's how I remember it."

"It's okay, Marco, go ahead. There was a fire?"

"Yeah, it started in the back of the school somewhere. It could have been burning for a while before we caught on. And then there was smoke. Thick, moving over the school like rain clouds." He pinches his eyes shut, remembering. "We all started yelling, pointing. I remember . . . remember the principal and, and . . . his secretary maybe. They came running out the front door. Cars stopped to watch. And the guys, we all scattered. Some of us ran toward the fire. The others ran away."

"What did you do?" Jake asks.

Marco's eyes open now. Crisp. Clear. "I ran toward the fire, around the school, to the back where the smoke was coming from. The guys with bikes had gotten there just before I did. Olivia had a bike."

Marco turns his face toward the empty train tracks and the horizon beyond. His tears are gone, his voice steady, but he's not here. Not with us. He's there. At that school. Watching it burn.

"I think Olivia went in after her mom."

"What makes you think that?"

"The burns. Her legs were burned. Bad. The backs of her calves, her feet. It's something I'd forgotten about. But they took her away in an ambulance. I remember that. I remember the ambulance."

I think back to the Fourth of July, to the barbecue. She was wearing shorts that day and I didn't see any scars on her legs, but I won't ask Marco about that now.

"You said you saw Brielle die," Jake says.

"The fire trucks arrived and were dousing the place in water. They'd removed the body—Olivia's mom—and another ambulance took it away. Most of the drama had died down."

"When . . ."

"I saw a face. In a corner room, through the window. I don't know if I really saw it that day. I don't think I did. If I had, it would have haunted me my whole life, I think. I would have remembered that. But yesterday, with the . . . halo . . . on, I saw her." His eyes find mine. "I saw you."

I lick my lips, not wanting to belittle his experience, not wanting to hurt him further, but knowing the impossibility of it. "I would have been—what?—three years old, Marco. It couldn't have been me."

"But it was. I ran toward the window, but before I could get there, the window shattered. Glass flew everywhere, stopping me. Keeping me from reaching you. But you were there. Staring back at me, your . . ." His face contorts and he buries it in his hands, his words spooked and muffled. "Your blond hair was on fire, and your white dress. Your eyes were so blue, and they looked right through me. And then . . ."

"And then what?" Kaylee asks, climbing onto the bench next to him.

He drops his hands, his green face tortured, like some sort of tragic swamp thing.

"You disappeared."

26

Brielle

Saluting Teddy the Elk, I push my way out of the community center. The sun's no longer in sight, hiding somewhere below the low-sitting buildings of downtown Stratus. The sky's still streaked with light, the windows fronting the community center reflecting a blue expanse dewy with the promise of a summer rain.

I cut behind the community center and through the alley connecting it to Main Street. It's darker here—secluded—and worry flutters through me once again. Before it can settle in my gut, a prayer whispers across my lips.

I pray all the time now. When I'm walking. When I'm sitting. When I'm eating.

I wake up praying.

All this unease has driven me to seek answers—real answers—and as infuriating as these dreams are, the only place that's ever provided me completely satisfying answers has been the Throne Room.

So I pray.

My prayers aren't particularly eloquent. They're more of the desperate variety, and I don't always feel heard. But saying the words, asking my Creator for answers, for direction, is right.

I know it is.

Even if I don't feel it.

Feelings can't be trusted. That's something else I'm learning.

I round the corner, stepping onto Main. The Donut Factory is down the street from here, but its sugary smell dances down the street, smelling an awful lot like Jake. It reminds me of an encounter we had there, in front of the theatre, the very first time I saw Damien.

The thought is mostly pleasant, and I relive it as I meander down the street. I pass the Auto Body and wave at Grace, an old classmate of mine. She started working there just after Dimples was arrested.

Dimples. The super-nerd who kidnapped Kaylee and dragged her into the mess at the warehouse.

Just beyond the Auto Body is a real estate office and then the Photo Depot where I'm to meet Jake. He doesn't get off for another few minutes, but I can wait.

And stare.

I haven't had time to adequately stare at him lately.

But just as I'm crossing in front of the real estate office, the world flashes orange.

Celestial orange.

What the . . .

Sweat breaks out along my neck and chest, and I stop. The street and the sidewalk, the ramshackle old buildings, the few cars parked along the storefronts—all of them shine with the light of the Celestial.

And then the summer night folds in around me once again.

My hands fall to my left wrist, to the halo thrumming there.

Did I just see the Celestial without the halo on my head?

I blink and blink at the blue sky. I will it to happen again, but only the stars wink back.

Both Jake and Canaan have warned me about this possibility—that I might one day see the Celestial without the halo.

Is this what they were talking about?

Will it come in strange flashes?

Or has the lack of sleep finally gotten to me?

A gust of wind blows against my bare knees. It's colder than it should be, but that's the Northwest for you. I hear the footsteps of another pedestrian, but when I look left and right, there's no one there. I'm alone on this small strip of Main.

I *so* need to sleep.

I rub life back into my arms and continue on.

But another step forward and I feel a tug on my head, like fingernails raking through my hair. I whip around, a flash of shimmering apricot sky hurling past me.

And I'm not alone on the sidewalk any longer.

It's Damien. On Main Street.

His wings are black and tattered, his form rife with thick, pink scars. Jagged fangs hang over his charred, scabby lips, but it's his eyes that frighten me.

They're wide open. Two black moonstones mounted in a melted face.

I stumble backward, colliding with a newspaper stand. On impact, the Celestial disappears along with Damien and his frightening stare.

I gasp and gasp. My elbow stings and my hands tremble, but now I'm certain.

It's the lack of sleep or the anxiety brought on by the nightmares or . . . or . . . something.

Because Jake assured me Damien was long gone. That Canaan's sword of light banished that demon to the pit of hell, where the Prince would leave him sweltering and burning—punishment for all the mistakes he made pursuing Jake.

Pursuing me.

I push away from the newspaper stand.

Jake wouldn't lie to me.

There aren't many things I'm certain of as I step into the Photo Depot, but that's one of them. Jake's integrity. His constancy.

"What happened to your arm?"

Fluorescent lights buzz overhead; a computerized photo sorter churns away behind Jake.

"My arm?" It takes my brain a second to register the question, but eventually I look down. That's right. It does sting. Blood runs in several small streams from my elbow to my wrist, looking like the pole outside Fancy Hill's Barber Shop.

We're alone. No other customers. No fellow employees. Jake pushes through the swinging door that separates the front counter from the lobby of the Photo Depot.

"What did you do?" he asks.

"I'm okay," I say, my brain sluggish. "Ran into the newspaper stand outside. Clumsy, I guess."

"I think Kaylee's rubbing off on you. You need to spend some time with the coordinated."

I laugh, but it's stiff and unnatural. "Are you offering?"

"Here, sit," Jake says, lightly shoving me into a chair by the door. "We've got a first-aid kit in back."

Seven and a half steps take him through a swinging door and behind the counter. Another two take him into a staff room.

"Jake?"

"Yeah?"

"Do you really need a first-aid kit?"

His head pops into view again. He stands there for a minute, thinking, staring.

Blinking.

He's been skittish to use his gift. In the six months since the warehouse, I've not seen him use it once. It's not like he's gone out of his way to avoid the injured, but he hasn't gone search-ing for them either, and right now I need to see it. I need to be reminded that I'm not the only one gifted.

His face brightens, and a smile emerges. A small one, the one that sits there at the corner asking for a kiss. "No, I guess I don't."

He walks to the door and flips the sign to Closed. Then he reaches behind me and drops the blinds. Fleetingly, I wonder if there's any chance Damien's there. Any chance that this small act could cost us something. But Jake wouldn't keep that from me. Wouldn't risk something like that.

He walks back to my chair and lowers himself to his knees. He has an apron around his waist, which he unties and dumps on the carpet. An ink pen, a notepad, and a couple film canis-ters topple to the ground. He folds the apron into a square and wipes the blood from my arm.

Then he drops it between us and wraps a single hand around my bicep just above the elbow.

He's warm. So very warm.

And I'm tired.

My eyes flutter and my head seems to have doubled in

weight. I lean my forehead against his shoulder, his temple pressing against my cheek. His pulse quickens, and my arm burns. And then . . .

"It's done," Jake says. He runs his fingers down my arm and over my elbow. "Good as new."

I don't want to move.

I've missed this closeness.

I've needed it.

"Your dad came in today," Jake says.

"You are so good at ruining these moments, you know that?"

"Sorry," Jake says, picking up his apron and the things he emptied onto the floor.

I flex my arm, feeling the wholeness of it, the strength I didn't know had gone. "What did Dad want?"

"Dropped off some film. Old stuff. 35mm. Demanded that Phil take his order, though. Wouldn't look me in the face. It was kind of funny."

My stomach rolls. "I don't think that's funny."

"Anyway, he dropped off an order—hour photo—but he never came back to pick it up." Jake stands. "I'll get it and you can take it home to him. Just tell him it's on me."

"Like that's not asking for a fight."

"Kill 'em with kindness, right?"

Jake disappears again, and when he emerges he has his keys in one hand and an envelope in the other. He hands me the latter.

I wonder what Dad got developed.

"Was he sober?" I ask, tucking the envelope into my purse.

"Looked sober."

"You know that's not the definitive litmus test."

Jake snorts. "Well, I didn't sniff him, but he seemed all right."

I cock an eye. "I'm going to need you to sniff him next time."

"You're serious?"

"As an empty grave."

By the time we get to my place, Dad neither looks nor smells sober.

Neither does the kitchen.

"Dinner at my place?" Jake asks.

Dad's fallen asleep at the granite island. He's sitting on a barstool, his hefty upper body sprawled across the countertop, which is littered with beer bottles.

What a waste.

"I don't think I have an appetite."

Jake grabs my hand. "Bet I can change your mind."

And he's right. Seven minutes later we're sitting cross-legged on his living room floor with two spoons and a gallon of Tin Roof Sundae. A Portland band, Pink Martini, vibrates through the gigantic speakers next to us. It's something Latin, something lively, and it's easy to forget the strain that has me seeing rogue demons on the streets of Stratus.

We talk for hours. He tells me what he's heard from Canaan: That Henry seems to be in better physical condition. That, as suspected, Olivia is overseeing the charity in his absence, and rumor has it she'll continue to do so from here on out.

He tells me Canaan hasn't seen any sign of demonic activity, and I grow more and more certain that the apparition I saw on Main was just that. A phantom of my imagination and nothing more.

The longer we talk, the more relaxed I feel. It's not sleeping, but being with Jake is the next best thing. When all that remains in the ice cream bucket are the two spoons, I stand and take it to the kitchen. I've just dropped the spoons in the sink when the whole house flashes golden yellow. It's fast, so fast, but I swear I see something in the brightness. Something scarring it. Blackening the corner of the image. I stand and stare, praying for another glimpse.

Nothing.

"Shane & Shane?"

"Huh?" I turn my eyes to Jake's.

They're a piercing white. The rest of the house has returned to the Terrestrial, but Jake's eyes . . . Jake's eyes retain their celestial glow. When people's eyes glow white in the Celestial, it means they've decided, either consciously or subconsciously, that they'd give their life for the person they gaze upon. That's the significance of the white eyes staring back at me. Jake would die for me if he had to.

It's such a disturbing visual against the comparatively mundane, ordinary living room that I yank the halo off my wrist and drop it on the counter. It spins like a top—like Marco's bottle top—finally settling.

Jake watches it from across the room.

"You okay?"

"Yeah," I say. "I just . . ."

Is it too much to ask for a normal night? A night without crazy, supernatural stuff happening every time I turn around?

"Need a break from the halo is all."

He looks at me. His eyes are hazel once again, and full of questions I really don't want to answer.

"Shane & Shane, you said? 'May the vision of You be the death of me.' I love that song. Put it in," I say.

I raise my eyebrows, nod my head, and do my best to appear normal.

He narrows his eyes, doubtful, but slides the disc in and cranks it up. The bass rattles the windows some, and I wonder if it'll wake Dad across the way.

Not that I care.

Jake closes his eyes and leans against the entertainment center, soaking up the music. It didn't take me long to understand the excessive stereo and the overlarge speakers. Jake loves music. Especially the kind that glorifies God. He loves everything about it. The instruments, the vocals. He told me once that he has a secret ambition to learn to play guitar but is terrified he'll be awful at it.

I decide then and there what this year's Christmas present will be.

We move to the study and settle in, Jake at his computer and me at Canaan's. Jake's been telling me about the Sabres. He says that whenever a cluster of miracles and healings occur, there's usually a thinning of the Terrestrial veil. Like the other night. And a thinning of the Terrestrial veil always means Sabre activity.

"Elle," Jake says. "Do you know much about the history of Stratus?"

I spin my chair toward him. "I know that Kaylee's great-great-great something was one of the first mayors, and that Dad's mom's dad drew up the plans for Crooked Leg Bridge."

Jake's back is still to me, his fingers moving over the keyboard. "No, I mean the spiritual history?"

I shake my head. "Never thought about it before."

"Look at this," he says, printing out a document. I roll my chair over, parking it next to his as he pulls the paper from the tray.

"Where'd you get this?" I ask, taking it from him.

It's the scan of an old church bulletin. A sixteen-year-old bulletin from Stratus Presbyterian. The little church in town. Our church.

"Off their website. According to the info here, Pastor Noah's been doing what he can to get old sermon transcripts, answered prayer reports, and church bulletins uploaded onto the site." Jake reads off the screen. "He says here, 'Our history is a part of who we are. A part of Stratus, Oregon. It would do us well to remember where we once were and what God has done for us.'"

"Smart guy," I say, continuing to scan the page.

This document is not unfamiliar to me. I'm handed one every Sunday morning by Sister Pat, a white-haired lady in sparkly heels. A sheet of letter-sized paper, normally folded in half with some sort of flower or cross design on the front. This scan is of the inside, so I can't see the image on the front, but the layout is nearly identical to what I receive each week.

Below the headline is the date. *Sunday, July 14, 1996.* As always, the right-hand side is a weekly calendar. Monday night Bible study, Wednesday night prayer, Saturday afternoon pot-luck, Sunday morning church.

I shake my head as I read. It's amazing how little has changed.

Below the calendar is a festive-looking box labeled Answered Prayers. Our bulletins still have this box, though the contents here are different from any kind of prayer report I've ever read. I'm used to seeing things like "Lanie Simpkins got that job we've been praying for!" and "James Childer is expected to make a full recovery after falling from his own apple tree."

Stratus in July of 1996 was an entirely different place.

The awning has been repaired after the building was shaken following Wednesday's prayer meeting. We thank Danny Jones for the repair, and our Heavenly Father for the shaking.

Thomas Grady has been healed. The cancer is gone! His doctor will be here next Sunday to speak about this miraculous event.

High school sophomore Ashley Carroll reports that seven of her girlfriends gave their hearts to the Lord at a birthday sleepover.

"Have you ever seen anything like this?" I ask.

"I might be the wrong person to ask," Jake says. "But this kind of activity tells me something was going on back then. Here, read this one."

Jake hands me another bulletin he's printed. Same weekly calendar, two weeks earlier.

The Banderas family sends their love and thanks for prayers. They've had several new converts and yesterday watched as an entire family was healed of Chagas disease.

"I know this name," I say.

"Chagas? It's awful. It's transmitted by insects—"

"No, not the disease. The family. The church still supports these missionaries. I saw their picture in the foyer."

We read through the bulletins for the entire summer of that year. Every single one claiming supernatural activity of some sort.

"What do you think it means?"

"I don't know. Maybe nothing. Maybe everything. I think

we need to keep looking. But at the very least, we know that the year your mother went missing there seemed to be some supernatural activity here."

"Sabres?"

"That'd be my guess. But we should talk to Pastor Noah. He'd be able to give us a better idea of what that year was like."

He continues on, researching other area churches. I return to Canaan's desk and my investigation into the Benson Elementary School fire. The details online are pretty sparse, but nothing in my dreams contradicts what I find on the Internet. One person was killed, a Susanne Holt, who was survived by her daughter. She was graciously taken in by her paternal grandfather, Henry Madison, of the Ingenui Foundation.

Graciously. Taken. In.

I've been yawning for hours, but around eleven o'clock Jake follows suit, and we stumble into a vicious cycle we can't seem to stop. A few minutes later Jake disappears. He returns with a mug of coffee the size of Crescent Lake. He sets it in front of me.

"I need sugar," I say, pushing to my feet.

He shoves me lightly back to my seat and places the entire sugar bowl in my hands.

"You really are divine," I say.

"I know."

I set the spoon aside and dump a good quarter cup of the grainy goodness into my mug. He returns to his side of the study, and our fingers pound away at our respective keyboards. As mellow as the night's become, and as horrific my findings, it's a pleasant way to spend an evening. Working together. Quiet. Focused on the same thing.

The idea of spending many, many nights this way is so far

beyond pleasant that I get a second wind, typing faster, my brain clearing. Of course, it could be the coffee.

The clock on Canaan's desk has just chimed midnight when our companionable quiet is shaken. The music in the living room masks his approach, so we don't hear Marco until he's standing in the doorway of the study.

"Hey," he says. I look him over. He looks clean, fresh. Well fed. Delia's been taking good care of him. He decided to stay in her spare room for a while. I think being near the halo terrifies him. I stand and pull him into a hug. He accepts the gesture and pats me softly on the back.

"You wanna stay here tonight, Marco? You're welcome to," Jake says. "Canaan's room is just sitting there."

"I appreciate it," Marco says, his eyes lingering on my empty wrist, on the spot where the halo normally rests, "but Olivia's waiting outside. Just came back for my stuff."

Olivia? I want to sit him down. Tell him we can explain. Rope him into our research. Anything but let him leave with her. She may have been victimized as a child, but I don't like her here. I don't like her near Dad or Marco. And something in Marco's demeanor tells me I'm right to worry.

"Marco," I say, tipping his chin up so his eyes meet mine. "You're not going after Henry, are you?"

"You should have told me he was Olivia's grandfather," he says. His tone takes me off guard, but Jake steps in.

"We haven't known for very long, man. We're just putting the pieces together now. How did you find out?"

"Olivia."

"How much time have you been spending with her?" I ask.

"We're old friends. Remember?"

He turns on his heel and crosses the hall to Canaan's room, abruptly ending the conversation.

Jake drags his hands through his hair. "Do you think he's going after Henry?"

"I don't know," I say, shaking my head. "I mean, I know he hates Henry, but Marco's not a killer. Is he?"

"We're all capable of horrible things, Elle."

Talk about an awful thought. "Okay, what do you want to do?"

Jake steps closer. "I think we should stop him. Make him stay. Get the PowerPoint out and explain angels and demons if we have to. Tell him what we know about Olivia. About Canaan and Helene. Tell him he doesn't have to be afraid of the halo."

Pixie dust!

"Jake, I left the halo on the kitchen counter. Maybe we should . . ."

"No, it's okay," he says, a hand to my hip. "I put it in my bag."

Relief washes over me.

"Thank you," I say. "I won't . . . won't leave it lying around like that anymore."

"I'm not worried about it," Jake says, squeezing my side. "So what do you think? We tell him?"

His hands are on both of my hips now, and really, what I'm thinking about has nothing to do with Marco. But another glance in Jake's eyes and I can tell he has no idea what his touch is doing to me. I force myself to focus.

"If you're okay with it," I say, clearing my throat. "I'm all in."

"I don't think we have much of a choice," he says.

He's right. I know he is. Still, as Jake takes my hand and leads me down the hall, I pray that Marco will handle this information a tad better than he handled the sight of the morphing halo and tremendously better than he handled the vision of me dying in that fire.

We stick our heads into Canaan's room, but it's empty.

"His bag's still here," Jake says, nodding at the far wall. Marco's backpack leans against the closet door.

"Probably just getting his stuff together," I say. "He had some books in the living room."

But when we reach the living room, Marco's not there. Just Shane & Shane, singing, strumming, worshiping through the speakers. I release Jake's hand and cross to the front door, opening it and stepping onto the porch. The night is cool and smells of wilting wildflowers. I inhale and lean out over the railing. I stretch past the post, looking up and down the highway.

Deserted.

Huh.

"Olivia's car's gone," I say over the blaring music, stepping back inside and closing the door behind me.

"So is my bag," Jake calls.

He's staring at the empty kitchen table, his face pale, his hands clenched in a chaos of sandy hair.

"What?"

Surely I heard him wrong.

"My bag. It was on the table and now it's . . ."

Did he just say . . .

I run over to the stereo and silence both of the Shanes with a slap of my palm.

"Your bag is gone?"

"Gone."

"And the halo?" I say, fear bouncing from lung to lung, shortening each breath.

"Gone," Jake says, letting his hands drop.

The icy hammer of panic pounds at my stomach and it folds in on itself in response. But Jake starts to laugh. He leans forward, his hands on his knees, and cackles loud and childlike.

He's lost it.

Completely and utterly.

It was only a matter of time, right? I'm seeing rogue demons, Marco thinks I'm going to die in a fire that happened sixteen years ago, and Jake's losing his mind.

"Jaaaake," I whine. "What are we going to do?"

His voice slowly quiets, but not before releasing another high-pitched sigh.

"What are we going to do?" I ask again.

At last he turns his face to mine. His eyes are white again. Celestial white. My hands shake. The halo's nowhere to be found, but Jake's eyes shine back at me, promising to die in my place should occasion call for it. I rub my eyes, but when my hands fall away and I open them again, Jake's white eyes remain. The same frightening, wonderful white that terrifies me every time I see it.

I have to tell him.

"Jake . . ."

But his long legs bring him toward me until he's so close I can smell the coffee on his breath, feel the fire radiating from his eyes. He grabs my hands and together we drop to our knees. Before I can say a thing, Jake answers my earlier question.

"We pray."

27

Brielle

I think we should check the chest," I say.

Canaan called not long ago from the city. He's been following the foundation's money and keeping an eye on Henry. He promised to keep an eye out for Marco and Olivia, but the phone's been silent for hours, and our prayers have dwindled to whispers. A quick glance at the clock tells me it's nearly four in the morning.

Jake jumps to his feet. "I'll do it."

He jogs down the hall and I head to the kitchen, underwhelmed by the silence of the Father. I fill a glass with water and down it like a shot. Unanswered prayers are still hard for me to understand.

From my perch at the kitchen counter, I see Jake emerge from Canaan's room down the hall. He has something in his hand. Small, thin, rectangular. It looks like a picture.

"What is it?" I ask, my pulse quickening at the thought of a way forward.

"A tattoo," Jake says, coming back down the hall. His steps are slow, measured. His face ashen. Jake shows me the picture.

It's one of those snapshots they hang in tattoo shops showing off their work. The top and bottom of the picture still has tape residue left on it. It's brittle with age and faded, but the photo is of the back of a man's neck.

Scrolling artwork creates an oval of sorts, just below his hairline. It's about three inches wide, all told. Within the oval, inked in heavy cursive, is the name Jessica Rose.

It means nothing to me. I flip the picture over. "Evil Deeds Tattoo Parlor" is stamped on the back along with an address in northwest Portland.

Men loved darkness instead of light, because their deeds were evil.

I've just guzzled a glass of water, but my mouth goes dry, my tongue like sandpaper. I tell myself I'm okay. I've seen crazy stuff before. This isn't anything to be shocked by. But I drain another glass of water, and another.

"This was in the chest?"

Jake nods, his hands in tight fists upon the counter.

"You know this tattoo parlor? You recognize the name?"

"No," he says. "I don't think so."

"Then what?"

But Jake says nothing. I lift his arm and step between him and the counter, forcing him to look at me. The celestial light that had shone there is gone, and it's those green and brown eyes that stare back at me. Flesh. Not spirit.

But they still give me butterflies.

"Jessica Rose was my mother."

My stomach clenches. It's like a miniature hunter just fired buckshot at the butterflies flitting about inside.

"I thought you didn't know your last name."

"I don't. I mean, if Rose was her last name, she listed

something else on my birth certificate. There's no record of a Jessica Rose giving birth in Oregon the year I was born."

"Then how do you know she's your mother?"

"It's one of the few things I remember. My dad slamming doors, screaming "Jessica Rose" whenever he was angry. Maybe it was her middle name or a nickname. I don't know."

Of all the things the Throne Room could have sent, of all the ways He could have answered our prayers for Marco, *this* is what we're given: a picture of a man's neck with Jake's mother's name tattooed on it.

I shake my head, trying to rid myself of the thought growing there. Of the certainty that this is our way forward. They're ridiculous, the words I'm about to say—because I need him here. I'm on unsteady ground as it is. With my dad and these nightmares. With the halo gone and Marco gallivanting about with Olivia. With the Celestial sliding in and out of view.

But I say them anyway.

"You have to go." I flip the photo again and read. "Evil Deeds Tattoo Parlor, NW 23rd. We prayed, and God gave us this."

"I don't want to leave you here without Canaan or the halo. Not with the nightmares, Elle."

"I adore the halo and Canaan's a rock star, but neither of them can stop the dreams. You need to go. And Helene's here."

"Are you sure? You'll be okay if I leave?"

I want to tell him, "No, stupid. Of course I won't be okay if you leave." But I don't. I remind him about the sketch in Ali's journal and the scripture written on the page.

"You have to go," I say again.

Jake leans in and presses his face to mine, the contours of our cheekbones curving perfectly together. "I'll go because it's the answer we've been praying for. But so you know, I'd rather stay."

I can't go with him. We both know that. Not with my dad so unstable and the possibility that Marco could return.

"I'd rather you stay too."

My heart bangs in my chest at his closeness, at the heat between us, at the promise of a future together. I think it's trying to break through—my heart—trying to be closer to the man in front of me.

I know just how it feels.

Close just doesn't seem close enough anymore.

It's another few minutes before he moves, but it's still far too soon.

He grazes my bottom lip with his thumb. "I'm going to go throw a few things in my bag."

"Marco's bag, you mean?"

"Yeah, Marco's bag."

He kisses me lightly and leaves me leaning against the kitchen counter. I'm still standing there holding the photo when he crosses the hall with Marco's bag and heads to his room.

I follow him down the hall, wanting to savor the last few minutes before he leaves. I'd help him pack, but I can't ever find a thing in his room. Still, I can sit in the mess and watch.

I pass Canaan's room, and that woodsy, outdoor smell tickles my nose. I stop and take two steps backward. It's coming from the chest. Jake must've left the lid ajar. I step into the room and take the five and a half steps necessary to reach the end of the bed.

I look down, but the chest's not open.

Huh.

Still, the fragrance is stronger than ever before, and an overwhelming need to see inside the thing pulls me to my knees. My hands are slick with sweat, so I rub them on my shorts before I shove the lid to the ground.

The first time I had the lead in a ballet was when I was eight years old. I was confident, bordering on cocky, really, and I had zero fear. But when that spotlight hit me and the world faded to black, when I could see nothing beyond that small circle, the terror crept in.

Just as it's doing now.

There is nothing beyond this circle of fear. Nothing in the world but me and Damien's dagger—Damien's bloody dagger—and the unmistakable absence of a sterling silver jewelry box.

A jewelry box with my initials on it.

With my . . . my ring inside it.

Tremors shake my body, but I reach inside the black chest. I wrap my hand around the dagger and lift it.

And I see with celestial eyes. But just the fear. It curls down my arm in chilling lines of black dread.

"I can explain," Jake says.

"Where's the ring?" I ask, biting my lip to keep it from trembling.

"Elle . . ."

"Where's the ring?"

There's so much fear in the room. It drips from Jake and crawls toward me, and I know the answer before he's said it.

"It's gone."

I drop the dagger. It falls into the chest, but I don't hear it hit the bottom. I hear nothing but the rushing of blood in my ears, the thundering of my own heart.

It's gone.

Like the halo. Like Marco.

Like Ali.

Like my mom.

Like her body.

So this is what he's been hiding. This is what has fear nesting in his heart.

"When?" I ask.

"December."

Just after the warehouse, then. I shove away from the chest and draw my knees up under my chin.

"You've been lying to me for seven months?"

"I haven't lied . . ."

"Don't even . . . ," I say, staring at him with every bit of vehemence I can muster.

"Elle," he says, bravely stepping toward me.

"'I haven't lied,'" I mock, doing an awful impression of Jake. "And my dad didn't actually *say* that my mother was in the casket he buried either. But I assumed. We've talked about it, Jake! About the ring. About . . . us. I believed you."

"I should have told you."

Understatement. Of. The. Year.

"And the dagger?"

"I noticed it the same day the ring disappeared."

I curl into a ball, hugging my knees to my chest. Before I can stop them, tears roll down my cheeks.

"I didn't know things could disappear from the chest."

Jake kneels in front of me and takes my face in his hands. "Neither did I. Neither did Canaan."

I let myself sob. I shouldn't. I should be strong. But I'm so tired of being strong.

"What does it mean?"

He doesn't answer right away, and I pinch my eyes shut, willing him to speak. These quiet, thoughtful moments of his drive me crazy sometimes. But when I open my eyes, I see the fear. With celestial eyes I see it. Crawling like a train of conjoined ants from my chin, up his arm, and across his chest.

I've unleashed fear on him.

And I hate myself for it. But he lied to me.

Jake lied to me.

"I don't know," Jake says. "I don't know what it means. Nothing, I hope."

"It has to mean something," I say.

"I just hoped they'd put it back. The Thrones. That whatever we'd done or didn't do would somehow get undone, and when I opened the chest one day the ring would be right there where it belongs."

"Is that possible?" I ask, my mind reeling at the thought. "Did we do something to . . . change the Throne Room's mind?"

"I don't know," he says, his voice raw. "And I hate not knowing."

I see the truth of it in his eyes. How much he hates that he can't fix this.

"Why didn't you tell me?"

"I didn't want you to worry," he says. "I didn't want you to be afraid."

I take a breath. Deep and rattling.

"But I am. I am afraid. Every day. And now I know you can lie to me. You. The one person I thought would never mess with my emotions."

"I didn't mean—"

"But you did. The truth is supposed to set you free, right? Isn't that what you told me?"

He's crying now, his face red, his eyes pleading. But he's broken me, and I don't know how to undo that. How do I trust him when I know he can lie so easily? So expertly.

I stand, needing to move, needing to shake the fear from my body.

"All you had to do was tell the truth, Jake. That the Thrones made a mistake. That God changed His mind. That we don't get a happily-ever-after."

"It may not mean that."

"I think it does. And so do you. Because if you didn't, you would have told me."

I want him to have an answer. I need him to. But the only thing pouring from Jake is fear, and I have enough of my own to deal with.

I leave him there on the floor and walk out the door with the tattered remains of my heart. I may never piece it all back together, but I don't have to give it to a liar either.

It's mine. And I'll take it with me.

28

Brielle

The remnants of a nightmare tumble around in my brain when I wake the next morning, but it's not the girl I think of. Not Olivia. I think of Jake—of the fear spilling onto the floor and the tears falling from his eyes. I think of all the angry words I threw at him last night and crawl back under the covers.

The ring is gone.

And Damien's dagger . . .

Why would the Throne Room send that? Why?

It's a warning, it has to be. Like the halo flaming at Olivia's touch, the dagger is a terrible warning. And Jake's kept it from me for . . . well, for far too long.

And now Damien's here, in Stratus. I know he is. The strange flashes I've been getting of the Celestial, Damien behind me on Main, fingers dragging through my hair. How could he have gotten that close?

I kick the covers off the bed and reach for my phone. Where is my phone? It's not on my bedside table. Not on my windowsill. I drop to the floor and search under my bed, under the desk, in last night's pants.

I need to call Helene.

"Elle!"

Dad is yelling, pounding around the kitchen, opening and closing cupboards, banging down cups or bowls or . . . hammers on the counter.

I'll use his phone.

"Elle, you up?"

"Yeah, Dad. Be there in a sec!" I rummage through my drawers, coming up with a pair of black shorts and a slouchy tank I'd worn once for a photo shoot. It's wrinkled from my poor treatment of it, but I feel more pulled together, more in control now that I'm out of my jammies and wearing something that was designed with such care.

Like me.

I run my hands over my stomach, willing it to unclench.

I'm fine. I am. If Damien had wanted me he could have had me. I was there for the taking. I close my eyes and breathe. I think of Canaan and Helene. I think of the Sabres, whose presence I hear from time to time.

There are more fighting for me than those fighting against.

I think of Jake. How can I not? He's the one who introduced me to this world, but thinking of him makes my hands shake, so I shove that thought aside and walk to the kitchen. I'm not going to panic. I'm not going to freak out my dad. I'm going to find a phone and call Helene.

But one sight of Dad and I remember I'm fighting battles on multiple fronts.

"*What* are you doing?" I ask.

He looks like death. He hasn't shaved in ages, his face pale and frantic, his hair greasy and matted in thick patches.

"Making my lunch," he says. "What's it look like I'm doing?"

"Remodeling?"

"Can't find my lunch box. You know where it is?"

I step closer, squinting at him through sleep-crusted eyes.

"Are you sober?" I ask.

"What kind of question is that?"

"A logical one."

"Yes, smarty-pants, I am sober." He leans against the fridge, both hands pressing into it. "I'm a little hungover, maybe, but I'm sober."

I stare at him for a few more seconds, and pity gets the better of me.

"Go," I say. "Shower. I'll pack your lunch."

"Thank you," he says. He pushes off the fridge and looks at me.

Is he going to cry?

He'd better not. I'm not dealing with that this morning.

"It's just a boxed lunch, Dad. You're not off the hook."

But it does feel kind of like a peace offering.

"No Pop-Tarts," he says.

He starts toward the bathroom, and I grab the phone from the living room. I dial Helene, but her phone goes straight to voice mail. I leave a message telling her to call me back, telling her I've seen Damien. No use in cryptic codes. If Damien's here, we're past that.

I dig Dad's lunch box—a small ice chest, really—out of the cupboard, and I jam in one of everything we have in the fridge. Except, of course, for the liquor. He'll have to settle for Gatorade—and a blue one at that. He hates the blue. Says it reminds him of maxi pad commercials—and yes, he calls them maxi pads. But I drop in the blue Gatorade and a strawberry Pop-Tart for good measure.

Beggars can't be choosers.

"Brielle."

I scream. It's impossible not to when Helene just appears in front of you.

She clamps a hand over my mouth, her voice hushed. "Your dad's here, yes?"

I nod, and she releases me. "In the shower. What's going on?"

"Damien."

The name barrels into my chest like a bulldozer.

How close is he? Is he here at my house or just here in Stratus?

But the questions die on my tongue. Her head turns violently to the right, and she disappears. Instinct pulls my head up and around, looking, looking. Wishing I could command my eyes to see the world as it really is.

But I can't.

The second hand on the clock twitches seventeen times before I make a decision. I run to the bathroom door and bang on it. I've got to get him out of here. The closer he is to me, the more danger he's likely to be in. "Dad! You're gonna be late. Hurry up!"

He hollers something back and turns off the water, but I'm already running through the house, looking for my phone.

Where is it?!

I lift the couch cushions and then shake out the blankets. I brush the curtains aside to check the window seat where I sat early this morning and watched Jake drive away. My phone's not there, but I catch sight of something else beyond the window.

Kaylee.

You have got to be kidding me!

She's pulling into my drive looking even more harried than normal. I dash back into the kitchen, colliding with Dad, who's standing in the arched entryway wearing nothing but a towel wrapped around his waist, brushing his teeth and staring at me like I've lost my mind.

"What are you looking for, kiddo?"

"My phone," I say. "Kaylee just pulled up, Dad, and you're naked! In the kitchen!"

"All right," he huffs. "I'm going. What's the herbivore doing here this early?"

I don't answer, but I notice he sounds better. Definitely smells better. Still, I have got to get him out of here.

And Kaylee too.

". . . don't have time for you to answer the door. Brielle, did you hear a word I just said?"

Kaylee's so close I can smell her cool mint toothpaste. She's still in her jammies, her hair tucked into a baseball bat, Tasmanian Devil slippers on her feet, hot-pink mascara lining her lashes.

"I'm sorry, what?"

"Have you seen Helene?" she asks.

I lick my lips. "Why?"

"Because she showed up at my door—at the butt crack of dawn, by the way—asking if I'd seen Olivia and telling me we had to go. And then I, like, blinked or something, and she was gone."

"I don't . . ."

"I tried to call you, Elle. Where's your phone?"

I scrape my nails across my scalp. "That is a very good question."

And then I can see. Into the Celestial.

A wing dips low through the roof. White. Shining.

I duck.

Kaylee makes a face. "Whatcha doin'?"

I look up and I *see*.

Not the entirety of the Celestial.

Just Helene.

Just Damien.

Just their swords!

I duck again.

"You gonna tell me what's going on, homegirl, or would you rather I drive you to the sanitarium?"

Helene swings her blade again, spinning, spinning toward him. He's so much bigger than she is, but she's fast—wicked fast—her sword nothing but a blur against the morning sky.

I grab Kaylee's hand and drag her toward the door, yelling over my shoulder.

"Daaaad!"

And that's when my heart explodes.

Two white wings and a tiny body fall through the roof, and I shove Kaylee aside.

"Whoa, turbo!" she says, colliding with the counter.

But I can't concentrate on Kaylee now. Helene connects with the linoleum, her wings useless, her limbs splayed like pickup sticks on the floor.

"Helene!" I scream.

A smoking wound of black ice cuts across the thick cords of shimmering white that wrap her torso. I drop to the ground, to my knees, and wrap my trembling hand around hers. Her white eyes find mine, and I hear her voice in my head.

"The Palatine are coming."

Before I can ask what in Neverland she's talking about, she vanishes, her fading eyes the last thing I see.

29

Brielle

The Palatine are coming."

"You've said that no less than twenty times, and I still have no idea what you're talking about."

I'm kneeling on the floor, the linoleum squares swimming before me.

"The Palatine—"

"Are coming," Kay says flippantly. "I got it. What exactly would you like me to do about it?"

"Who are they?" I whisper.

"I *know* you're not talking to me."

I'm not. I'm talking to Helene. My Shield. My beautiful, powerful, wounded Shield. How many times will that little angel be mangled in front of me?

"Kaylee?"

"Right here. On Planet Sanity, by the way. Whenever you're ready for a return trip."

"What happened?" I ask.

Kaylee's slippers purr along the linoleum, and two Tasmanian Devils move into my line of sight. "Okay, that didn't sound like a rhetorical question, but let's just say I'm a little short on details myself."

"Tell me anyway."

Kaylee's hands find my shoulders, and she pulls me to my feet. She doesn't stumble, she doesn't stutter. She looks at me with those gigantic brown eyes of hers and says, "I'll tell *you* if you'll tell me."

Her eyes are a little too knowing, her lips a little too tight. And I understand that this is that moment. The one Canaan said would come. *The mind can't be forced.*

But now she's asking.

"Are you sure you want to know, Kay? 'Cause once you do, you can't unknow. It's just . . . infuriating like that."

"Infuriating like a halo that gives mysterious boys visions of you dying?"

"Yeah," I say. "Just like that."

"Then yeah. I think I can handle it."

"*This* is my lunch?" Dad stands in the doorway of the kitchen, staring at the contents of his lunch littering the floor, but I'm still staring at Kaylee. Still considering her words. She did handle the halo far better than I expected.

"Okay," I say.

"Okay?" Dad says. Out of the corner of my eye, I see Dad kneel to the floor and start scooping his lunch back into the ice chest. "It's not okay."

"Okay," Kaylee says with a nod.

"I just, I've got to do something first." But even as I say it, I have no idea what I'm going to do.

Damien's out there.

And the Palatine.

Whatever the heck that is.

Maybe it's good. Maybe I want the Palatine here.

Jake would know.

But he's gone and I have no idea where I left my phone.

I stare through the entryway into the living room. I stare at the landline phone sitting next to Dad's recliner and I try to conjure up Jake's number, but all I come up with is speed dial 5.

Speed dial 5.

So not helpful.

All of this flies through my head in a matter of seconds, and then I see Damien.

Yes, Damien.

His talons appear first. They wrap around the entryway between the living room and the kitchen. He's taken some damage during his fight with Helene and bears a series of festering sear marks across his arms and chest.

Still, he's lethal. And I have no idea how long I'll be able to see him.

My hands shake. And my legs.

My stomach roils, and I know I'm going to be sick.

God, are You there?

Please, please help me.

A bead of subzero sweat rolls down my spine, and it's not God who answers. It's Damien.

His voice snakes into my head, and it's not melodic like Helene's or soothing like Canaan's. It's gritty and toxic and cold.

"The Palatine are coming? Now?"

He's asking me?

I don't nod. I don't answer.

Why is he asking me?

I try to look away, but his presence in my house is jarring.

His chest is slick with fear. It blackens his talons further and pours liberally down my walls.

Is he frightened? Or does he just produce the stuff in vast quantities?

If the idea of the Palatine in Stratus frightens him, maybe they're on my side. Maybe their presence will send him to the skies.

"Brielle, baby, are you okay?" It's Dad, and I don't know what to say. He stands and closes the ice chest. "Brielle?"

Kaylee takes my hand and tugs. Her breath flutters the hair at my ear as she hisses, "You're doing it again."

I break eye contact with the monster and look at my dad.

"I'm okay," I tell him, trying to smile. "Just a little out of sorts, I guess."

"Maybe you should head back to bed? It's still early, kid."

Damien slides down the wall and crouches in the entryway now. Massive shoulders, frayed wings, bulky arms with razor-sharp talons pressing into the linoleum flooring that Dad laid himself.

My father's huge, but this beast dwarfs him.

It seems he's willing to wait for a response, though, which baffles me. Will he hurt my father to get one? The thought makes my knees weak. Damien's just feet from Dad now, and I try to warn him, try to say anything, but my throat just gurgles.

Dad's brow knots.

Kaylee laughs, but it's forced, and still I can't take my eyes from the demon in my house.

"Your dad's totally right, Elle. You're a space cadet, and we have tons to do today. I'll get her to bed, Mr. Matthews. You go. We'll be fine."

But leaving me in Kaylee's "capable" hands does not calm

Dad, and he walks toward me. He hefts the ice chest in one hand and takes my chin in the other.

"Tell me you're all right, baby."

I can't avoid his gaze now. He's there. Blocking everything else with his ruddy beard and his dripping hair. He looks cleaner, younger—the dad of my childhood almost—and for a moment I consider crawling into his arms, asking him to tell me there's no monster. That it's just my imagination. He would too. He'd tell me that. He'd do it just because I ask him to. Because I'm scared.

But it would be false.

Like the years of lies he told to protect me.

Like the one Jake told.

"I'm fine, Dad. Sorry. Kaylee's right. You should go. I'm fine."

I'm not fine, not by a long shot, but if Dad can lie to protect me, then I can return the favor.

He narrows his eyes at me, a bear scrutinizing his cub. At last he kisses my nose and pulls me in for a hug. "Sleep, okay? Let this little vegan—"

"Vegetarian."

"—take care of you. You've got me all freaked out here."

You're not the only one.

The door closes behind him with a hollow rattle, and Kaylee yanks me toward her.

"You've lost the privilege of deferring till the second half, Elle. Talk. Now. *What* is going on?"

I'm out of ideas, and nothing but the truth makes sense. So I open my mouth and I tell her. "There's a demon behind you," I say. "In the archway between the living room and the kitchen."

Her face goes white, her eyes shifting left and right.

"Demon, like that hot guy who used to be on *Buffy* but has that *Bones* show now? That kind of demon?"

"Nothing like that guy."

"Fiddlesticks," she breathes. She stands stick straight, the thin muscles in her neck taut. "What's he doing?"

"He's talking to me. Asking me about the Palatine."

"Wh-What are you going to tell him?"

"I'm going to tell him the truth. That I don't know anything about the Palatine. You hear me?" I yell toward Damien, "I don't know anything."

Kaylee flinches at my outburst.

Damien does not.

"But they're coming now?" His voice is acidic, chewing away at my courage. "The Palatine are coming?"

"I don't know," I say, frustrated. "Are you not hearing me? I don't know a thing."

"Do not lie to me, human. I heard you say, 'The Palatine are coming,' and we still have days before that should happen. I still have days."

He *is* frightened.

Dear Jesus, please let this be the right thing to say.

Please, please.

"I was repeating Helene," I say. "That's all. Maybe she was wrong."

"Helene." Damien's face contorts at the word. I think he's smiling. He turns his face to the sky, his fangs flashing, reflecting some unseen celestial light. And then he leaps through the roof and I lose sight of him.

Which terrifies me more than seeing him.

Still, I breathe deep. The air feels cleaner without him

here. Kaylee's grip is an anaconda on my wrist, her eyes glued to my face.

"Helene," she whispers. "And the warehouse." Tears clump in her hot-pink lashes.

I want to ask her what she remembers, what haunts her, but we'll have to play catch-up later.

"Listen, Kay. Look at me. Good. I can't see him now, but that doesn't mean he's gone."

Her lip trembles. "Why? Why can't you see him?"

"I'm not entirely sure."

"Why could you see him before?"

"That's another tough one to answer."

She's giving me that look. The same look I'm sure I gave Jake when he was struggling to explain. "Look, there *are* answers, Kay. Kind of. But we have to get hold of Jake. Now. Do you have your cell?"

Her mouth opens, and her eyes glaze over.

I grab her shoulders and shake. "Kay!"

"Yes. I'm sorry." She pinches her eyes shut and shakes her head. "My phone is in the car."

Outside. Ugh.

I look at the door like it's a mutinous traitor. The reality is we're not any safer here than we'd be outside. These walls, this roof over our heads—they offer nothing in the way of protection from invisible forces.

But I won't get separated from Kaylee. That would be a mistake. Damien knows I care about her, knows I wouldn't let her die. So to leave her without celestial eyes would be dangerous.

"Okay, then. Let's go." I step to the door and twist the handle. "You have your keys."

Kaylee pats down her pockets and pulls a bedazzled key ring out of her pajama pants.

I take her hand in mine and we run down the stairs and to her car. The day is warm and bright, a glorious northwest summer day, but there's a chill in my chest. I stay at Kaylee's side while she jams the key in the lock and flings open the door. She reaches inside and pulls out her phone, shoving it into my hands.

I fumble with her phone, but it's newer than mine, fancier, and I can't find Jake's number.

"Can you . . ."

She takes it from me and slides her finger along the screen. A few taps and the phone is ringing.

Ringing.

Ringing.

Pick up, pick up.

PICK. UP.

30

Jake

The neon sign in the window says Open, but it's a lie. Two hours ago Jake climbed out of his car and shook the door handle. He succeeded only in dislodging the sign that declared the tattoo shop was open from eight to midnight daily. The clock hanging just inside the window says it's half past eight now, and still Evil Deeds is nothing but shadows and glare.

On its left is a hair salon—very girlie, very bright. Above the red brick storefront, a swirly sign in red and orange guarantees you'll love your locks when they're through with them. Something about the place screams *Kaylee*.

To the right of the tattoo shop is an awning with vibrant swatches of material decorating it. The sign above this door says New Age Books, but not a single book is visible from where Jake is standing. Through the window he can see display cases of candles and perfumes. Baskets of rocks and crystals line the front counter. The doors are thrown open, welcoming, beckoning morning shoppers. The smell of incense irritates his nose, and he steps sideways to avoid it.

As annoying as the incense is, the bookstore is far more

welcoming than the dark hole of a tattoo shop next to it. Yet Jake stands in front of its windows staring at the artwork painted there. A snarling lion emerges from a heart styled of scrolling loops and curves. His heart feels an awful lot like a lion is trying to claw its way out of it, and as the minutes pass he develops a fascination for the artwork.

He reaches out a hand and runs it along the twisting lines merging with the lion's mane. If he can figure this out, figure out why the Throne Room sent him here, maybe he'll understand why they took the ring. Maybe, just maybe, it'll be enough to convince Brielle to hear him out.

In his back pocket is the picture of the tattoo—the one they found in the chest—but he doesn't need to pull it out to recognize just how similar the styling is to this. To this lion and its evil heart.

"Sorry, sorry, sorry."

Hurrying toward Jake from the south side of the street is a man wearing threadbare jeans and a Rolling Stones T-shirt with the sleeves shredded. A cigarette dangles from his lip, unlit, more decoration than anything else. He's easily in his fifties, but his gray hair is plastered into a series of little spikes and he's wearing thick black eyeliner. A chain of keys slaps against his thigh, making his approach sound like a chorus of bell-wielding children. His arms and neck bear hundreds of tattoos, his hands are decorated with an array of rings. Thick bands, silver skulls, gaudy gemstones.

He lifts the jangling keychain from his hip, finds the correct key with remarkable ease, and jams it into the lock. He spins the key around and thrusts himself into the building.

"Bike broke," he says by way of apology. "You here for some ink?"

The man drops his keys on the counter and tucks the cigarette behind his ear. He busies himself—flipping switches, turning on computers.

"Actually, I have a question," Jake says.

"Little early for pop quizzes, ain't it?" The man slides onto a barstool behind the counter and looks Jake in the eye for the first time. He must see something there he likes, because his demeanor softens. "Go ahead, kid. I'm just messing with ya."

Jake hesitates. The idea of knowing what this guy knows is suddenly terrifying. Still, he pulls the picture from his pocket and slides it across the counter.

"You know this?"

The guy picks it up and swears. "Where'd you get this, kid?"

"So you know it?"

"Sure, I know it. I did it, didn't I? Haven't seen this in forever."

"Can you tell me who it is?"

"Doctor Doom," he says.

"Excuse me?"

He laughs again. It's weasely, this man's laugh. Kind of shrill, kind of devious. But his face is kind.

"Doctor Doom, ha! Yeah, that's what we called him." He taps the corner of the picture against his lip. "What *was* his real name? Bud, maybe? Billy? I don't know. It's been too long now. Don't rightly remember."

Brian, Jake thinks. *If it's my dad, his first name was Brian.*

Jake's lips have never felt so dry. He licks them, and then once more before he asks, "Do you know his last name?"

"Nah. Just Doom, you know? He was Doom to those of us around here."

"Did you know Jessica? Was she his . . . wife?"

"I don't know if they were hitched or not, but they were together all the time. Before the fire, she worked at a pub on Burnside. Still there, if you wanna check it out. Ringlers."

"There was a fire at the pub?"

"Not at the pub, but there was definitely a fire."

Jake's hands are slick. He wipes them on his pants. "When?"

"Details aren't really my thing either. At least a decade ago, maybe more. Doctor Doom himself set the thing. Accident, by all accounts, but there's no shirking it. The blame lies with him."

Jake feels the sweat break out along his hairline and down his spine. He's never believed much in coincidences, and his stomach is sick at the scenario placed before him.

"What happened?"

"Well, you know that copper stuff inside of wiring? It's worth an awful lot of money to the right people. And Doctor Doom, well, he never had a real job. Quick buck here and there. Just stuff like that, ya know? That's all he was ever looking for. Somehow he got into this whole copper deal and started scaling buildings for the stuff. Breaking apart AC and heater units for it. Awful hard work for a guy who didn't want a job."

Jake rubs at his neck, tense—tells himself it's the lack of sleep, the long drive, but it's more than that and he knows it.

"And he started a fire?" he asks.

"Yeah, man. Huge thing too."

"How?"

"Well, I don't rightly know all the details, but if I remember correctly, the police found a soldering iron there in the rubble. If he used that, it'd been far too easy to get the sparks flying. It was an old school. Couple sparks is probably all it took before the place went up in flames."

It's not just his lips now; Jake's mouth goes dry. The morning sun beats through the glass windows pressing against his back, drawing sweat that slips down his chin.

"Was anybody hurt?"

"Lady, I think."

Jake is trembling, the pieces sliding into place, creating a horrible, horrible picture. If what this guy's saying is true, his dad killed Olivia's mom.

"You okay, kid?"

"Yeah, just . . . What happened to him—to Doctor Doom?"

"Arrested, man. Caught all burnt and blistered. Never saw him after that. Last I remember, he got sent up on charges for what he done. That school wasn't his first, so who knows."

But Jake's mind is a step ahead. There are articles online about the fire. Brielle was reading them last night. Doctor Doom's last name has to be in there, and if it's not there will be arrest reports. Jake's last name could be in those reports.

The guy checks his watch and then stands, moving toward the back of the small shop. "You can keep asking, kid, if you got more questions, but I gotta get set up. Appointment in a few."

Jake follows him back, his mind moving like a trap, his eyes absently wandering the walls and the pictures plastered there. Photos of tattoos done in the shop, of clients with dragons and tigers and flowers. Lots and lots of flowers.

"Can you tell me what happened to Jessica?"

"Disappeared when Doctor Doom did, I think," the guy says, setting the picture on the tray before him. He lays out a series of metal tools on a white terry cloth.

"Was she was involved in the copper theft?"

"Nah," he says. "I doubt it. She was a sweet gal. Pity she

got mixed up with him. Don't get me wrong, he was a nice guy—Doctor Doom—fun to be around, threw a great party. But Jessica, well, she was special. Had something of a temper, but with Doctor Doom, ya know, probably a necessary thing. She needed someone in a suit and tie, you know? Someone who could get her out of waiting tables."

Jake watches him prepare his workstation, his mind taking a beating, moving slow. Eventually his eyes settle on the picture.

"How do you know them, kid—Doctor Doom and pretty little Jessica?"

"I think they were my parents."

"Whoa. Didn't know they had a kid. Here," he says, lifting the picture off the tray and handing it back. "You keep it."

"Thank you." He's not sure how he feels about this picture now. About what his . . . dad . . . did. He doesn't look at it as he slides it into his pocket. "I appreciate it. And your time. I know it's early."

Jake extends his hand, and the guy shakes it.

"You come back, kid, all right? Pick anything you like. Ink's on me."

Jake can't decide if he's tempted or not. "I appreciate it."

"Anything for Doctor Doom's kid."

Jake steps onto the sidewalk, the glorious summer day at war with the cold winter taking up residence in his chest.

The son of Doctor Doom.

Go figure.

31

Brielle

Redial.

Pick up, pick up, pick up.

Voice mail.

Again.

"So he's invisible? This demon?"

"Kind of, yes," I say. "Invisible to you."

She picks at her eyelashes. I redial again. "Why can you see him, Elle?"

I don't have time to consider the consequences of telling her. I don't even have time to weigh my options. It's not ideal, not as I imagined it would be: sipping coffee and eating cookies, poring over Scripture. But what about my life is ideal these days?

I'll answer her questions. Truthfully. There's no other way to explain this morning anyway. No other way to explain my crazy response to Damien and Helene.

"The halo. It's not just a halo in the figurative sense. It's an actual, literal halo. An angel's halo."

Her jaw drops open, making a sucking, popping sound, but she doesn't question my claim.

"Where is it?" she asks, searching my wrists.

"Marco has it," I say. The phone at my ear rings again and again.

"Marco's an—"

"No, no, no. It was in Jake's bag—the halo—and Marco grabbed the wrong bag when he left," I say quickly. "Pick up!"

"Marco left?"

"Pick up!"

But Jake doesn't pick up. I jam my finger on End and hand the phone back to Kaylee.

"I might kill that boyfriend of yours," she says.

"Not if I kill him first."

I search the sky, but there's nothing to see. Not even a cloud.

"So he flies, then," Kaylee says, shooting darting glances upward.

"Yeah," I say. "Yeah. Big black wings and all."

"So, if there are demons . . ." Her voice has gotten all gulpy.

"Then there are also angels," I say, placing my hands on her shoulders. "Good guys."

"Jake?"

I shake my head. "Canaan."

"Oh." She's computing. I see it—her brain working, her eyes twitching as this new information slides into place.

"So Jake, then. He's the son of an angel?"

I shake my head. "Jake's parents abandoned him when he was young. Canaan raised him."

More info. More computing.

"You have way too many secrets. Okay, then what about this demon-guy? What does he want?"

"That's a very, very good question."

"You don't know?" Shrill. Gulpy.

"Well, the idea of the Palatine being here freaked him out."

"Have we decided what the Palatine is?"

"No," I say, "but just before Damien—"

"Damien? That's his name? The demon's name is Damien? You're kidding, right?"

"Not kidding. Before he asked me about the Palatine, Helene fell through my roof and told me that the Palatine are coming."

"Helene too?"

"Yes."

"And she fell through your roof?" Kaylee stumbles back a step and slides down the door of her Honda. Her Tazmanian Devil slippers kick up dust as they slip out from under her, and she plops down in the gravel. I squat beside her.

"She'll be okay. She heals."

"She heals?"

"Look," I say, tugging on the brim of her hat. "I know this isn't a good time to dump more info on you, but you need to know something, okay? Damien—this demon—he was the author of the whole warehouse thing. It wasn't that Juan guy or Eddie."

Her face puckers at my reference to Eddie. Dimples. The guy who kidnapped her last December; he tied her up and hauled her to Damien's warehouse intending to sell her. I hate bringing him up, but she wanted the truth and I don't have time for a soft version of it.

"They were just a couple goons he worked with. Damien is the real nightmare."

She just stares. I hope—hope—that she's getting this. That she's understanding, because I have no idea where Damien is or whether he's coming back, and I want her to be prepared.

"He has the ability to cloak people, Kay. Make us invisible

like him. He can pick us up—fly us around—do bad things to us, but you need to know this. Are you listening? Because if you don't hear anything else I'm telling you, you need to hear this: there are more fighting for us than there are fighting against us."

I give it a second to sink in, but she just blinks back at me.

"Listen, I'm going to do my best to talk to him. To understand what he wants and why he's here."

"Why *is* he here?" And now tears pour down her face. They're pink, her mascara running, dripping from her chin onto her pajamas.

"He shouldn't be. He messed up big at the warehouse, and my understanding is that his punishment should have lasted longer than this."

Her eyes widen.

"We'll talk, okay?" I tell her. "Later. All about demon punishment and . . . stuff. But promise me you won't freak out. Promise me you'll stay calm if he comes back."

"If he's invisible, how will I know?"

"If I can see him, I'll tell you."

"If?"

"Without the halo my sight is . . . inconsistent. I don't know why. You don't have Canaan's number, do you?"

She shakes her head. It was a long shot anyway.

"I have Helene's."

I think of Helene's mangled body. I think of her disappearing from sight. She needs time to heal, but how long will that take? I think back to the warehouse. To the extent of her wounds there.

"Okay," I say. "Here's the plan. You keep calling. Jake and Helene. Just call until one of them answers. Leave a message on their voice mail too. And text your heart out, Kay."

She clenches her phone to her chest. "I can do that."

I laugh. It's too loud, out of place here with a demon circling, but I do it anyway.

"Yes, I believe you can."

"What are you going to do?"

"I'm going to pray."

Her face is already pale, but now it looks all green and sickly.

"That's it. That's all? I'm going to text and you're going to pray?"

I nod, her fear grabbing hold of me as well.

"No offense, Elle, but that's a crappy plan."

She may be right.

"Yeah, but it's all I've got right now," I say, pulling her to her feet. "You with me?"

"Okay," she says. "I'm in, but what are we going to tell your dad?"

I twist around, and there, walking up the road back toward the house, is Dad.

"Holy heck. What is he doing back here?"

"I don't know, but he doesn't look happy to see you outside. You're supposed to be in bed, remember? We're going to have to tell him something."

"Sitting Dad down and telling him we had a little visit from a demon this morning might not be the best way to handle this."

"It's what you did with me."

"Yeah, well, you're not as crazy as my dad. Or as hungover."

"That's saying something at least."

Dad crunches through the gravel toward us, his ice chest swinging against his leg, his eyes squinting in the morning light. I hold my arms out, questioning.

"Truck broke down," he says.

Of course it did.

"They're towing it to the Auto Body."

"So, no work for you today," I say, glancing at the sky once more.

"I'm expecting an angry call from Cliff anytime now. What are you girls doing out here? Thought you were going back to bed, Elle."

"I was. I am. Kaylee needed something from her car."

"My phone," she says. "Forgot it out here."

"And you needed an escort?"

"You know girls," she says. "Gotta do it all together. In fact, I think, yup, I have to pee. You wanna come, Elle?"

"Yes!" I say. "The bathroom. Yes."

Dad narrows his eyes at us, but we're around her car in a flash. We run up the porch stairs and back inside, through the kitchen and into the bathroom. I slam the door, and she falls onto the closed toilet.

"Okay, what now?"

I stare at my reflection in the mirror. Holy golden haloes, Batman. I'm hideous.

"You start dialing," I say. "I'm going to brush my teeth and pray at the same time."

"Does that work?"

"Sure. Why not?"

"You don't, like, need to be on your knees or holding beads or something?"

"I'll be talking to an invisible God," I tell her. "He's all right with me brushing up while I do it."

I pull my toothpaste from the drawer. "But, Kay?"

"Yeah?"

"I'm new at this whole praying thing, so I'm going to do it silent-like, okay? In my head."

"Whatever sharpens your pencil, girl. I'm pretending this is all in your head."

32

Jake

When he exits the tattoo parlor, Jake finds Canaan leaning against his car door, his face hanging with emotion.

"I'm sorry, Jake."

"You heard, then? Doctor Doom."

"I heard," Canaan says.

"Do you think that's why Olivia's come to Stratus? For some sort of generational revenge?"

"I'm not certain *Olivia* knows why she came to Stratus. I expect only time will tell."

"And you haven't seen her or Marco?"

"No," Canaan says. "But I'll keep an eye out for them."

"And the halo?"

Canaan shrugs. Even on the phone he was strangely serene about the missing halo.

"We have no control over that now," he says. "You're more like him than I, Jake. If you stumbled upon it like he did, would you let it out of your sight?"

Jake thinks back. "No," he says. "The security it brought

me—the peace—it's addicting. But, Canaan, I may not be as much like Marco as you think. First off, he's with Olivia, whose intentions are already suspect. And you didn't see Marco when he touched it. He lost it, completely freaked out. The halo didn't bring him peace. Not even a measure of it."

"We don't get to choose how others respond to God or His gifts; we can only pray they'll be open. And, Jake, we may serve the Prince of Peace, but He is also a warrior."

They've had this discussion before, and Jake rehearses a phrase he's heard Canaan say many times. "War may end with peace, but it rarely starts there."

"So we exercise faith, Jake. Faith that God has a plan and that His will is perfect."

With a pang that has him looking away, Jake considers the missing engagement ring and can't stop himself from wondering, *Is God's will always perfect? Always?*

He doesn't want to talk about that now. Not with Canaan, whose faith can't be shaken. Jake tips his head to the sky, willing the tears to stay put.

There's not a cloud in sight, hardly any wind. The sun bounces off hundreds of city windows, turning the urban setting into a trove of gemstones. But Jake needs to get back to Stratus. To Brielle.

"Are you staying?" he asks.

"For a while. There's been some activity at Henry's place. Not demonic, but I'd like to see what's going on."

Jake opens his driver's side door and drops into his seat. He shifts, feeling something beneath him: his phone.

Canaan lowers his face to the window. "Drive safely," he says. "I'll call soon."

But Jake's ill. His hands shake, and he can't quite focus on the message before him.

Canaan yanks the phone from his hands and reads.

And then, without discussion, he crouches next to the car, and Jake watches the Terrestrial swallow his guardian. A blink later and Jake is lifted from his seat and secured against Canaan's chest. If he were to open his eyes, he'd see the city of Portland passing below them in a conglomeration of light and color, but his eyes are closed in prayer.

He utters nothingness, pained fears, desperate pleas, terrified gibberish.

Is today the day?

The day he loses Brielle?

33

Brielle

Anything?"

"No," Kaylee says, her fingers jumping like spastic crickets over the smooth face of her phone. Her slippered feet are drawn up, crossed on the toilet seat, her back curled against the tank. She looks small.

She looks scared.

I want to say something to reassure her, but I could use some comforting words myself.

Where is Jake?

"You girls done in there? I need to pee."

"We're done," I say, opening the door and stepping past Dad into the hall.

I bump the beer he's holding. It sloshes down his hand and onto the blue carpet.

"It's not even nine o'clock, Dad."

He casts a quick glance at Kaylee, but she looks away.

"Just leave it, Elle," he growls.

"You know I won't."

I'm steaming, but Dad closes the bathroom door and the

conversation ends. Kaylee follows me to my room and crawls up onto my bed while I pace.

"You okay?" she asks.

"I will be."

"What's that mean?"

I don't answer. I'm too busy plotting. Kaylee's phone vibrates with a low purr.

"Who is it?" I ask, lurching to a stop.

She reads the screen, her face a smear of pink mascara and resignation.

"Delia." She sighs. "I left the faucet on. Flooded the bathroom. She's not very happy about it."

"Lucky thing you're here then."

"Yeah. Lucky me. Palpable father-daughter tension and invisible demons."

She has a point.

Another sigh from Kay. A big, fat, end-of-the-world kind of sigh. "Since I seem to have nothing, Elle, what about you? How'd that whole praying thing work out?"

I start walking again, back and forth, searching for words. For the right words. I know I'm supposed to be a good example—supposed to know what to say—but I don't. I don't know anything. And Dad's beer—the one he's holding right now—feels like the final straw. Not the one that breaks me, but the last one I'm willing to suffer.

"I'm glad I prayed," I say, "and I'm going to keep praying, because I don't know what else to do."

"Where are you going?"

I don't answer. I'm afraid saying the words out loud will dampen my resolve.

"Elle?"

I fling open the door and step into the hall. Three steps more and I'm in the kitchen. I grab the plastic trash can as I pass it. Three more steps take me to the door of the fridge. I take one more deep breath and then I open the door and count. Fourteen blue-labeled bottles stare back at me. Laughing.

They've got my dad, and we all know it.

Indignation makes my muscles and bones ache. I let it take control, let it swipe my arm across the middle shelf. I press the trash can closer, catching every last bottle. Glass shatters, and the smell of misery fills the air.

"*What* are you doing?" Dad stands in the arched entryway between the kitchen and the living room. His mouth gapes. The television chatters behind him, making him look like a character in one of those foreign films whose words have been dubbed in. Unimportant. What is important is Dad's face.

He's mad. More than that, he looks disappointed.

In me.

That's fine.

I hug the trash can to my chest and walk to the kitchen door.

"Gabrielle!" His face is red, his hand white around the neck of the half-empty bottle in his hand.

"That's your last one today," I say. My words are empty of conviction, but my legs aren't. They take me away from him. Toward the door.

"Brielle!"

I fling the door open and step into the sunlight. I don't check the skies. I don't look around for Damien. If he's there, I don't want to know. Not now. Not until I've got this done. Twelve steps take me around the house and to the large garbage can pressed against its side. It's awkward, but I lift the lid and heft the plastic trash can in. The whole thing.

Glass breaks, amber liquid sloshing like a choppy sea as the bottles collide, but I'm relieved.

Demons from without are one thing.

In my house—in my father's hand—they're impossible to fight.

Adrenaline shakes my body, but I close the lid on the wet, sopping mess and fling myself against the side of the house. A sob gurgles in my throat, but I refuse to let it free.

God, be my peace. There won't be any inside after what I've done.

A soft breeze tugs at my hair, at the shirt hanging loose against my body. The wind rushes faster and faster, pushing past me, and then as quickly as it arrived it abandons me to the hot sun.

It leaves behind a song—high voices that whisper soft unintelligible things and low notes that rattle my chest.

The Sabres.

I step away from the smell of alcohol and toward the voices. The melody is louder here, coming from this direction, but though I squint and crane around I see nothing. Nothing but the decaying apple orchard in the distance. The music pulls me closer, and I step carefully with my bare feet, doing my best to avoid fallen pinecones and dry prickly weeds.

And then I see it.

Spiraling from the tops of the apple trees, I see worship. Like the pianist's song on Christmas, the melody trills in loops of colored incense toward the heavens. Greens and blues. Shades I have trouble naming, but they're thrilling and awe inspiring. My eyes follow the streaming tendrils higher and higher, my heart swelling with the sound. With the sight of it all.

I tip my chin up, wishing my fingers could touch the ribbons of worship high above.

And then fear smacks me in the chest. It wraps me tight and pulls me to my knees.

I gasp and gasp, my eyes glued to the heavens. Rocks and gravel bite at my bare legs, but the pain is nothing to the fear pressing down on me.

My eyes—celestial eyes that have just seen worship—now see a sky black with writhing bodies. A mass of twitching wings and claws, their swords of ice steaming in the hot celestial sky.

"The Palatine. They weren't supposed to be here for two more days. And now we're out of time."

Damien's voice is in my head again. I have no idea what he's talking about, but he's here and that's enough.

If the frigid cold climbing up my back is any indication, he's close.

But I don't turn. I don't move. One monster is not nearly so frightening as a sky full of them. My gaze arches across the sky from horizon to horizon, but I see nothing beyond the army. Not to the east or to the west. I look north and south, panic coating my arms in chilling sweat. I thought there were more fighting for *us*, but I was wrong.

We're hemmed in.

Stratus is surrounded.

34

Pearla

A Shield, Commander, approaching from the west."

Loyal snorts and shakes his mane, melting into the celestial sky as Michael flies to Pearla's side.

"You've good eyes, Pearla. Let us see what he has to say."

The two of them hover, one great and one small, several hundred yards in front of the army, watching as the Shield advances on their position.

"He flies with only one set of wings, Commander."

"Well noted, little one. I do not believe our comrade is alone."

Pearla encounters members of the Shield often enough, but it's rare for her to see one with a charge tucked beneath his wings. It's a curious thing to behold, and she continues to watch. He's taller than most men—a common enough thing for Shields—but not nearly so large as Michael and the other archangels. She's seen this Shield moving in and out of Stratus, but she's kept her distance. Cherubic protocol. She's to observe and report, not engage. It's why her relationship with Michael is so strong. He's nearly the only true friend she has.

"Canaan!" the Commander calls, his mind full of recognition. "It has been too long."

The one called Canaan pulls up just feet from them, the smile on his face strained. "Commander, you approach Stratus?"

"We do. It's a slow approach. The Palatine have just arrived. We mean to surround them."

Canaan's white eyes close. Pearla hears his mind thinking, turning over the thought again and again. Trying to make sense of it. "The Palatine are in Stratus."

"In the skies above it."

"Can you tell me why?"

"I can tell you what I know. Pearla"—he places a large hand on her shoulder—"a spy of the cherubic order, has been to Abaddon. In her presence the Prince received word that the Sabres had been released. He believes they've been asked to rend the veil over Stratus."

"Yes, we've heard them, seen them. Will they rend the veil, then?"

"I've heard nothing from the Throne Room, but they've lingered here longer than would be expected if that wasn't their aim."

Canaan's mind is quiet, his white eyes still.

"I've a charge inside. In Stratus."

Michael indicates the boy secured in the safety of Canaan's wings.

"Is this not your charge?"

Pearla watches the boy through Canaan's wings. He appears to be sleeping, but even unconscious he fascinates her. Humans fascinate her. Has this one any idea the price that was paid for him? The sacrifice that was made?

"He is. They both are. And both of them have been targeted before."

It's a moment before the Commander's mind speaks. "You aren't under my command, Canaan, but I suggest you keep him out. The Palatine stand between us and the town. If they see you approaching, they will not hesitate to attack."

Canaan's wings push him closer, his voice tight. "We've heard from her, Commander. A demon stands guard over her house. One named Damien."

The name is a light thrown into the confusion tickling Pearla's mind. It draws her into the discussion.

"You are the boy then!" Her eyes alight on Jake once again. "The boy with healing in his hands."

His eyes, closed until this very moment, open. His face shines with understanding, and he presses his fingers to Canaan's wings.

"I am," he says, his voice muffled.

"And the girl," Pearla's mind says. "The girl in Stratus . . ."

"Brielle," Jake says, his eyes frantic. "Her name is Brielle."

Pearla looks to Michael.

"She's the one, Commander. Brielle Matthews. The girl who can see into the Celestial."

"Well done, Pearla." Michael turns back to Canaan. "What can you tell me about him? About this Damien?"

"Not so long ago, he was responsible for orchestrating a child trafficking ring, was responsible for the corruption of several men. One of them took the life of a young woman. His attraction to Jake seems to be based on the healing in Jake's hands. His initial plans included corrupting the gift. Using it for darkness. I can only assume he wants the same for Brielle. For the gift instilled in her eyes."

"Weaknesses?"

"He suffers. His eyes were damaged years ago."

Pearla interrupts with a shake of her head. "He's been

healed. Not long ago, by the Prince himself. The Prince sent him to Stratus. Demanded he bring your two charges to Danakil."

Canaan flashes red with anger.

The Commander's face turns hard, but his words are measured. "Cold-blooded creatures like the desert, friend. The dragon is no exception."

Pearla knows Michael was one of the angels who ministered to Christ after his own time in the desert. After his own time of testing. Does the Prince have similar designs for the boy before her? For the girl with celestial eyes?

"It's true he was sent here for the two of you, but I think Damien has designs of his own as well," Pearla continues.

Canaan's golden brow creases. "Do you know what they are?"

"He's expressed interest in a bracelet. He's engaged help to secure it. A woman by the name of . . ."

"Olivia," Jake says, his eyes wide. "Olivia Holt."

Pearla nods.

Jake's voice is so very human, desperate. Pearla's never understood such desperation. "They have the halo, Canaan. Olivia has it. They'll be after us next. We can't leave her. Canaan, we can't."

Pearla doesn't understand Jake's reference to the halo, but she dare not interrupt. Emotions are running high, and she's only a Cherub. She's to observe and report, not engage.

Canaan's wings tighten around his charge. "We'll leave you, Commander. It seems Jake and I have things to discuss."

The Commander clasps Canaan on the shoulder. "Blessings, friend. If you find yourself needing a demon to destroy, you are welcome in our ranks."

"Perhaps I will take you up on that one day. For now, God be with you."

"And you."

Pearla watches as Canaan turns away, his face pointed to the ground. He falls hard and fast toward the earth below. Toward the terra firma humans are so comfortable inhabiting.

"Follow them, Pearla."

Michael's instruction confuses her. "Commander?"

Emerging from the celestial sky, Loyal appears at Michael's side, snorting, ready for battle. The Commander's wings lift him high above the animal before lowering him onto the warhorse's back.

"That boy's face told me everything I need to know. Canaan may counsel against it, but Jake's going after the girl."

"But he could die . . ."

The Commander's face takes on a soft glow. "He loves her, Cherub. Her life is worth more to him than his own."

"Yes, sir." It seems Pearla will have a chance to engage after all. She rather likes the idea.

"My prayers go with you, little one. Fly fast."

Pearla nods and dives after the Shield, her mind sorting through this new assignment. It's the greatest expression of love, she knows, to lay one's life down. But she wonders if humans know just how unique the ability is to do that. Death is not something an angel has to offer her loved ones. How glorious it must be to have one's days numbered by the Father.

How precious it makes each and every one.

35

Brielle

lle?"

Kaylee stands on the porch stairs, her phone in her hand, her face white. And though it's my name lingering in the air, her eyes are not on me. She's staring at Damien—who, for reasons passing all understanding, is standing between us in his human form.

"Go back inside," I tell her.

It's a stupid thing to say. She's no safer there, but at least I won't have to see the terror bubbling from her eyes, snaking like an adder down her cheeks.

Dad steps onto the porch. Damien is three feet from me, but the thing that grabs my attention is Dad's empty hand. He's relinquished his death grip on the beer bottle's neck. I hope he chose to do so before downing the last few gulps.

"Who are you?" he says, looking Damien up and down.

"Dad . . ."

"Inside," Damien growls. "All of you."

"Says who?" Dad is indignant.

Damien strides to the porch. Kaylee tries to back away, but

trips over the top stair. She lands on her backside, her elbows smacking the wood flooring. The fear running down her face multiplies, and I see Damien sniff at the air and grin as he bends and yanks the phone from her hands.

"Hey!" Dad says. "What do you think you're doing?"

Damien jerks upright and slides Kaylee's phone into his pocket.

"I said *inside*. If you want either of these girls to survive the day, you'll comply."

Dad's ruddy face is splotchy now, red and white and ticked all over. Indignant, he's unpredictable, but tipsy *and* indignant, Dad is just plain stupid. He takes a swing at Damien.

I groan and squeal all at once, but Damien avoids the blow. He steps back, his black dress shoes crunching in the gravel. Dad tumbles past Kaylee and down the stairs. He lands on his hands and knees at Damien's feet.

I rush to his side, but Dad's on his feet again before I can intervene.

"I wouldn't, Mr. Matthews." Damien's use of our last name is too intimate, too real.

I wrap my fingers—all ten of them—around Dad's forearm, praying he'll see reason. Praying he'll tame his temper for a few brief moments. But he shrugs me off, more irrational than ever. He curses and shoves passed me, but I throw myself between him and Damien. I'm sure it looks like I'm protecting Damien—this demon-man who just assaulted my father—but really, the opposite is true.

Life would be unbearable if Damien took Dad from me.

"Please, Dad. For me. For Kaylee. Let's just go inside. See what he wants. What he has to say."

Dad glances at me, but it seems to be Kaylee's sobs that move him to sanity. She's shuddering now, trying to breathe, but her large, gulping breaths succeed only in sucking copious amounts of black fear into her mouth and down her throat.

She gags, and Dad grunts his begrudging assent.

Damien stands at the door now, smiling, gesturing us inside like we're his dinner guests. The thought itself is disturbing and I don't linger on it. Instead, I focus on the good example thing and stomp up the stairs, my bare feet making dull nothings on the steps.

I pull Kaylee up as I go, and Dad follows us inside, cursing. Always cursing. Damien shoves Dad as he passes, sending him into the island. His face is a furry tomato now, but before Dad can turn his ham-sized fist into a ball, before he can swing again at Damien, I grab his hand and twist my fingers into it.

"Dad," I say, clearing my throat. I need to be clear. Dad must hear me. "This is Damien. He kidnaps children and sells them to pedophiles. Ali found out, and one of his men killed her. He was the mastermind behind the scenario at the warehouse this winter."

The blood drains from Dad's face—a tomato no more. "But you said—"

"Regardless of what you thought—"

"Of what I was told—"

"Regardless," I say firmly, "this guy is—"

"Capable of anything," Damien finishes, pulling a gun from his waistband. He points it at Dad's head. "Now sit."

It's a gun. I know it is, but all I see is a dagger. Sharp and bloody. And I know this guy will not hesitate to deal out death today.

Dad steps forward—*stupid, stupid*—his forehead bumping the barrel.

"Daddy, please." The words pour like tears from my lips.

"Yes, Daddy," Damien growls. "Please."

Dad doesn't move, doesn't back down, so I grab his hand and pull him away. I know he's letting me pull him, and I'm grateful for this small concession.

Kaylee walks in front of us. Her sobs are silent now—it seems she's gained some semblance of control. She curls onto the sofa, and I sit next to her, Dad on my other side.

"Where's your boyfriend?" Damien asks.

Dad's grip on my hand becomes vise-like, and I have to struggle out of it.

"I should have known this had something to do with him," Dad says, moving to stand again.

Damien stops Dad with the barrel of his gun. He presses it into Dad's shoulder, his lips curling back to reveal two rows of impossibly white teeth. "Mr. Matthews, I am out of patience now, and since your own life seems to matter little to you, let me make this clear: I've killed your daughter once. I will not hesitate to do it again."

Dad looks to me, his beard a prickly creature standing out from puffed, angry cheeks.

"He's not lying, Dad." I nod, trying to convey every bit of my own terror. He could use a little fear right now. After a second he sinks against the cushion, silent.

"Brielle," Damien says. "I asked you a question. Where is Jake?"

I pray an angel falls through the roof, a thousand of them maybe. But after a moment, I know the answer to my prayer won't be that simple. Kaylee's hand is suddenly on my knee. She squeezes, but I answer before Damien notices her movement.

"He's not here," I say.

"I'm aware of that." His head tips down, and his eyes constrict like a croc peering at me over still waters. "New eyes, see. Where has he gone?"

I shake my head.

I can't tell him.

I won't.

Damien points the gun at me. He yells, "Where is Jake?"

Dad throws his arm across my chest. I feel it tremble against my rib cage. "If you want the kid, find him yourself. She has no idea where to find him. She told you as much."

Damien's gun hand falls to the side, and he takes a knee before me. Dad's arm tightens across my waist, and I pull my feet off the floor—anything to get away from Damien. But he doesn't touch me. He just stares. And then I hear his voice in my head.

It's cold. So very cold. My eyes glaze over at the assault, and the room crystallizes before me—everything chilled, everything locked in ice.

"There are things even white eyes can't overlook," he says. "Humans don't stay where they're not wanted. And your father's made it clear Jake's not wanted here. He'll leave you. One day, he will."

A hot, round tear spills over my lashes and races down my cheek. The crystals dissolve. The room is bright and alive again. Still I say nothing.

"Oh, she knows where to find him," Damien says. "I'm certain of it."

"She doesn't, though," Kaylee says. I want to clamp a hand

over her mouth, keep her quiet. Keep her invisible to Damien, but his crocodile eyes settle on her. "Check the phone," she says. "The one you took from me."

His eyes are slits now, disbelief narrowing them.

"Dude, just check the phone!" Her voice is shrill, agitated. "We've been trying to get ahold of him. He hasn't . . . hasn't been answering."

He pulls Kaylee's phone from his pocket and throws it at her. "Show me."

Her deft fingers scroll and click. "Here," she says, shoving it at him. "I told you."

Damien takes the phone and reads. His face is unreadable. Is he angry? Is he scared?

And then it vibrates. The phone in his hand. Kaylee's phone. We gasp as one.

"One new message," Damien says.

He presses the face with his gigantic index finger.

And then he smiles. Those white teeth glare back at us. "It seems your boyfriend's on his way, Brielle. These things are good to know."

"You can't . . . don't . . ." The words are jumbled on my tongue.

"Oh, I can," Damien says. "And I'll enjoy it."

Dad's off the couch and on top of Damien before I can move—before the demon realizes what's happening. Kaylee and I scream. We grab for Dad, his shoulders, his shirt, but Damien's faster than both of us. And he's stronger. He leans back, his hands buried in Dad's chest, and throws all two hundred and fifty pounds of him over his head and into the television. I'm sure there's a crash, some kind of loud collision, but the world goes silent and all I hear is that singing again.

My eyes are on Dad, on the mass of electronics and denim, but I don't move. I can't. Kaylee's there now, at his side, and I'm grateful because I can't move. I'm paralyzed by the Sabres' song. So much louder. So much closer than I've ever heard it.

And it seems I'm not the only one. Damien stands to his feet, blocking my view of Dad. His head is cocked, his dead eyes boring into mine.

We stare at one another and we listen.

Eight . . . nine . . . ten seconds of heart-stirring melody. And then Damien's eyes open wide—wider than I've ever seen them—and he vanishes.

"Brielle!" Kaylee's voice breaks through the music and brings me back to the living room. "Brielle!"

She's trying to heft the television off Dad, but she's nowhere near strong enough. I slide to my knees at her side, and we lift the television off his chest and onto the floor. Dad lies faceup, unconscious, his forehead bleeding onto the blue carpet. I press my ear to his mouth—he's breathing—and to his chest—heart's beating. Other than the gash on his head, he seems okay.

I grab my favorite quilt off the ottoman and press the corner of it to his wound.

"Here," I tell Kaylee. "Hold this."

She does, her hands remarkably still after what we've just seen.

I stand and turn my eyes to the ceiling.

"Are you okay?" I ask her.

"No," she says. "But if we get out of this, I'm *so* going to church with you on Sunday."

I laugh, a bizarre vibration that seems to erupt from my throat, but in my frustration it dies quickly.

"Where did he go?" Kaylee asks, her head whipping around.

"I don't know."

Try as I may, I can't see through the ceiling.

Why can't I control this angel eyes thing?

I scan the house, looking high and low, but there's no sign of the Celestial in here. Even the sludge of fear on Kaylee's face has disappeared from sight.

"I'll be right back," I say, diving over Dad and out the front door.

I stumble into the clearing between Jake's house and mine. The sun kisses my neck and face, thawing my skin. The smells of hot pine and mowed grass tickle my nostrils as I turn my eyes here and there praying for celestial sight, for something to indicate where Damien went and what he's up to.

And that's when a thousand daggers come tumbling toward me.

36

Jake

I'm going after her," Jake says.

He and Canaan are about a half mile from the cemetery, just outside the border of Stratus, surrounded by redwoods and pines. Canaan's taken on his human form beneath the dense covering of trees. The branches are full with summer life, pressing against their backs, pushing them closer to one another as they speak.

"You'll be walking into a trap, Jake. Damien wants you both. He'll keep her there as bait. He knows you won't leave her."

Jake speaks through clenched teeth. "He's right."

"And what then? He takes you both to Danakil? To the Prince?"

"We'll be together," Jake says, his voice catching. "That's what matters."

"No," Canaan counters, "that's not what matters. Your souls matter. Proximity makes you easier to use against one another. Makes your will pliable, your heart emotional, your flesh weak."

"Then what? What do we do?"

"*You* do nothing. *You* wait. I'll go. I'll get Brielle out of Stratus."

Jake shakes his head. "You're a much bigger, much brighter target than I am. I can get in and out . . ."

"You might be able to get in, Jake, but with Damien there, you're not getting out."

Jake's jaw snaps shut.

"I can help." A tiny girl appears next to them on the forest floor. Black skin, black hair knotted at her neck, bright brown eyes. She looks no more than eight years old. A dark orange cloth is tied at one shoulder and hangs to her knees. Her feet are bare.

"Pearla, yes?" Canaan says, kneeling before her. "The Commander's Cherub?"

"Yes, sir, I am, and I've been sent to help."

Jake's open to anything right now. Anything except standing here talking.

"Go ahead, Pearla," he says. "Tell us."

"Your charge is right, Canaan; you're far too bright to enter unnoticed."

"Do you believe the Palatine will abandon their posts to attack a single Shield?"

"It's possible. The Palatine are vicious fighters, but they aren't known for their ability to follow commands. But more to the point is that they've been given incentive to capture Jake or the girl themselves. The Prince has promised a reward."

Jake's heart flips.

"General Maka's made it clear that the Sabres are their first priority, so while he won't command the legion to pursue a single Shield, you may attract the attention of a few who are more interested in reward than fearful of General Maka's wrath."

"Fair assessment, little Cherub."

"The Prince wants Jake. Wants Brielle. But he did not send

the Palatine for that task. They are here to ensure the Sabres do not succeed."

"So your plan, Pearla?"

"I suggest you both enter, but in your human form, Canaan. That way your entrance will not be so conspicuous."

"My celestial form won't be hidden entirely from the eyes of the Fallen."

"No," she says, "but you'll have a chance—a much better chance—that way. I'll stay near, in the Celestial. I'll warn you if there's anything to fear."

"Won't they see you?" Jake asks.

"Not if I'm careful. I'm created for such purposes. Darkness was given to me as a gift, and the Fallen often mistake me for one of their own."

"But your eyes . . . ," Jake says.

"Will give me away if I'm not careful."

"So . . ."

"So, I'll be careful."

So matter-of-fact. So light. So carefree. Her plan, her presence fill Jake with confidence.

"This will work," he says, standing.

It's a long second before Canaan joins him. "It could."

"We have to try!"

"Okay," Canaan says, his hand on Jake's chest, his eyes on Pearla. "Let's do it. Let's try."

37

Brielle

I dive to the ground, my palms scratching against the rough
grass, my check pressed to a pinecone. And that's when I
hear the music. It crawls in through my ears, but it doesn't
settle there. It moves through my body, through the invisible
spirit part of it. It's a wave that moves over every part of me,
pulling me into myself and out of myself.

I long to stand. I long to stretch my limbs and dance to this
song, to worship with my arms and my legs, with my whole
body. I'm on the verge of giving into this craving when the
memory of a single dagger slicing through my chest floats to
the surface of my mind. It hangs there, terrifying me, keeping
me frozen. The idea of a thousand daggers is enough to keep me
huddled on the grass a moment longer.

Maybe many moments longer.

I curl tighter into myself, listening to the music. To the
sound of instruments I can't name and voices so familiar they
sound like fractured parts of myself. And then the fragrance
reaches me. The smell of worship. I breathe it in. It's joy and life,

and it's not long before my desire to understand trumps the fear blossoming in my chest.

Why are they here?

I sit up. Dried grass has woven itself into my hair, itching my face and neck, but I can't make myself care. Before me the world is in sharp focus, and I see it all with celestial eyes.

Damien faces my direction, hovering about thirty feet off the ground. He's armed with his scimitar, but he is small compared to the angel opposite him. Virtue stands on the ground, between Damien and me. Silver light is thrown about, reflecting off his body and his wings, but he's not nearly as bright as he was in the graveyard.

His wings continue to play, the dagger-like blades moving back and forth, a symphony on his back. I look at Damien, at the ridiculous scimitar shaking in his blackened hand, and I know: he's no match for Virtue.

Damien must know this as well. He flies backward several paces, and Virtue turns toward me. Thousands of blades stand at attention, aimed now at Damien. Virtue's white eyes rest on me, compelling me to speak.

"Your song," I say. "It's beautiful."

He steps toward me, dazzling in his splendor. My eyes water, but I brush the tears away, refusing to close my eyes on him.

"Not nearly so beautiful as yours."

I choke. He's obviously never heard me sing.

"Believe me, child. It's the song of the Redeemed that terrifies darkness. It's your song, not mine."

The idea that I, all emotion and fear and confusion, could terrify my enemy—could terrify Darkness—seems senseless.

"I don't terrify anyone."

"Oh, but you do. Only humans can know the joy of being redeemed. Of being lost and then found. It is your song that reminds the Prince of Darkness that he's already been defeated. That the day will come when even Abaddon won't be able to protect him from the light he's rejected."

Virtue's words are a salve in my mind and in my heart, and though I've no idea how a song can help me now, I'd stand and talk to him forever if I could. But above Virtue's strong chin, his smile turns hard and thin. He glances over his shoulder at Damien and then back at me.

"I've not been given authority to destroy this one," his mind says to mine, "and I have my own assignment to complete. But remember well what I have told you."

I think about nodding or saying okay or something equally insufficient, but in the end I just stand there and watch. He squats, his enormous legs flexing and shoving him into the air. The sky looks almost neon against the imposing hoards above. Virtue's wings beat against it, releasing music and lightning that tear across the expanse. Even the closest of the demons—still miles away—skitter for cover, their strange forms melding like waves into sinking sand.

Virtue flies off to the north, his silver light going with him. I stare at the demonic forces above and watch their lines re-form.

The song of an angel.

That's all it took to frighten hundreds. To scatter them.

I see the enemy in a new way. As frightened children. Terrified of what we'll see. And of what we'll do with the knowledge it brings.

God's children are stronger than we know.

I've lost track of Damien, but with each passing minute he

concerns me less. What concerns me most is not the army above or the demon using me as bait for Jake. What concerns me most is that of the three of us—Kaylee, Dad, and me—I'm the only one with a song.

A redeemed song.

I'm the only one who can fight against our enemies.

The thought starts me trembling again, and I turn away from the demonic ranks high above and storm up the stairs. The moment I cross the threshold, the Celestial implodes before me and I'm left with only our living room in shades of brown and blue.

Dad is conscious. He's propped against his La-Z-Boy, Kaylee wrapping an Ace bandage around his head. I drop in front of him, shoving aside displaced cords and what looks like the corner of the television.

"Time to talk, Dad."

He stops moaning and blinks back at me. Kaylee chews her lip, but her hands are steady, her eyes dry. I hate that I've put her in this situation, hate it. But the only thing I can do now is make sure she can fight.

But Dad first.

My gaze is unflinching, and to my great surprise he looks embarrassed.

"I should have told you before," he says.

I rub my scraped hands against my thighs. There's a world of things he's left unsaid. Which one is he talking about?

"You should have told me what before?"

"I should have told you about the music."

I go still. Kaylee too.

"What music, Dad?"

He doesn't answer, but his eyes close and he leans his head back against the chair, his face pointed at the ceiling. Kaylee secures the bandage and steps away.

"You hear it, Elle. I know you do."

It's Virtue and maybe another like him. The music seeps through the walls. I imagine it curling around us, filling the room. But I thought I was the only one who could . . .

The idea strikes hard and fast, like a bird colliding with an unseen window.

"You can hear that?"

He grunts. "Wish I couldn't."

"Kay?"

She's sitting on the couch, looking lost without her phone. "I don't hear anything, Elle. Should I?"

I shake my head. "No, you're good." I turn my attention back to Dad. "When . . . when did you first . . . ?"

"The day your mother disappeared."

The air whooshes from my lungs, but when I next inhale, I realize he's just given me a puzzle piece. I open my eyes wider, not wanting to miss a single one.

"That was it, kid. Just the once. Thought I was going crazy, but it faded. It left not long after your mom."

I'm still, so still, afraid to move. Dad has seven, eight, nine gray hairs in his beard.

"That was it. Just the one time until . . ."

And then I begin to understand.

"That Sunday, in the house," I say.

Dad keeps his eyes shut, his head tilted back on the seat of the chair. "I'd been hearing it for a couple days by then, but yeah, I know you heard it too that day. And then at the lake—at the blasted lake. It was all I could hear. And then Canaan started whistling that same miserable song. The one I heard in the house. The one I hear when I'm trying to sleep or work. The same one that disappeared with your mom. The same song that follows me everywhere."

Tears slip down my face now. No warning. Just tears.

And understanding.

"I should have told you, Elle. But how could I, without telling you about your mom? That she disappeared. That I . . ."

"That you buried an empty casket."

He clears his throat, his face splotchy again. "And now I can't stop hearing it. It's everywhere. The noise. The music. I can't *not* hear it. And I know that whoever took your mother—whoever it was—I know they've returned. They're the ones responsible for desecrating her grave."

My head aches and my eyes burn. Dad might not be wrong. It's the first thing he's said in weeks that makes any sense. And yet . . .

"You know Canaan had nothing to do with it, right?"

Dad looks past me.

"Tell me you know that. Tell me you understand that Jake and Canaan were just as surprised by Mom's empty grave as I was."

Dad remains stubbornly silent.

"Dad!"

Kaylee climbs off the couch and wraps her arms around me.

"He was whistling the same song, Gabrielle." He says *whistling* like it's a nasty word.

I look to my friend, to the helpful expression on her face. She's not accusing. She's giving me an opportunity. I see it in the lift of her brows, in the encouragement behind her weak smile. *Tell him,* her face says. *Tell him what you told me.*

The air is sticky and uncomfortable—it reeks of the alcohol on Dad's breath and the dirt caking my clothes—but I take a deep swig of it and press a hand to Dad's knee.

"I bet all the angels know that song."

Dad's eyes narrow and his mouth drops open. "Wh—"

But he doesn't get to ask his question. Blood explodes on his shoulder, a bright red firework against his white undershirt.

He yells out, lashing, but that just makes the blood run faster. It drips down his arm and Kaylee screams out.

"Dad!" I cry. "Dad!"

But Dad's head lolls and he drops back, unconscious.

And then Damien's there, crouching in Dad's chair, his wings too big for our living room, his body wholly unwelcome in Dad's favorite seat. He withdraws the talon he's driven into Dad's shoulder and leans into my face.

"There's a reason we're invisible, girl. You can't think we'd let you destroy that."

38

Jake

They reach Main Street unscathed. Jake's about three strides behind Canaan, and they move fast. Only someone who's really seen Canaan run would know he's working hard to keep his pace reasonable. Pearla, for her part, has stayed invisible to their human eyes. Jake's not seen her since they left the covering of the trees, but he knows she's there. Believes it with all his heart.

They catch several wary glances as they hurl themselves down Main. Jake ducks his head and presses on, veering into the road to avoid the ever-present table of old men enjoying their donuts and coffee.

"Donut, Jake?" Bob yells.

"Not today, gents."

Canaan turns down a side street, his pace quickening as they enter the thin alley backing the stores on Main. Jake pumps his legs harder as they pass the rear of Jelly's. He hops a stack of flattened cardboard boxes and clips his knee on a discarded street sign. And that's when Canaan skids to a stop. The rubber tears free of the toe on Jake's right Chuck as he slides through the dry dust on the alley floor, but he manages to stop just short of Canaan's left shoulder, coughing with exertion.

Pearla stands before him in her human form, her dark face ashen. He catches only one word. "Transfer."

Jake doesn't have time to steel himself before he's wrapped in Canaan's wings and lifted into the sky. He sees Jelly's, its neon lights strangely magnified in the Celestial. The enormous grape jelly jar is there, a smear of violet against a backdrop of orange marmalade. Canaan continues toward the diner, toward the very end of Main Street. From there it's just a short flight up the highway to Brielle's.

Below Jake the Photo Depot, The Donut Factory, Miss Macy's, the community center—they all glow bright, a variety of occupants within shading the skies with various hues. To his right, beyond the community center, the small church is nestled in a rainbow of color.

He loves the sight of Stratus lit up with God's glory, but the anxiety eating away at his gut leaves little room for adoration. Especially when a blotch of darkness skates across his line of sight.

His heart redoubles its efforts, but a second glance shows him a familiar face.

Pearla.

Her wings are fast. Faster even than Helene's.

She tucks them close and falls away, her voice ringing in Jake's head.

"Behind you."

Jake's stomach is in his mouth as they tumble after her. Canaan collapses his large outer wings, covering Jake's body and erasing the world from sight. His stomach tells him they're cartwheeling through the sky, but he sees the underside of Canaan's wings. Nothing more.

And then with a jolt that vibrates through his bones, Canaan's outer wings slam open to reveal a set of snapping fangs. Jake tries to backpedal, but he's immovable against Canaan's chest. Fangs flash and talons reach, but before they can find purchase, Jake is lifted up and away as Canaan soars over the demon's head.

The demon turns, but he's not nearly fast enough. With a flash of white light, Canaan draws his sword and drags it down the demon, separating the fallen one in two.

Ash fills the air as the demon is reduced to sparking embers.

Canaan turns toward Jelly's once again.

Hang on, Elle, Jake thinks. *We're almost there.*

But the thought shatters like a tray of dropped ice. The roof of Jelly's is graced with two demons, their scimitars drawn and smoking in the hot celestial air. The larger of the two has a hand clamped around the neon tubing of the jelly jar. The other hunches below on the roof, his wings hanging at his sides, black and tattered. Canaan doesn't slow, and Jake presses against him, nearly climbing up his chest to be free of danger. Scripture leaps from his tongue.

"He will cover you with His feathers, and under His wings you will find refuge; His faithfulness will be your shield."

The two demons lunge at once, and Canaan swipes in a wide arc. His sword catches the wing joint of the smaller demon, and he spins, trying to regain control. The larger one loses half a leg. Sulfur spews into the atmosphere, stinging Jake's nostrils and sending tears streaming down his cheeks.

Both demons mount a second attack. The one with the broken wing is gimpy, flying lopsided and angry, but he presses closer as Canaan focuses on his companion. Jake's hands ball into fists and he prays harder.

A black smear speeds into his vision.

Pearla!

But she's so small. No weapon. Two delicate wings.

What is she doing?

She dives between the demons and Canaan. Her presence seems to confuse the Fallen, and they pull up.

They think she's one of theirs!

The larger of the two tilts his head, ape-like, and lowers his sword. It's just a momentary lapse, but it's all the time Canaan needs. He shoots forward, grabbing the demon's lowered scimitar in his left hand and shoving it upward. With his right hand, Canaan swings his own sword wide. Simultaneously, the demons are sliced through—one through the chest, the smaller one losing his head. Their forms hiss and smoke, but Canaan's past them already, leaving Jelly's and Main Street behind.

39

Brielle

amien's here, isn't he?" Kaylee is huddled behind me, her breath ragged. "He did that to your dad."

I nod. Afraid to do more than that. My fingers find the quilt on the couch, and I tug it toward me. It's still wet with the blood from Dad's head, but I find a clean corner and press it to his shoulder. He remains still. Deathly still.

My hands tremble.

"What do you want?" I whisper to the demon hanging over me.

I hate that my voice sounds subservient, hate that he's reduced me to that. I hate his voice in my head and the simple answer he gives me.

"I want you. I want Jake."

His chest is slick with fear. I've never noticed how thick it is on him. Is everything he does motivated by it?

I look at my dad's face, white and clammy, hear Kaylee's stifled cries, and I wonder what Damien sees when he looks at me. I wonder if the fear is just as thick on my skin as it is on his.

I'm afraid, but my soul is safe.

"I don't know where Jake is," I say. "But take me. Leave my dad and Kaylee. Leave them alone and take me."

For a second I think he considers the option. Am I worth that much? And is this how I die? Maybe that's why the ring disappeared from the chest. Maybe I won't be alive to wear it.

But then his wings snap, all irritation and resolve.

"It may come to that, but not yet."

"Not ever."

I spin toward the kitchen, and there he stands.

Canaan, in all his celestial glory. Jake is there too, his face anxious, fear like pinpricks along his arms and neck.

"Elle?" Kaylee's voice reminds me that she can't see any of this. That her emotions are surfing on every move of my head, on every twitch of my face.

"It's okay," I tell her. "Canaan's here. And Jake."

She turns toward the kitchen, to the spot I stare at hungrily.

"I can't . . . can't see them."

"I know, but I can."

Jake presses against Canaan's inner wings, his eyes as hot as ever, and I can't help thinking of the first time I saw him. Of the chill that held me captive the day I caught him staring at me through Miss Macy's window.

"Keith's hurt, Canaan," Jake says.

Canaan draws his sword. Behind me, Damien rises to his full height, the talons on his feet digging into the arms of Dad's chair. He draws his own sword. And then something I really should have anticipated: he grabs the back of my shirt and lifts me into the chair before him. His massive arm circles my waist, and I feel the fear creep from his arms to my stomach. It burrows inside, turning my gut into a lake of frozen ice.

"Elle . . ." Kaylee's sobbing now, shaking and staring at me. "Elle."

From behind Canaan, a ball of frenetic black energy appears. Another demon? But no, her eyes shine bright and pure. It's an angel! A very small, very dark angel. Silky wings propel her forward, and she lands on Damien's chest. Her wings flap hard and fast, and I'm reminded of the time I came face-to-face with a confused bat while rock climbing.

She seems to have the same effect on Damien. He releases my waist, his hands flying high to fight the onslaught. The flat edge of his sword connects with her abdomen, and he swats her away. But it's too late; I've tumbled to the floor now. I land on Dad's shins and quickly push away, crawling as fast as humanly possible. I grab Kaylee's hand and drag her with me behind Canaan's legs, where we huddle beneath his outer wings.

Canaan's mind speaks to Damien's. "Your sight has been restored."

"By the Prince himself." Damien lifts his chin, puffs out his broad chest, but Canaan's face shows only sorrow.

"The Prince's hands no longer possess a healing that can last, old friend. I do hope you know that."

Damien's face contorts, and he lunges. And then I feel the hot wind of the Celestial blowing against my back. In one swift motion, Canaan pushes off from the ground and swats at Damien with his sword. Damien blocks the blow, but it takes the strength of both his hands to hold his blade steady. He shoves back, but Canaan seems to be the stronger of the two. Canaan realizes this too and opens his inner wings, releasing Jake. He tumbles to the ground next to me, sending Kaylee into a fit of startled shrieks.

But her voice is quickly drowned out by the sound tearing from Damien's lips. Like a hawk going in for the kill, he cries out, his eyes on me. I want to hide, but I can't look away. Canaan smacks him in the face with the hilt of his sword, and Damien's cry turns brutal. His wings pull him backward, putting distance between the two of them. He lifts his scimitar high and then . . .

And then they disappear from sight.

My chest rises and falls, my eyes open and shut, again and again. But they're gone. The Celestial is gone. I'm both relieved and terrified.

Jake moves away, toward Dad. He removes the quilt that hangs like a veil over Dad's face. He doesn't hesitate, doesn't pause to consider the consequences, he just presses both hands to the wound. I crawl on my hands and knees until I'm next to him. Dad looks . . . well, he looks awful. His hair is matted to his head, a dirty mess of sweat and blood. I push a clumpy strand out of his eyes.

"Are they gone?" Kaylee asks.

"For now." I grab her hand and pull her toward me.

"Is he . . ." But Kaylee's voice catches and she can't even finish the thought.

"He'll be okay," Jake says. "He's just lost some blood is all."

I have complete confidence in Jake's healing ability. What I don't have is an assurance that Dad won't murder Jake the minute he wakes.

"I told him, Jake. I told him about Canaan."

Jake looks at me, his face inscrutable. "How did he take it?"

"I don't really know. Damien's talon interrupted things."

"It's better that he knows," Kaylee says. "Way better. His head was super messed up about this whole thing. About your mom.

Thinking Canaan had something to do with her disappearance. You had to tell him, Elle."

Jake bumps Kaylee with his shoulder. "Looks like this one knows too."

"No choice," I say, smiling at her. "She was here when Damien showed up. And Helene."

Helene! This is the first free moment I've had to consider her.

Kaylee seems to be thinking the same thing. "Do we know what happened to her?"

I shake my head.

"Don't worry about Helene," Jake says. "She's immortal. If she's hurt, she'll heal."

His hands are occupied, but I take his face in mine and I kiss him. Hard. It's awkward, with his hands still on Dad's shoulder, but he's warm and he's close, and I kiss him again.

"Oh, come on! Demons *and* make-out sessions? Unless you're getting *me* one of these," Kaylee says, gesturing to Jake, "save it for later."

"Fair enough," Jake says, blushing.

"Speak for yourself," I say, and press my lips to his once more.

"Barf," Kay says.

"Yeah, barf." It's Dad.

We jerk apart, but it's too late. His eyes are open, his mouth set in a frown.

"Sorry, Dad. I just . . ."

But he's moving his shoulder now. Jake's hands fall away, and Dad rotates his arm. He winces, pressing his fingers to the spot Damien's talon punctured.

"I'm not sure if it's done, sir," Jake says.

"Feels a heck of a lot better than it did before." He looks at

Jake. I know that look. It's the same one he gets when he's trying to decide if he's going to eat his dinner steak rare, or bloody and mooing. "What did you do?"

Jake swallows. Audibly. "My hands can . . . God uses my hands to heal. Sometimes."

And just like that, Dad lets out a sob. Loud and awkward. He sniffs and jams his fist into his eyes, one at a time.

"Thought you said Canaan was the angel."

Jake is quick to speak. "I'm not an angel, sir."

"No?" Dad barks. "Then what are you?"

I slide my hand into Jake's. It's wet with Dad's blood, but it's warm. I squeeze, hoping to convey something encouraging.

"I'm human, sir. Like you. I just have a gift."

"And Hannah, my wife, is that what happened to her? Did she have a gift? Is that why they took her?"

With celestial eyes I see the waters of misery break over my dad. Murky and cold, they run from his scalp down his chest, puddling into the carpet around him. I didn't know my lungs could stretch so tight. Didn't know they could survive the weight of so much emotion. Of so much sadness.

"I wish I knew," Jake says. "I wish I had answers for you."

Dad blows out a puff of air, grumbling, cursing under his breath.

"Dad, I told you. Canaan and Jake don't know anything about Mom."

Dad rolls his shoulder again, his expression the fuming side of doubtful. I'm readying myself for an angry outburst, for a barrage of questions, when the room fills with music. Louder than I've ever heard it. It's everywhere. It's between us and under us. It dances around us. I see the tendrils of incense swirling about, see it wrap Kaylee and Dad tight, see them both gasp and blink and turn their heads left and right.

"Okay," Kaylee says. "I hear *that*."

"They both do," Jake says, mesmerized. "They both hear it."

And then from outside, Canaan calls.

"Jake! Brielle!" His voice is strained, desperate, and Jake pulls me to my feet.

Dad tries to stand, but he's still weak.

"Don't even think about it, Dad. You're hurt."

Dad's face is purple with the strain of trying to stand, but he's still stubborn. "You telling me what to do, baby?"

"Yes, I am." I shove him down, taking no satisfaction in watching him wince. "Kay, stay with him, please. Keep him here."

The last thing in the world I need is Dad getting attacked again.

She nods and Dad protests, but Jake's pulling me with him, and I turn my focus away. We run hand in hand out the front door and into the field and then we're standing next to Canaan, the three of us staring into the apple orchard behind the house.

"What *is* that?"

"Is that . . . ?"

"Do you . . . ?"

"How . . . ?"

Jake and I start to formulate questions, but our lips won't finish them. The orchard is on fire, but it's not burning. The trees, the mangled overgrown shrubs, the weeds protruding everywhere—it's all a bright red. Not the frightening bloodred of violence, not that terrifying crimson shade, but dazzling, luminous.

The music continues to swell, piping louder and louder.

Violins and pianos. And voices, so many voices. Flutes and the deep swell of a bass. And I *see* the music. See it with celestial eyes, just as I saw it in the house. Curling ribbons of worship in color after color, wrapping the orchard and then rising above it higher and higher until it disappears into the army of death above.

The blood racing through my veins turns hot with desire. I want to touch it, to be part of whatever is making the orchard flame. I want to be inside those trees, inside that life.

I release Jake's hand and I run, flying through the grass, dropping down onto the orchard floor. I shove aside branches, needing to find the source. My hair catches on a limb, but I press forward, ignoring the pain tearing at my scalp. The fragrance of worship surrounds me: flowers and fruit, salty sunlight and the smell of Gram's front yard. It's all so familiar, so achingly familiar.

And then Jake is next to me. I smell the coffee on his skin, the sugar of his touch as it brushes my shoulder.

Sweat pours down my arms, down my back. "This isn't the Celestial, is it?"

"I don't know," he says, looking around. "I don't know what it is."

I look at his face, at his eyes. He's on overload trying to take it all in, as confused as I am.

"The Terrestrial veil is thinning," Canaan says. "Here, in Stratus, as it did on the mountaintops above. They're doing it slowly, carefully."

Jake and I turn at his approach. He steps off the grass and onto the orchard floor. As he walks toward us, flickers of his celestial self come into view. A thread of light wrapping his waist and then disappearing. A white wing there and then gone. His eyes, silver then white, then silver again. One half of his face yellow with a celestial glow, and then fading again to the olive of his human form.

"What does that mean?" Jake asks.

"It means that if the Sabres continue to do their job, if they're not stopped by the army above, eventually the veil will tear."

"Is that good or bad?" I ask, the thought both wonderful and terrible in my mind.

And then for the briefest of seconds I see Canaan in his full celestial regalia: alabaster wings, cords of light that wrap his legs and waist, his feet and chest bare, his silver hair floating on waves of celestial heat. The red orchard surrounding us is glorious, but it's nothing to his beauty.

He smiles. "Wasn't it Hamlet who said, 'There is nothing either good or bad, but thinking makes it so'?"

I turn my eyes back to the trees—back to the red, mottled trees—and I try to understand what Canaan's just said. He helps me.

"For the man drowning, rain is only another helping of tragedy, Elle, but to the man on fire, that same rain is the last hope he has."

Proverbial truth. An orchard on fire. Fragrance and music. Light and life. My senses are on overload. What will happen if this veil actually tears? What will happen to those who don't understand? To those who do?

My heart hammers my ribs, the *thud-thud* of it quivering outward from my chest, filling my arms, my legs, my neck and face. And then I realize it isn't my heart. It's the sound of drums.

"Do you hear that?" I ask Jake.

He shakes his head, and I turn my eyes to Canaan. His head

is cocked, the intensity of his gaze tells me I'm not alone in what I hear.

"What is it, Canaan?"

He listens for a moment more and then stands taller.

"The drums of war," he says. "The Palatine attack."

I turn my eyes to the sky but I can't see past the trees. Can't see past the beauty, and that terrifies me. I'm claustrophobic, panicky. What does this attack mean for my dad? For Kaylee? How will they fight? They don't have a song.

Canaan strides toward us, and Jake's hand finds mine. Canaan steps behind us, but he does not cloak us, he does not take us into the safety of his wings. He remains in his human form, a hand on both our shoulders, and together we listen.

The drums are closer now, and I hear strange, violent voices. Like animals. Like angry, raging animals, they approach. I step closer to Jake, squeeze his hand tighter.

And then Jake is quoting Scripture. "He who dwells in the secret place of the Most High shall abide under the shadow of the Almighty. I will say of the Lord, 'He is my refuge and my fortress; my God, in Him I will trust.'"

I know this one. It's a psalm, written by King David. I join in, and Canaan does as well.

"He shall cover you with His feathers, and under His wings you shall take refuge; His truth shall be your shield and buckler. You shall not be afraid of the terror by night, nor of the arrow that flies by day, nor of the pestilence that walks in darkness, nor of the destruction that lays waste at noonday. A thousand may fall at your side, and ten thousand at your right hand; but it shall not come near you. Only with your eyes shall you look, and see the reward of the wicked."

And then a silver light invades the orchard and we're surrounded.

I scream out, but Canaan's grip on my shoulder tightens, and I understand we're in the presence of friends. Of allies. Of the angelic. Their backs are to us. Their forms are so bright I have to squint to see, but I make out wings of blade on every single one of them. We stand within a circle of gigantic winged men, their swords drawn, the metal-like feathers of their wings vibrating one against the other, encasing us in song.

I resist the urge to count. I don't need to. Helene told me. There are twelve of them. Twelve Sabres, and not a single one of them is cloaked.

"Some things were never meant to be secret," Helene told me.

Virtue turns toward us, his silver form vibrant against the red limbs that surround us.

"It's time to remember," he says to me.

"Remember what?"

"Why the grave is empty."

He steps closer, his white eyes mesmerizing. I watch them closely for some sign of what I'm to do, of what I'm to say. And then I'm falling into them, into his eyes. Into the purity of love's greatest expression.

And I remember.

40

Brielle

The room is small with Mom's hospital bed here, with the machines whirring and the medicine dripping down a tube and into her thin hands. The sight shakes me, but I still feel disconnected, like I'm nothing but a fly on the wall watching, observing.

It's my room, I realize, not Dad's. She lived out her last few days here.

A toddler bed is pressed against the wall, low to the ground, covered with the quilt my Grams made me when I was born. Pink with a large purple octopus stitched on. I still have that blanket, tucked away at the top of my closet. But here, in this memory, it's spread across my bed, covered with stuffed animals and sticker books. A pair of ballet slippers hangs from the wall, pictures of flowers and fairy kingdoms, but mostly the room is filled with Mom.

Mom's bed, Mom's machines, Mom's medicine, Mom's cancer.

I look at her now, in all her illness, and I see my mother as she was. She's thinner than any of the pictures I remember seeing. Obviously frail. Her head is full of flaxen hair, but it's brittle, dying.

Like everything else about her.

She's propped up on large white pillows, and there, lying in her arms, is me.

Three-year-old me.

I don't remember this. Don't remember it occurring, but seeing it brings a small sense of peace. It's good to know it really happened.

That my mommy held me, that she stroked my hair.

And then the strangest thing happens. I'm aware that I'm still in the orchard, can still hear the Sabres and their music, can still feel Jake's hand in mine, but for the first time ever I remember. It's like something explodes in my mind.

I don't remember her touch or her voice. I don't remember the room or the bed or even the brush in my hand. What I remember crawls inside me and twists itself around my heart, squeezing until I'm just sure it will burst.

For the first time ever, I remember what that moment smelled like, what my mother smelled like. I choke and sob at the memory. The first real memory I've ever had of my mother.

She smelled like worship. She smelled like curling, fragrant tendrils of adoration. My three-year-old self breathes her in, again and again.

Standing in the orchard, watching this memory in the eyes of Virtue, I do the same. Inhale, exhale, and again. Remembering, remembering.

I watch as my three-year-old eyelids grow heavy and the hairbrush in my hand falls to the mattress next to my mommy's shoulder. She lies there, her thin fingers tangled in my hair, her mouth whispering praises. In broken sentences and stuttering pauses, her cancer-wracked body thanks her Lord and Maker for every moment she has left with me. With Dad.

"I'm not ready to leave," she says. "To leave my husband. To leave my little girl." These are the first full sentences I've caught. The first words I've fully understood. "But You're taking me, I know that."

Her eyes are open, her pale face soft in the yellow light pressing against the blinds.

"If there's anything I can do for You, Father, before I die, anything I can do here, I am willing."

And then Virtue stands before her. Uncloaked, unhidden from her human eyes. She doesn't gasp. She doesn't flinch.

He's expected.

"Hello, Hannah," he says, his lips still, his wings rubbing one against the other, their music filling the room.

Her eyes fill with tears. They run down her face, wetting the hair at her temples, dampening her pillow. "Are you here to take me? Am I to see my Father now?"

Virtue smiles. "Not quite yet," he says. He gestures to my sleeping figure, the tiny three-year-old body curled around my mother's. "May I?"

She pulls me tighter to her chest. "Will I see her again?"

Virtue runs a silver hand along Mom's brow, and she takes a deep, shuddering breath.

"Will such an answer help you say good-bye?"

The tears fall fast now, her voice thin and weak. "No," she says. "I don't think so."

She squeezes me, her arms straining against the tubes in her hands, and she kisses my blond hair, her eyes pinched shut. Her chest shakes and her lips move against my head. I wish I could make out the words, but I can't. It seems they were for the Father alone. After a moment she nods at Virtue, who takes me in his arms and lays me at the foot of the bed. I watch my three-year-old self sprawl on the quilt, my arms spread wide, my tiny chest moving up and down. There, next to my heart, is Olivia's necklace.

"Please," Mom says to Virtue, "take care of her, protect her. And my husband. I want him to know the Father like I do. Give them eyes to see and ears to hear. Can you do that?"

"A beautiful request, Hannah. It is not within my power to grant such things, but your Heavenly Father hears and answers His children. You can be certain of that," he says, his hand still upon her brow. "Are you ready?"

"Where are we going?"

Another smile from the Sabre as he removes the tubes from Mom's arms and lifts her from the bed as easily as he'd lifted three-year-old me.

"You are needed elsewhere."

41

Brielle

The orchard comes into focus one twisted limb at a time. Virtue is gone, as are the other Sabres. And Canaan. Jake and I stand alone, my hand trembling inside the warmth of his.

"Are you okay?" he says.

If I feel anything right now, I feel numb.

"Dad was right," I say. "He took her. Virtue did."

Jake turns me toward him, a look that would quell the darkest storm on his face. "Then I know without a doubt that she was well looked after."

"He's big," I say. It's a stupid thing to say, a stupid thought, but his size brings me comfort.

Jake seems to understand. "Really big."

And then we laugh. And cry. It's all so jumbled, but there's relief there. And pain. We sink to the ground, the red trees surrounding us, and I tell Jake about my mom's final moments in Stratus.

"I have a memory of her now," I say, my mouth quivering, my nose running. "Maybe it'll be enough to help us find her."

"I hope so, Elle. I do, and we'll look. I promise." Jake wipes at my face, soaking up tears with his index finger. His mouth curves into that little crescent moon I love so much.

"What?"

"I just smeared mud across your cheek."

We laugh again.

Understanding why Mom's grave was empty didn't solve a thing, but it gave me a way forward, and my heart is lighter for it.

"Where are the Sabres?" I ask.

"Fighting," he says.

"And Canaan?"

"Looking for Damien," Jake says. "He made a grab for us just as you started your trip down memory lane."

"He tried to attack while we were surrounded by Sabres?"

Jake nods, his face serious. "Tells you how desperate he is to have us, Elle. The Sabres hurt him, but he kept coming. With his sight restored, he's a dangerous specimen."

I think of the dagger that punctured my chest last December, of my life leaking down the ridges of an aluminum building.

"He was dangerous before," I say.

"And now he's worse. Much worse."

I want to tell him I'm sorry about last night. I want him to know that I understand he was trying to protect me, just as I was trying to protect Dad, but before I can voice either of those things, I'm pulled into the Celestial.

I gasp for air as my kneeling body is yanked straight and pressed against a hot, soft form and flown backward through the orchard. She's singing, loud and fierce. It's Helene! She's here! She's whole.

But relief is short-lived. We're flying fast and low through the trees, my eyes trained on the spot I've just left. On Jake. Just beyond

the orchard, there is a flurry of activity. I see Sabre wings flashing.
I hear music droning from them, smell the fragrance of worship as
they fight. I see darkness as the Fallen close in. And then Canaan
dips into the orchard, shaking a demon off as he does. With his inner
wings he pulls Jake to his chest, and I watch as they fly skyward.
Four demons abandon the Sabre they're fighting for an easier target.
A smaller angel, slowed by a charge, and carrying only one sword.

They fly at Canaan.

I cry out, but it's nothing save unintelligible hysterics,
and there's too much noise. Too many demons screaming like
animals, too many Sabres singing violently. Blade rings loud
against blade, demons dissolve with hissing sputters into the
Celestial around them.

Hot tears sting my eyes, but I force them open.

The demons attack. All four of them, slicing away at Canaan.
At his wings. He's fast, so fast, and his skill with a sword is staggering. For a moment I think he has the situation under control, that
he and Jake are fine, but then a fifth demon joins the fray. Canaan
manages to dispatch three of the Fallen before another slices open
his inner wings.

I scream, and Helene dives toward them.

Toward Jake tumbling to the ground.

And then I see him.

Damien.

He's flying at Jake. Fast and precise, his untainted eyes guiding him through the battle. I scream again and again. Helene
flies hard, but Damien gets there first. With razor-sharp talons
he snatches Jake from the air. I catch just a glimpse of his white
eyes before they disappear into a mass of Fallen warriors.

I don't think I'll ever stop screaming.

42

Brielle

There's a new nightmare now. I'm looking through my mom's eyes. I know they're her eyes because I'm sick and dying, but Virtue is there. He's holding me tight, his wings singing, his chest warm. My eyes are closed, but I think we're flying. I feel the wind on my face, pressing against us. I wonder where we're going, but I haven't the energy to ask.

And then Virtue sets us down, and I open my eyes. The building around us crumbles, flames licking the walls, charring them, turning them black. The smoke makes me gag, my legs weak from the disease ravaging it. But at my feet is a woman, dead already. Her nurse's scrubs are stained with smoke, her left side burnt.

Mom groans at the sight. She knows her. I know her.

"One more thing," Virtue says. "One more thing before you go."

And then I hear a voice crying, panicked. It screams and screams.

"Mother! Mama! Where are you? Please, Mom, please!"

I recognize the voice. More than that, my mom recognizes it. With energy she doesn't possess, she runs out the open door and into the hall. It's full of smoke, classrooms on either side. Ten-year-old Olivia runs down the hall, limping, injured. She opens one door after another, screaming for her mom.

My heart breaks at her agony, but she shouldn't see this. She needn't see her mother burnt and dead. Seeing won't change a thing. So I run—Mom runs—down the hall. She grabs Olivia by the hand, spinning her toward the exit.

"Hannah?" Olivia asks, tears streaking the smoke on her face. "What are you doing here? Where's my mom?"

Mom doesn't answer. There's not enough energy for that, just enough to pull the screaming, flailing girl through a corner classroom and shove her out an emergency exit door.

The door swings shut, closing Olivia out. Hannah slams her fist against the knob, locking it, keeping the girl from the flames that killed her mother. And then she stumbles to the center of the room, sucking raspy breaths of smoke-saturated air.

Virtue steps through the flames and takes her hand. He rubs his wings together, releasing wave after wave of worship.

"You could have done that," Mom says, swaying on dying legs. "You could have saved her. Why bring me here?"

"Because you asked. You wanted to be useful to the Father, Hannah, and you have been. Your saving her now will pave the way for your daughter to save her later. And one day Olivia will need saving."

The idea is confusing, but there's peace in it for Mom. Peace that her last minutes have made a difference. They're the last words she hears—the last words I hear before Mom takes one last breath. Before Virtue wraps her in his arms and spreads his wings wide, shattering the classroom windows and lifting her into the heavens.

43

Brielle

*M*iss Macy arrived a half hour ago. She spent two minutes talking to Dad and twenty minutes cleaning the kitchen. When I couldn't watch her scrub another dish, I left her there and retreated to the orchard.

To the red orchard.

The battle continues to rage overhead, but the Sabres have kept Maka and the Palatine from taking Stratus. Their song has all but torn the veil, and the orchard is brighter than ever. Helene is never far, tells me the Army of Light has arrived. She says they'll surround the Palatine, engage them on multiple fronts.

The Fallen will take me if they can—I know that—but I'm as safe in the orchard as I am inside.

I sink to the ground amidst the rotting fruit and weeds. The Sabres' song surrounds me. It's as loud as ever, but not everyone can hear it, it seems. Miss Macy can't, but Dad and I can. I think it's the only reason I was able to find sleep last night. As it turns out, my cell was under the couch. I press and hold the number five, my hand trembling to keep the phone in place.

But it doesn't matter. Jake's phone goes straight to voice mail.

I leave a message telling him to call me. I try not to cry while I'm talking, but there's no stopping the tears once they start. And they haven't really stopped since yesterday. I tell Jake I'm not mad. That I don't care about the ring. That it's not important. A life together isn't even the most important thing, I tell him. It's his soul. Whole, untarnished, uncorrupted. That's the important thing.

I hang up, but I don't release the phone. Jake might call. Or Canaan even. He followed Damien into the distance and never returned. I don't know how long he'll follow the demon, but I pray he'll follow him to the ends of the earth. That he'll bring Jake back safe.

And if he can't do that, I pray that I'll have a chance to see Jake again.

If not on this side of heaven, then on the other.

Like my mom and Ali.

With my phone still in my hand, I pull the envelope of pictures from my back pocket. The pictures Dad had developed the other day. I find strange comfort in them, the envelope already worn because I've opened and closed it so often.

They're pictures of Mom. Of Mom and Olivia, actually. It seems their encounter at the hospital wasn't their last. As a girl, Olivia visited Mom at the hospital. I imagine she came when her mother was working. There are a few pictures of the three of them. There are even some of Mom and Dad. Of Miss Macy. Of Pastor Noah and Becky. I need to talk to them. They can tell me about Stratus all those years ago. About the miracles and the healings.

I slide the top picture to the back and find my favorite of the bunch. Mom's reading to me—Dr. Seuss, by the looks of it—and we're on her hospital bed. I'm wearing the flowered necklace. Olivia's necklace. I can only guess she gave it to Mom, and Mom gave it to me. How it ended up in her grave is anyone's guess, but I'm sure Dad had something to do with it.

He had to bury something, after all.

I'm still not sure what Mom was doing in a Portland hospital, but it's something else I'll ask Dad later. For now, I'm done asking questions. The answers don't satisfy, and they won't help me fight.

And if I'm ever going to get Jake back, I need to fight.

I tuck the pictures away, closing the envelope again. And then I stand as the tendrils of sound and light surround me. I breathe them in and let the music take me. I let myself dance.

I may not have the confidence to sing my redemption song, but I can wield it anyway. My arms and legs can fight even when I don't have the courage to move my mouth. The orchard doesn't provide the easiest dance floor, but my heart doesn't care. The Sabres sing somewhere beyond the veil. Their voices sing of an almighty, all-knowing God, and I let my body join them. I let myself believe that He knows best, even though it hurts. Even though everything I love has been taken.

I'm broken, but here in the red orchard, surrounded by the sweet smell of worship, I raise my hands above my head, and I believe.

Reading Group Guide

1. After the chaos of her senior year, Brielle is anxious about what to do after high school. Can you relate to that? Do you have post-graduation plans?
2. Both Brielle and Jake struggle with believing that God's plan is best. Do you believe that? Have you ever faced a situation where God's plan seemed less than desirable? What did you do?
3. Kaylee really blossoms in this book. She sticks by Brielle even when things get rough. Do you have a friend like that? Are *you* a friend like that?
4. Brielle learns that there are ways to fight evil: prayer, worship, Scripture. Are you quick to recognize a spiritual attack? Do you know how to fight?
5. It seems the Throne Room is choosing to communicate with Brielle through her dreams. Do you think God uses dreams to talk to us? Do you have an example to share?
6. Brielle is a crier and she knows it. How do you respond to heartbreak? Do you get angry? Do you withdraw? Are you prone to tears like Brielle?

7. Marco's response to the halo is very different than Brielle's. Why do you think that is?

8. In the Celestial, worship is seen as smoke or incense, ribbons of color. What do you think worship looks like to God? What do you think it smells like?

9. One of the hardest things for Brielle to cope with is the fact that Jake lied to her. Do you find it difficult to forgive when you're lied to? What does the Bible say about forgiving others?

10. This series is full of imaginative descriptions of angels. What do you think angels look like? How are they described in Scripture?

11. The halo has given Brielle the ability to see the Celestial. It's given Jake the ability to heal. And thus far, it's given Marco horrible memories. If the halo was given to you, what gift do you think you'd receive? Is there a gift you'd prefer—or despise?

12. When Brielle uncovers the truth about her mother's death, it makes her question everything. Have you had a moment like that—a moment that shakes the very foundation of your world? How did you react? What advice would you give a friend walking through a similar situation?

Acknowledgments

There are so many amazing people who deserve my thanks. Friends and family who've invested in my stories and my journey. Your support means more than I could ever say. Please know I'm grateful.

I would like to give a huge shout-out to my church family at Living Way. You watched my kids, you covered my Sunday school classes, and you let me ditch when the deadlines got scary. You've also provided me with an amazing place to worship, something that shows up all over these novels. Without you, they wouldn't be what they are. Every time we gather together, I get to be surrounded by the incense of worship and I never leave unchanged. So, thank you. Your love and prayers mean the world.

Thanks to Becky and Jodi, to Katie and Ruthie, to Daisy and the rest of the team at Thomas Nelson Fiction. Your commitment to my work is staggering. I'm blessed to be working alongside you.

To my agent, Holly, and all the writers on Team Root, you rock. Your friendship keeps me sane and your stories remind me that words really can change the world.

I would also like to thank my husband, Matt. By the time this book hits shelves, we'll be finishing our tenth year of marriage. In every way, you've been my partner and my friend. And you're hot. So, I'm blessed. SHMILY.

And to my kids. Thank you, Justus, for letting me share my love of story with you. One of these days I really will let you read these books. And Jazlyn, thank you for doodling on all my index cards. You keep my days delightful and interesting. I love you both to infinity and beyond.

One halo brought sight to
Brielle. Another offers sweet
relief from what she sees.

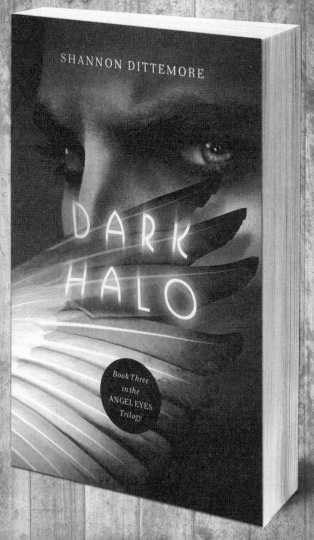

SHANNON DITTEMORE

DARK
HALO

Book Three
in the
ANGEL EYES
Trilogy

Available August 2013

For the latest news about the
Angel Eyes Trilogy, visit

ShannonDittemore.com

Connect with Shannon through
Facebook and Twitter:

Facebook: Shannon Dittemore – Author

Twitter: @ShanDitty

About the Author

Author photo by Amy Schuff Photography

Shannon Dittemore is the author of the Angel Eyes Trilogy and has an overactive imagination and a passion for truth. Her lifelong journey to combine the two is responsible for a stint at Portland Bible College, performances with local theater companies, and a focus on youth and young adult ministry. When she isn't writing, she spends her days with her husband, Matt, chasing their two children around their home in Northern California.